To Dodge a Duke

by

Naomi Boom

Entangled Nobility, Book 2

To Dodge a Duke

Cover Art by *RJ Morris*

The Wild Rose Press, Inc.
PO Box 708
Adams Basin, NY 14410-0708
Visit us at www.thewildrosepress.com

Publishing History
First Tea Rose Edition, 2017
Print ISBN 978-1-5092-1468-6
Digital ISBN 978-1-5092-1469-3

Entangled Nobility, Book 2
Published in the United States of America

Logan smirked and stood to tower over her.
"I think you welcomed my advances very much. I would prove it if you ask."

Eleanor glared at him and took a step back. "That is unnecessary. I already know I did not appreciate the first example." Besides, even if she had enjoyed it, it would be inadvisable for her to allow another kiss to transpire. His smirk remained glued to his handsome face, and she said, "Oh, stop it. You think much too highly of yourself."

He chuckled in response and took a step closer. Eleanor, naturally, took another step back until he reached out and pulled her to him in a rough embrace. Incensed, Eleanor asked, "Who do you think you are? There is never an acceptable time for you to behave so impudently toward me!"

His arm imprisoned her as he smiled down on her. "Isn't there? Would it have been preferable to fall into the ravine?"

She swung her head around to find they stood mere steps from the rushing waters. She gulped and turned to face him. Obviously, it was best to stay away from the ravine, but she would not concede his point. "Yes. It would have been much more desirable."

Dedication

Thank you to those who continue to support me,
and to my husband: Go Dawgs.

Chapter 1

"Why me?" Eleanor sighed as she made a valiant attempt to focus past the rain pouring down around her. Her half boots made sucking sounds with each step, and the only part of her that remained dry was, well, nothing. Her outing had turned quite bleak and, judging by the darkened sky, would not improve.

If she had known the weather would take such a drastic turn, she would have sent a servant to mail her letter, rather than make the journey on her own. On foot, no less. Fresh air and a bit of sunshine had lured her out of her warm, and dry, home, and she had foolishly followed its call.

The boom of thunder interrupted her thoughts, and she squinted through the rain to determine her location. She would never make it home at this rate. Granted, she had no options at present but to continue walking and to try to ignore the angry weather swirling about her.

As she trudged along, growing colder by the minute, the shape of a carriage materialized through the rain. She stepped to the side of the road and tried to arrange her sodden blonde hair into a bun, just in case the passerby stopped. Unfortunately, her hair was beyond repair, and she gave up her attempts to look presentable.

The unmarked carriage pulled to a halt as four matched bay horses pawed at the ground, chomping at their bits in annoyance. The coachman reined them in as he huddled beneath his greatcoat, not even bothering to spare her a glance. Suddenly, the coach door swung wide, revealing a gaping, dark cabin with nary a soul in sight.

She hitched up her skirts and eyed the driver once more. Rather than hop down from his perch to assist her, he continued to ignore her as if she weren't even present. After several moments, which seemed an eternity as the rain pelted her fair skin, a deep, cultured voice called from within, "Hurry up now. We do not have all day."

"Does the man have no manners?" Eleanor muttered as she attempted to pull herself up. Her dress was soaked, which made it more than double in weight and gave her added trouble as she clambered in, unassisted. She came precariously close to slipping and falling backward in the mud but caught herself in time.

Cursing under her breath, she hefted herself through the opening, finally taking her seat in the cozy conveyance. She arranged her skirts as best she could and then looked up to find the most handsome man she had ever seen staring back at her.

The pleasant warmth of the carriage blazed into an inferno as Eleanor found herself immobilized by the sight of him. Not one to feel overcome at the sight of a man, she was unprepared for the excitement of such an overwhelming attraction. He was blessed with dark brown hair and the most vivid green eyes she had ever seen set over an aquiline nose and full lips. He appeared quite tall and had very little excess weight on his lithe frame.

She mentally shook herself. Unless he was wealthy

and titled, she had no interest in him. She did not recognize him and could only assume he was one of the local gentry she had somehow failed to meet.

She hid her physical attraction with false bravado and attempted to ignore his casual, assessing look as she said, "Tell your driver to turn around. He can stop in about half a mile."

His eyes met hers again, and she was astounded at the cold indifference held there. No one ever looked at her that way. At least, no gentleman. She cocked her head to the side and looked down her nose at him, hoping to cow him with an air of superiority.

"No," he said with a dismissive flick of his hand. "I can drop you off in town, and you should be thankful for that much." The carriage rocked into motion, going in the opposite direction from which Eleanor directed, and she glared in response.

"Do you not know who I am?" Her voice was a bit shrill, not the dulcet tones she typically employed. As a lady of unparalleled beauty, Eleanor was unused to gentlemen contradicting her orders. No, all other gentlemen fawned over her in a humiliating fashion.

"Should I?" he asked, his gaze drifting over her with a look of derision as if finding it hard to believe she was someone important.

As his gaze perused her figure, Eleanor became uncomfortably aware of how she must look. When she was not soaked, she had light blonde hair that shone, blue eyes, and a much-sought-after figure. With her drenched hair hanging in a knot down her back, she must look like the most downtrodden of wenches. Even her hem was caked with mud.

She squared her shoulders and gazed back at him

without betraying the slightest bit of emotion. Despite her sodden appearance, she was still a noted beauty, and he needn't act like such a cad. "Yes, you should. I am Miss Eleanor Ashford, and you, sir, are no gentleman. Otherwise, you would turn the carriage around as bidden."

"Hmm." He tapped his chin and tilted his head to the side as if lost in thought. "It would appear I have two options. First, I could ignore you, but that almost guarantees you will pester me until we reach Rotsdale. Or I choose the second option, which almost ensures your silence." He continued to tap his chin, and she tried desperately to ignore his impertinent statement. His finger dropped, and he smirked at her. "Fine, Miss Ashford. I will have the coachman turn around. I do not believe I can endure your irritable overtures much longer."

Eleanor gasped, but he ignored her as he rapped on the ceiling of the coach. He yelled over the din of the rain. "Take us to the Ashford estate."

Every muscle in her body tensed at his words, and her hands trembled in anger. She was thoroughly annoyed with the man, but he did as she wished so she would not take him to task. The carriage slowed to a stop, began to back up, and then rocked in place as it halted. Eleanor waited for the motion to resume, but it never happened. After several moments, a knock sounded, and the coach door swung open.

The unknown gentleman rushed through the entryway before the coachman could say anything and, several minutes later, poked his head back in. "Would you prefer to wait here or walk with me to town?"

Eleanor jumped up and moved to the doorway. She

had forgotten about her soaked skirts, and as she moved, they became entangled in her legs. She threw out her arms in an attempt to grab any sort of handhold that would avail itself to her. This action proved futile as she flew out of the coach into a very solid, very warm body. Her hands gripped his arms, holding on to him in a tight grip.

The feeling of falling was not something Eleanor experienced often, nor was a man's body pressed against hers. He obviously was not prepared for her onslaught either, because her descent caused him to fall back with her, careening into the mud.

A surprised *oomph* issued from the man's mouth as she landed on him. She was acutely aware of his body beneath hers as she lay stunned and unmoving on top of him. Warm and muscular, it was not the most comfortable landing spot, both physically and emotionally. Mere contact with him sent sparks flying through her, and she needed to get distance between herself and him. Now. As she picked her head up from his chest, she blushed and tried to sit up, only to find her skirts were trapped under his legs.

"Do you mind?" he asked with a grim frown.

His warm, large hands rested on the small of her back, which added a pleasant warmth to her predicament despite the chilling rain. Judging by the puddle underneath him and the rain falling from above, he was now as sodden as she. He would have appeared frightening in his anger, except a small green frog sat beside his head and blinked at her. The image was too much for Eleanor, who couldn't help the tinkling laugh of delight from pouring forth.

Her laugh prompted his scowl to intensify, and she

smiled down at him as she said, "Oh, do calm down. You are on top of my skirts."

"What a likely excuse."

Eleanor's cheeks heated at the gentleman's accusation. The little green frog chose that moment to turn and hop away, disappearing into the downpour in mere moments. If she could, she would hop away as well. After all, the man thought she used her skirts as an excuse to lie on top of him. She attempted to remove the fabric that was trapped by jerking it out from under him in one swift motion. Her progress was minuscule, as her prone position did not allow for much movement.

Trying to pull her skirts harder, she began to slide into the mud, only to have him catch her. As his hold on her tightened, she gasped with the realization of how strong and how completely at his mercy she was. She glared at him as he waited beneath her. He did not offer any sort of aid in her plight, aside from keeping her on top of him, and judging by the light in his eyes and smile on his lips, he just might be enjoying this.

Finally, he leaned forward, allowing her to pull her skirts free. She scrambled away and he stood. The warmth of his body had kept the cold at bay, but his absence allowed the sharp wind to hit her with a startling force, and she turned back to the carriage without sending him another glance.

"Do not enter that coach. We will walk to town."

"And why can't we ride?" She swept a hand across her face, attempting to wipe the rain away. Her actions proved futile, as the rain continued to beat down in a torrent.

"We cannot ride because the back wheels are mired in the mud."

She shielded her eyes and inspected the back of the rig. Sure enough, half of the wheel had disappeared into mud. She turned back to face him and asked, "Why ever did your coachman back us into a ditch?" She searched the surrounding area for signs of the man but found none. This coachman was proving rather useless. He had failed to help her enter the carriage or remove herself from the unknown gentleman when she fell on him and had even forced them to get stuck. "Where is he anyway?"

"He is untethering the horses." His voice lowered, and he said in a mocking tone, "As for your other question, he backed us up into a ditch because a certain high-handed female demanded he change direction in the rain."

"Well, I never—"

He ignored her protestations and brought his hand up. "Really now, we should be going."

Eleanor shook her head and wiped the rain from her face. She would not walk to town when she could wait in a warm coach. She ignored him and started to climb back into the vehicle with its enticing promise of warmth. Before she could enter, a pair of strong hands encircled her waist and effectively ignited her temper.

She whirled on the stranger. "What are you doing? You have no right to lay your hands on my person." She paused in surprise when he appeared unfazed by her tirade. "My father will have your head if he finds out you treated me this way."

He opened his mouth to speak, but she spoke first as she averted her eyes from his. "I suppose it's best if Father does not know I spent time with you unchaperoned, no matter the circumstances. I have no wish to marry landed gentry." In fact, the lowest she would settle for was a baron. An earl would be ideal, but those were not so easy to come by.

A small smile played on his lips as he assessed her. If anything, this unknown gentleman was even more attractive wet. A raindrop even now worked its way down his lips, and flurries immediately overtook her stomach. It was unfair, really.

He ignored the rain as he regarded her with his alluring green eyes. "We are near to town and might as well walk the distance rather than remain here, alone."

"In case you had not realized, it is raining. I do not wish to grow ill."

A wicked smile encompassed his face as he leaned toward her. "I would hate to think how your father would respond if he knew we were unchaperoned. Why, he could demand we marry."

She blanched. The notion of sitting alone with him in close confines for an extended period of time did not sound appealing, as his gaze alone did strange things to her stomach, and the man was right. Her father would be furious if he discovered she had been alone with any man, rain or no rain. There was one other option, though.

"Might I suggest I wait here while you and your man get help?"

"You may not." He crossed his arms over his chest and shook his head. "I will not leave a young lady out here alone." He turned from her and went to the other side of the carriage before she could respond.

"Of course he would act chivalrous now." She shivered as the wind picked up. He reemerged several moments later with the coachman and horses in tow.

"I suggest you come along now," he said over his shoulder.

With an indignant little huff, Eleanor scurried to catch up to the man. How was it this gentleman could be so immune to her charms? Most men would bend over backward to please her. He was a bit of an enigma and did not look even remotely familiar to her. She sneaked a glance at him and was once again struck by how attractive he was.

She shook herself as she caught up to him. Curiosity about him would do no good. He was not a prospect for her no matter how handsome he might be. In fact, no man was a prospect unless he held a seat in parliament, which a baronet or knight did not.

He scowled up at the almost black sky, and a shiver ran down her back as he asked, "Is there a house nearby? I worry we will not make it to town."

The rain impeded their progress in a most noteworthy way. Every step she took was met with mud that seemed to propel her backward. She stopped to consider her surroundings. "I believe the vicar lives over that ridge." She pointed eastward, although nothing could be seen from their vantage point but dark furious trees, rioting in the wind.

He nodded, and they resumed their walk. After a couple of silent minutes, the gentleman started to slide and almost fell into the mud. Eleanor could not help the laughter at the sight of him, flailing to keep his balance, but she managed to suppress her reaction when he sent her a dark glance. He clearly did not appreciate the humor in the situation as she did.

They topped the ridge to find a quaint house, obscured by the rain. The rain now resembled a waterfall more than a downpour, and the promise of shelter was a welcome sight. The vicar had a daughter around Eleanor's age who would likely lend her a dry dress and make her a hot cup of tea. Renewed vigor coursed through her, and Eleanor trudged along with a bit more energy.

They reached the humble entryway, and the gentleman lifted the brass door knocker. He knocked several times, waiting with more patience between knocks than Eleanor could ever manage. On the fourth knock, he dropped his hand as the door creaked open.

"Who's there?" The door swung wide, revealing Mrs. Platts, a middle-aged lady of large girth who was married to the vicar. "Oh, it's you, Miss Ashford. Whatever are you doing in the rain?" She moved from the entryway, and Eleanor hurried in. Warmth greeted her, along with the enticing scent of fresh flowers.

They stood in a small, bright foyer. Ahead of them stretched a hallway with multiple doors on both sides and a stairwell at the end of the hall. A large wooden cross hung on the wall over beige damask wallpaper, which ran down the length of the hall. The only color in the room came from the steel-blue runner on the floor and the vase of tulips arranged on a table by the door.

"Is there someplace my coachman can take the horses, my lady?"

Mrs. Platts nodded. "Of course, there is a barn around back."

The unknown gentleman stepped to his coachman's side, whispered a few words, and then sent him around the house. He closed the door behind him, and Mrs. Platts shook her head. "You both are soaked to the bone. We must get you out of those wet clothes immediately." She cast them a sympathetic look and rushed out of the room, calling over her shoulder as she left. "Wait here. I will return with dry garments."

Nothing could compare to the thought of clean, dry clothes. Well, maybe one thing could. Eleanor had appreciated lying on top of the stranger, feeling his masculinity all around her, but a repeat of such an act was not in her realm of possibility. Not for this gentleman, whom she would never again see after this day.

"Would you care to explain who our hostess is?"

Eleanor shook herself from her silent reverie. "She is the vicar's wife, Mrs. Platts."

"And you do not believe she will have questions?"

Her brows drew together in confusion.

He must have read her expression, because he said, "You worry how your father will react if he discovers we were alone together, yet you do not care what the vicar's wife thinks? Your logic is flawed, my little water nymph."

Stairs creaked, and Mrs. Platts materialized in the hall carrying two bundles of fabric. She extended one to the gentleman and the other to Eleanor. "Excuse us, my lord. Miss Ashford and I shall go to the kitchens, while you change in the sitting room." She nodded her head to the first door to the left, and he took his leave of the ladies.

His words rang in Eleanor's ears as Mrs. Platts led her down the long hallway. Now that she was away from him, she allowed her rigid posture to deflate. Had he called her a water nymph? She shook her head. It would be completely nonsensical for him to call her that.

They entered the kitchen where someone had recently made bread, as evidenced by the flour adorning the countertops and the lingering scent of yeast. Mrs. Platts turned Eleanor away from her, pushed aside Eleanor's bedraggled hair, and proceeded to undo the laces of her gown.

"I suppose you want to know how I wound up on your doorstep with that man." Eleanor's voice trailed off, unsure if she had taken the correct approach. She really should have determined the man's name, at least.

"Has he behaved the gentleman?" Mrs. Platts asked, finishing with the laces and helping Eleanor from her sodden garments.

"Of course." Eleanor pulled a worn, dry chemise over her head and said, "I was caught in the rain on the way back from Rotsdale when I happened upon the gentleman. We came here straight away." Omitting part of the story was not a lie, right?

"Precisely what I figured." Mrs. Platts helped Eleanor into a drab gown intended for someone much shorter and said, "You know I cannot stomach gossip. Our good Lord warned against it, so if you claim all is well, I will believe it."

Eleanor's heart stuttered. Had fate finally smiled upon her this dreary day? "You mean you won't tell anyone I was here? What about your daughter? Will she?"

"Beatrice better not spread any rumors!" Her voice quieted, and she smiled, turning Eleanor to face her. "My dear daughter is not here. She and my husband are visiting parishioners today. Of course, if anyone asks what happened, I will tell them, but I would never defy God's will in such a way as to spread malicious rumors."

"Of course." Eleanor smiled. The likelihood of someone asking the vicar's wife of Eleanor's whereabouts was slim indeed.

Mrs. Platts led Eleanor out of the kitchen, stopping before the room the gentleman occupied, and called out, "Are you finished dressing, my lord?"

"Yes."

She then led Eleanor into a small parlor where the gentleman was already seated on a rugged armchair. He stood as the ladies entered, although Eleanor ignored him. Her focus was on the roaring fire which would soon dry her hair. Sitting down with her back to the flames, she unwound what was left of her chignon and combed her fingers through the tangled mess. The heat from the fire was pure heaven, and she closed her eyes.

"Do you not prefer to sit on a chair?"

Eleanor peered through her thick lashes at Mrs. Platts. She shook her head, closing her eyes once more as her damp skin warmed. "I must dry my hair. I am a bit parched, though. Go fetch some tea."

"Of course, dear." Mrs. Platts turned on her heel and left them together, alone. The door remained cracked open, and Mrs. Platts's receding footsteps echoed down the hall, until they were swallowed by silence.

"You should have asked for tea, not demanded as if she were a mere servant."

Eleanor pried her eyes open and awarded his candor with a look of open hostility. He had resumed his seat on the armchair and made himself quite comfortable, judging by the way his large frame reclined against one of the arms. His features in the candlelight were exquisite, and she suddenly found herself at a loss for words.

He coughed as she continued to stare at him. Remembering herself, she tore her gaze from his only to recall her borrowed gown was too short. Her ankles were on blatant display. She brought her feet nearer to her torso and tucked her ankles under the available fabric, but not before he noticed. His eyes watched her ankles as they moved, and now, there was a definite glint of appreciation in their green depths.

His attention was nothing new. She had thwarted numerous advances, but this was different. She almost wanted to encourage him.

"Are you friends with the vicar and his family?"

She closed her eyes once more and ignored him. The warmth of the fire had a lulling effect, and she would not waste it by conversing in a tedious manner with him.

"You must not have heard me. Are you friends with the family?" His voice was deep and soothing. While the fire was pleasant, it was more pleasant when he was silent.

Despite her desire not to, she reopened her eyes. She would answer him this once. "Hmm, no. We are acquaintances, at best." She chuckled. "In fact, I believe the vicar's daughter dislikes me."

"I am not surprised. Do you treat her as you have treated me?"

Eleanor's eyes widened and she straightened. "First of all, that was rude of you to say. Secondly, I have treated you nicely, considering."

He growled. "Considering what?"

"Your rank is inferior. Under normal

circumstances, I would not give you the time of day, much less be as kind to you as I have been."

He smiled. No, not smiled, it was more of a smirk. A dangerous smirk, as if he enjoyed her statement. "Do you think that might be why the vicar's daughter dislikes you? You have hardly endeared yourself to me, you know."

His candor was not something she could appreciate, no matter how accurate. "You assume I care for either your, or the girl's, approval. I am capable of acting perfectly enchanting. I just choose to reserve that behavior for people worthy of the effort."

He took a moment to consider her words before asking, "Do you have any friends?"

"Of course!" she said in too loud a voice. Some of her fire left her as she admitted, "At least I did, until I muddled that up. My cousin, Laura, was my best friend. We were very close."

"What happened to her?" he asked as he shifted in his seat, causing the leather on the chair to creak.

She closed her eyes and uttered a soft sigh. "She married."

"I am sorry."

Reopening her eyes, she leveled a hard stare at him. He met her gaze, and the air heated around her. Who was this man that he did not back down from her? Everyone else did, but he appeared unaffected. His reaction intrigued her, even though she did not wish to feel intrigued.

A crackle sounded from the fire, and the room brightened. Eleanor pulled her legs toward her and leaned her head against her knees. She did not care that her ankles and feet showed, or that he looked.

She would never see him again, so why not allow herself to be frank? "Growing up, she was always the perfect one. Whenever I did something wrong, Mother would ask why I could not be more like Laura. Eventually, I learned how to behave myself, but I was never as good as her."

"That sounds more like a competition than a friendship."

"Yes, I believe that describes my relationship with Laura accurately, to an extent. She was always so perfect. Everything came naturally to her." Eleanor sighed and shook her head. She spoke of matters she never told anyone, ever. "I remember how easily she learned to dance, as if it were the same as walking. I, on the other hand, had to sneak in practices so everyone would think I was just as good." She inclined her head and looked at him as the firelight played across his strong features. His eyes seemed to glow as he returned her gaze, a soft warmth in them as if he understood her.

She rushed to speak before he could say anything, to express his pity for her. "I am, of course, above reproach in all things I do."

He laughed, and his pity was replaced with humor. "I expected no less. So aside from your cousin, do you have other family?"

"Oh yes. There is my mother and father and a dear widowed aunt."

He arched an eyebrow. "And are you close to them?"

Eleanor brushed a piece of lint off her skirt and said, "No. Father has never been involved, and Mother has always held me to an impossible standard. It is hard to be close to people like that." She smiled as she reflected inward. "My aunt, on the other hand, has always acted more like a mother to me than an aunt. She is not perfect, but who is?"

She turned her attention to the fire. She should never have spoken to him in such an unguarded manner, but his eyes were compelling, and he seemed to hold genuine interest in what she had to say. Most gentlemen she knew did not want to hear her speak, much less speak about herself.

"How sad."

"Yes, I suppose it is." She smiled a wistful little smile. "But Laura was always there, and my aunt gave me plenty of fond memories to ward off the bad."

He scowled and stood from his seated position. Walking over, he bent down and took her hand in his. "You have had an unfortunate family life. Luckily, you have the chance to turn that around by having a family of your own."

Of course she would have her own family, but he was delusional if he thought hers would be any different than her own parents. Dreams were best forgotten and realities focused on with forceful determination. Just as her mother taught her to do.

He smiled in sympathy until his eyes took on a darker light, and he leaned toward her. She threw up her hand and said, "Just so you are aware, you will not be the one I build that family with."

He stood and stepped back as she lowered her hand. No, her future marriage of convenience would never allow for such a picturesque idea. Such dreams were dangerous, and she could not allow them to spread like wildfire in her mind. Not when she needed to snare a titled gentleman.

"Tell me about yourself."

He rose and returned to his seat. "I grew up in the country without much family, as my father and mother had no other children and passed away at a young age from illness. I do, however, have a couple of cousins and an uncle."

"And you are close to them?"

"I am close to one, but he is an irritating fellow."

She smiled at the fire. Her relationship with Laura was similar. "I can understand. I am sure you love your cousin very much but sometimes cannot abide him."

He nodded, and she asked, "Where is your estate?"

His expression was unreadable as he shifted in his chair. "It is in the North. I am currently visiting a friend who lives nearby. Perhaps you know Lord and Lady Gammon?"

"So you are not from here, then?" That explained why she did not recognize him. "Where in the North?"

"My estate is called Briarthorn and is near the Scottish border."

How horrid, to live so far from London. Her hair had dried a sufficient amount, so she sat up and began to secure it in a quick bun.

"Stop."

Eleanor paused, and then continued to do her hair.

"Did you not hear me?" he asked in a mesmerizing, deep voice.

"Of course I heard you. You are only five feet from me." Eleanor laughed at the absurdity of his question.

"Your hair looked lovely unbound."

Their discussion stopped as footsteps rang out in the hall. She tore her gaze from his, sucking in a breath and trying to act unaffected. His words had hardly been the most eloquent, but he had meant what he said, not what he thought she wished to hear. She studied the sea-green walls as the footsteps drew nearer.

Mrs. Platts entered the room, bearing a tea tray and sandwiches. She set them down on a table and took a seat on the settee. "Did I miss anything?"

Eleanor stood and ran a hand down her skirt to smooth it. She then took a seat in the spot next to Mrs. Platts, who was in the process of pouring tea.

"Thank you," Eleanor said with a sweet smile as she accepted a cup from her hostess.

"Of course."

Eleanor sipped her tea, welcoming the warmth of the liquid as it spread through her. The stranger remained silent in his armchair, his gaze fixed on the window near him. He stood, and Eleanor was reminded of his considerable height as he towered over the two ladies.

He turned to Mrs. Platts and bowed. "Thank you for your generosity. I believe the rain has lessened a sufficient amount, and I should be on my way. I will return the clothes once I have had them laundered."

Mrs. Platts rushed to stand, but he held a hand up and smiled at her. "Please, remain seated. I can find my way out." His smile turned mocking as he regarded Eleanor. "Do you care to know my name, at least?"

"No." She straightened and turned her gaze from his to the window furthest from the door, hoping he would understand their interactions were finished. Forever. The outdoors looked so dreary, despite all the signs of spring. Even the tulips arranged in a straight row appeared drenched. She continued to look outside as she said, "No. In fact, I would prefer to forget I had met you altogether."

Silence descended on the room, broken only by the soft sound of the door as it opened and shut.

"That was not very nice of you, young lady."

Eleanor turned back to her hostess and smiled. "How I behave toward him hardly signifies. I doubt I shall see him again." Her words were confident, but why did she feel a twinge as she said them? She took another dainty sip of her tea. His type was unsuitable for her, and she had best remember that.

Chapter 2

Logan Eastworth, the tenth Duke of Waking, guided his white stallion over a small hedge and smiled as Raphael regained his footing. He followed a tree line which appeared to stop in front of him, melding into a veritable forest. He should return, but those trees beckoned to him, to discover what lay under their canopy.

He had gone on longer and longer rides since his rainy encounter with Miss Ashford in a futile attempt to erase her from his memory. How could he though? The look she had afforded him when he complimented her hair had spoken volumes. She found him as attractive as he found her, but somehow she was under the misguided notion that he was beneath her. Granted, he had thoroughly enjoyed being beneath her the night he met her, aside from the fact that he fell into a puddle of mud, but she was misguided. His rank was the superior one. Not hers.

No one had ever treated him the way she had. Yes, she acted superior to him, but she also desired him, and it was an honest desire. Not a false desire because of his station. He could grow accustomed to the way she made him feel, as if he was the most attractive man in the world and she just waited to do his bidding. Unfortunately, that fantasy was dashed whenever she opened her mouth, but her criticisms of his supposed station did not change the look in her eyes when she beheld him.

He entered the dense forest and eyed a stream as he flew by, appreciating the way it sparkled in the sunlight that trickled through the leaves. The moment he saw Miss Ashford, he had thought of the water nymphs of legend. Her beauty could rival any Greek goddess, no less a naiad. The way her clothes had clung to her body had been alluring, to put it mildly, and then, when he had beheld her ankles…He swallowed. Ankles should not have the power to excite him, yet hers did, with extraordinary force.

She had treated him in an increasingly frustrating manner throughout the day. Somehow, she had latched onto the idea that he was landed gentry, and who was he to say different? She had not been a simpering bundle of nerves, hoping to entice him into marriage, and he had appreciated her honesty. He doubted he would have enjoyed Miss Ashford's company as much if she understood just who she had spent an unchaperoned afternoon with.

He followed his path around a bend and pulled up on his reins as another rider appeared. Excitement coursed through him as he realized he had happened upon Miss Ashford. However, she looked far from pleased to see him.

"What are you doing here?" she asked, without offering a welcoming smile.

He surveyed her as he displayed his own impeccable manners by smiling. Dressed properly and dry, she was even more appealing. Yes, she was beautiful, but she would be even more so if she would smile.

Now that he was not soaked to the bone and covered in mud, his disposition had improved. "What does it look like I am doing?"

She rolled her eyes. "Oh, obviously I can see you are riding, but why are you riding on the Ashford estate?" Her piercing blue eyes narrowed, and she said, "My father will never believe you if you claim to have ruined me."

Exhaling a breath, Logan relished the irony. He was plagued by young ladies trying to trap him into marriage all the time. This was the first instance he had been accused of attempting to capture the lady's hand, and it amused him.

He had asked Lord Gammon about Miss Ashford and been apprised of all sorts of interesting things, including her sizeable dowry. He also had learned just what he had suspected when he first met her. She was a bit of a spoiled narcissist who tempted men like a siren to her at every turn. A bit of teasing would benefit her.

"Oh, I think I can be quite convincing when I tell him how you threw yourself at me, causing both of us to tumble onto the ground. He will not be pleased to hear how you refused to get off me." He smirked. An outraged blush suffused her face, and his smirk broadened.

"That is not at all what happened!" she shrieked as she looked panicked. "Besides, you would not want to marry me. I would make you a terrible wife, especially if I were forced to live so far north." She shuddered and paled.

"With your sizeable dowry, I hardly think your compliance important." Never mind the fact that her dowry would make very little impact to his coffers. And never mind his favorite estate, Briarthorn, was one of many. Frankly, she would be delighted to hear his ducal seat was located much further south.

"All I have to do is tell my father you are a fortune hunter, and he would not believe a word you said," she gloated with a smile and a lift of her brow.

"Well, in that case, I will just have to ensure I ruin you beyond redemption before presenting my case." He could not help adding that little jab, and besides, he would love to be the one to ruin her.

"As if that would ever happen." She laughed as her blue eyes turned glacial. "I am not stupid enough to be ruined by any man before marrying him." She turned and began to ride away, but when she noticed he followed, she asked over her shoulder, "What more could you want from me?"

Their interaction was quite exhilarating. "Well, in all honesty, I am not here to talk to your father." That might just soften her thorny mien.

"So you are not interested in marrying me?" she asked with relief etched through every inch of her slight frame.

Logan was not pleased with how happy she looked, although he did not wish to marry the lady. He had his pride, and this was the first time a lady had ever told him she was uninterested in him. "You could do worse than to marry me, but no, I am not interested."

She tossed her head in response. "I may be able to marry a worse man than you, but I certainly can do better."

Having returned from the continent to finally secure his lineage, Logan had fortified himself with the knowledge he would have to marry a lady after his title.

Under different circumstances, this lady might just have been the one he chose to marry. Now, however, she would hate him when she discovered he was a duke and had tricked her. Granted, she might still decide to pursue him. Titles had that effect on women.

She urged her mare to a trot, and he caught up to her before she could get far. He grinned and said, "You know, it is considered quite rude to leave in the middle of a conversation."

"I do not see the need to mind my manners around undeserving people."

Her flippant remark almost smarted. Almost. "And that is why you have no friends."

She whipped around to face him with a glare on her face. "You have no right to speak that way to me." She sneered. "You, a gentleman barely in an acceptable social class, should watch what you say around me."

He had to fight back the urge to tell her exactly what social class he was a member of but managed to quell his reaction. Logan's response was a calculated one she would hate. He simply lifted a reproving eyebrow, turned, and rode away. He had taunted her, but he would not put up with a woman lacking in basic manners.

He had to school his features, when, after several moments, she called out, "Oh, do come back. I may have spoken too harshly."

He turned and made his way back to her with a serene look of indifference on his face. Inwardly, he gloated. How could he not? He reached her side and said, "May have? Even landed gentry have feelings, you know."

She softened and smiled at him. "Do they? Who

knew." Her smile disappeared and she eyed him. "You may accompany me on my outing."

She kicked her mare into a trot. He trailed behind and enjoyed a most fortunate view of her. Not only was her waist tiny, but her hips flared out to a lush bottom. Her riding habit was a light blue which offset her eyes and emphasized her curves despite its austere cut. No wonder she had claimed to be a renowned beauty, for today, she deserved the honor.

He tore his gaze from the delightful sway of her hips to survey the landscape around them. When he rode, he did so to enjoy the scenery, which today was deserving of his attention. Everything around them had turned green from the recent rain, and even a few wildflowers were in bloom. Trees surrounded them, except for a small clearing ahead. They entered the clearing, and a large willow came into sight.

He swung off his horse, paused to survey their location, and was struck by its loveliness. They were situated on a grassy knoll next to a ravine. A weeping willow offered shade, and several patches of grass had sprung up through the mud. The recent rains had swollen the stream in the ravine and it rushed past them, creating a pleasant song of water dancing in its frenzy. The air smelled of rain and fresh earth, with the barest hint of warmth. The scent was redolent of spring.

"What a lovely spot," Logan said as he lifted her from her mare. He followed her beneath the willow to a large rock. She sat down under the cascading branches, and his breath caught. She was a magical creature.

"This is my secret spot." Her gaze was trained on the water as it flowed past, and her voice almost sounded shy. Shyness did not seem typical of her character, and he softened toward her. Her current behavior did not fit with Lord Gammon's description. Not at all.

A strand of her blonde hair escaped from its confines and fell to her shoulder. She averted her gaze and said, "You are the first person to ever come here with me."

His hand itched to touch that tendril of hair, but he ignored the urge and asked, "Your cousin has not?"

"No."

"Why is that?"

"Sometimes I need time to myself, in a place free from scrutiny." She gave him a pointed look and smiled a wry smile. "Now would be such a time, if you had not insisted on joining me."

He barked out a laugh. Her response seemed more flirtatious than cutting and was ample reward for choosing to follow her.

She appeared surprised at his honest laugh. Surprised and appreciative, and with that look, he could not hold back from saying, "You could have let me leave."

She responded quickly, without thought. "Yes, but—" Then, she clamped her mouth shut, all humor vanishing in an instant.

"But what?" He grinned. She had betrayed a unique sparkle of personality that exhilarated him and made him want more.

Her eyes narrowed. "I suppose it doesn't matter if I tell you." With an inhale, she squared her shoulders and said, "I kind of—well, enjoy talking to you."

"Oh?" His heart beat at roughly the same rhythm Raphael's hooves made at a gallop. What was he?

Some boy to grow agog over a woman's interest?

The most charming of blushes rose to her cheeks. Her tone turned icy, which belied her words. "Yes. You listen well and are useful."

According to rumors, Miss Ashford was a shrewish young lady. Yet now she complimented him. His lips itched to smile, but he stopped them. He did not need to scare her away. "Is there anything else you would like to confide, my lady?"

"Of course not." Her words were sharp, but the most fleeting of sparks shifted through her eyes. The spark looked eerily similar to the humorous glance she afforded him earlier.

A sudden urge to see her laugh filled him. He was no jester, so a mere sparkle might have to suffice. "In the future, if you enjoy someone's company, perhaps you should be pleasant. Not so pleasant as you were on our first meeting, though. Throwing yourself on top of a gentleman gives the wrong message."

"Oh, for heaven's sake." She threw up her hands in exasperation but stopped when he grinned at her. The corners of her mouth tilted, and his heart soared. "I will take your words under advisement."

"See that you do. I should hate to see how a less chivalrous gentleman would react." At his words, her demeanor shifted to her normal look of reserve. He had lost her.

She returned her attention to the water. "What is your name?"

He needed to see her smile again, and admitting his identity would not help. He had several titles to choose from but decided to say, "My name is Logan."

"Logan suits you."

"Thank you." The rushing waters commanded her attention, and he searched for a way to win her back. Anything would suffice. "Tell me more of your aunt."

She did not turn back to him, but her voice carried to where he stood. "She was widowed at a young age. Widowed and poor. The two are an especially horrible combination as she wound up beholden to my parents." Anger laced her voice, and her hands shook. She clenched her hands into tight balls and dropped them to her sides. "Father allows her to live in a small cottage on the estate and, whenever they need her to chaperone me, trots her out as if she were chattel." She shook her head, slowly turning back to face him. Her voice grew louder, angrier. "They should have granted her a tidy income and a house of her choosing where she could have a life of her own."

Where had all that come from? Such conviction did not belong with a selfish, spoiled brat. She was chock full of surprises.

"I will see her situation changes once I wed." His brows rose in surprise, and she scowled at him. "I will, mark my words. She will live wherever she chooses, be it London, Brighton, Bath, or any other place of her liking. She will not rely on them any longer."

He remained immobile, his brain working hard to connect the woman who sat before him with the woman he thought he knew.

At his silence, she flexed her hands and lowered her gaze. "I do apologize. You hit a sore spot."

His surprise faded, and he whispered, "Don't apologize. Your intentions are noble. Far nobler than most."

She nodded slowly and exhaled a pent-up breath.

"You never told me what brought you out on your ride today."

People never questioned where he went, and he had not bothered to consider his whereabouts as he rode. "I enjoy riding and almost always engage in a ritual morning ride."

"I wish I could do the same." Her voice was as soft as a breeze, and the moment the words left her, she blushed and covered her mouth with her hand.

"What do you mean?" He leaned toward her, curious to understand what she unintentionally admitted. Her voice was quiet, but even more importantly, he wished to be near her.

"This is to be our little secret, but...I detest horses."

Trying to hide the surprise from his voice, Logan asked, "How is that possible? No one dislikes horses."

"You do not have to be so shocked by it. I just have always hated them. I am not certain why, maybe it is their size, or the fact that I have to sit atop them." She turned her face to her mare and looked at it with an impassive expression. "I might not mind them so much, but I have to ride at least once a week in order to stay in practice."

"You practice riding and dancing. How unusual," he murmured as he noted her quiet acceptance of her duties. "What else do you practice?" The thought had never occurred to him that some ladies might not excel at the ladylike activities they all engaged in. How many other ladies practiced little things like riding horses?

"I also play the pianoforte and paint, but those activities are much more enjoyable."

"Could you not just be honest about your distaste

for horses and avoid them?"

She laughed, but her laughter sounded brittle, rather than joyous. "Gentlemen do not care if a lady enjoys doing things. It is expected that all ladies ride, therefore I must ride well. Besides, honesty will never help me make an advantageous match."

Logan considered her words. Every lady in his acquaintance likely shared the same view as she, and the harsh reality was as long as a lady knew he was a duke, she would lie to him. "Why not just be yourself? Maybe some gentlemen will not like you, but others will."

"What a naïve thought. You know me better than most. Tell me, would you be interested despite my imperfections?" Her eyes were on his, and he could read the emotion in them. It was as if she willed him to contradict her, to tell her how wrong she was.

Logan took a step forward and kneeled at her side despite the soiled earth. The vulnerability on her face defied reason, and he fought the urge to pull her to him, to give her the comfort she required. How could she believe gentlemen would not like her for herself?

From what he had seen so far, he could do much worse than marry a woman such as Miss Ashford. He could imagine her carefree, unhindered by the expectations society placed on her. She might smile and say more of the kind, unbidden words she admitted to him. Then there was her very obvious love for her aunt. He had never witnessed such loyalty. How would it feel to inspire such devotion? Why, he would give most anything to have her love.

He sucked in a breath at the thought. Why not just pursue her instead of the other title-hungry maidens he would find in London? Imagine if he could make her fall in love with him, the unknown landed gentry, as opposed to the duke? Hiding his identity would not be easy, but if he could convince her to marry him without disclosing his title, he would find a woman he might cherish and befriend, one that he would also enjoy bedding. How could he possibly do better than that?

His mind made up, Logan focused his attention back on Miss Ashford. "What is your given name?" he asked as he searched her eyes.

"Eleanor."

"Eleanor." He paused to consider the sound of her name on his tongue and decided he quite liked it. "Eleanor, do you believe in love?"

She scoffed, and the vulnerability faded from her face. "Of course not. Love is an idiotic made-up emotion for the weak." She smirked. "My cousin married for love, but I remain unconvinced."

Well, that hindered his plans. He would just have to convince her to believe. "I have concluded love does exist. In fact, I believe if you were to be yourself, you could find a man to love you for you. In answer to your question, yes, I would be interested. Your quirks are trivial and rather endearing." Her face softened into an inviting smile, and he once again thought of a water nymph. She looked so much different when presentable, yet judging by her favored location to visit, she held an affinity for water. He added on a whisper as he kneeled by her side, "My dear water nymph."

****

Eleanor struggled to comprehend what he just said. Not only was his presence enough to eradicate all rational thought, but his nearness prompted her thoughts to veer toward sinful things such as kissing him. With a start, she realized he had stopped talking and was looking at her as if he wanted to eat her. Her stomach lurched in anticipation. No rational gentleman stared at a lady and then called her a water nymph. Before she could ask if he'd gone daft, he brought his lips to hers, which silenced her worries about his sanity and all other thoughts as well.

A shiver ran over her skin as she understood her sinful thoughts had been returned. His bold lips felt magical on her, as if he knew precisely how to kiss her. This interaction felt different from any she had experienced before. His lips were like silken caresses against hers, rather than the indifferent kiss of an unwanted suitor. Not only was his touch something of an elixir, but the knowledge that he found her true personality to be interesting filled her heart with lightness. She knew she would never act like herself around others, but his validation acted as a balm to her spirit.

Could this sort of feeling ever exist with another man? Her errant thoughts fled as his hands crept around to pull her closer to him. She sighed into him and placed her hand on his neck to ensure the embrace continued. His kiss ignited a fire within her, one that should have scared her but instead seemed to awaken desires she never knew existed. She wanted this moment to continue. No matter his rank or unsuitability, she longed for the caress of a gentleman with humor-filled eyes and a quick wit. One who understood her.

With a final caress, he halted the kiss. Keen disappointment engulfed her despite her sensible realization that it should end. Must end. Such traits remained unimportant in comparison to wealth and a title.

No, she had best remember herself. She stood and brought her emotions under control. His hand reached out to catch hers in his, and she pulled it away with a frown of disapproval. "Control yourself. No woman wants to be accosted in such a manner."

Logan smirked and stood to tower over her. "I think you welcomed my advances very much. I would prove it if you ask."

Eleanor glared at him and took a step back. "That is unnecessary. I already know I did not appreciate the first example." Besides, even if she had enjoyed it, it would be inadvisable for her to allow another kiss to transpire. His smirk remained glued to his handsome face, and she said, "Oh, stop it. You think much too highly of yourself."

He chuckled in response and took a step closer. Eleanor, naturally, took another step back until he reached out and pulled her to him in a rough embrace. Incensed, Eleanor asked, "Who do you think you are? There is never an acceptable time for you to behave so impudently toward me!"

His arm imprisoned her as he smiled down on her. "Isn't there? Would it have been preferable to fall into the ravine?"

She swung her head around to find they stood mere steps from the rushing waters. She gulped and turned to face him. Obviously, it was best to stay away from the ravine, but she would not concede his point. "Yes. It would have been much more desirable."

He threw his head back and laughed. She was not

sure why he found her so humorous, but she knew she had to get away from him. Now. Even the scent of him was enough to drive her to distraction, and distraction was not something she needed in her life. Her added glower of disapproval only elicited another chuckle from Logan, which did not exactly soothe her temper. "Get off me." She bristled while shoving his arms away from her. Not about to try backing up again, she stared up at him with a raised brow.

"May I help you with something?" Logan asked in mock innocence.

"You can move aside." She tapped her foot as he remained rooted in his position. "Any time now."

"You mean to tell me you do not wish to take a swim in the ravine?"

His gloating tone was enough to send her over the edge, and she could tell he knew it. If she wasn't such a lady, she would have hit him by now. She inhaled a calming breath and managed to say, "No, I do not."

"Ah." He acted surprised by her revelation and leaned in to murmur in her ear, "You seem angry, and you know what they say about anger. It is simply one step away from passion."

Eleanor shrieked and pushed him, despite her resolve to act like a lady. He chuckled and stepped back, which allowed her to depart from her location between him and the ravine. "Now, if you will excuse me," she said, moving to her horse with alacrity.

"Aren't we in a hurry? Are you afraid you will be unable to resist me if you stay, Nell?"

"Excuse me?" She turned to him and planted her hands on her hips. While some people used the nickname Nell for Eleanor, it was not a name she employed.

He shook his head. "Hmm. Maybe Nellie?"

Her lips parted, and she shook her head. Nellie was also unacceptable. "My name is Eleanor."

His ensuing smile disarmed her and her heart began to beat in staccato. "No, that one won't suit you either." He scratched his head and then smiled again as he held up his index finger. "Ellie."

"My name is Eleanor," she reiterated with a frown. Normally, she did not make such expressions, but drastic times called for drastic measures.

He walked up to her, and she began to back away. He was so very male, and that alone made it difficult to breathe around him.

"No, I think you are much more of an Ellie."

He placed his hands on her waist, and she tensed. "What are you doing?"

He raised his brow and asked, "Did you not wish to mount your horse?"

"Of course I did."

His hands tightened on her waist, and before she could say anything else, he swung her up on her mare. Once seated with her limbs properly arranged on her sidesaddle, she looked down on him and said, "Thank you. In the future, if you ever see me again, my name is Eleanor."

He chuckled, but before she could depart, asked, "Will you attend the Gammon soiree?"

"Yes. Mother demands it." In fact, her mother had warned her against faking an illness. No excuse would work, even a real one.

"Then I shall see you there."

She steered her mare away from her favorite spot

and, more importantly, him. She waited until she rounded a bend in the trail, and then brought her hand to her lips. That kiss had been magical, almost to the point she would have welcomed a second. If only he held a more acceptable rank. He was just the sort that she could dream of marrying.

****

The ride back to Lord Gammon's estate proved enjoyable for Logan. Every time he ran into Ellie, he was left with a pleasant, albeit unsettled, feeling, and the more he thought of his decision to marry her, the lighter his mood grew.

As a duke, there were certain things he required in a duchess. Impeccable lineage was a necessity, which he was positive Ellie possessed. Intelligence and decorum were two other important traits that seemed innate to the lady. Additionally, if there were any task she did not excel at, he was sure she would practice until she mastered it, although he doubted he would force her to participate in any activity she hated.

Logan's arrival at Lord Gammon's ample stables halted his musings, and he went in search of his friends. Luncheon had just been served when he entered the house, and his short search ended as he crossed the threshold into the dining room.

A simple spread lay in wait on the large mahogany table. Across the room, a sideboard in the same style as the table held a vase with fragrant lilac. The room would have been quite dark with its blue walls, except for the wall of windows which looked out on the gardens behind the house.

"Your Grace." Lady Opal Gammon stood and curtsied when she noticed his arrival. With dark brown hair and hazel eyes, she held an almost exotic beauty. Her skin was a shade darker than the typical Englishwoman's, but it served to make her more beautiful. She smiled a welcoming smile and indicated he should take a seat.

"Oh, do sit down, Opal. You needn't stand on my account." Nodding to Lord Reuben Gammon, Logan sat in a chair across from the couple. Reuben did not share many characteristics with his wife. With light brown hair and blue eyes, he was clearly English. "I have some interesting news for both of you, and an unusual request."

Lord and Lady Gammon exchanged a worried glance before Reuben asked, "Does it have something to do with Miss Ashford?"

Logan helped himself to some blood pudding and said, "Why yes. I ran into her again and decided she would make as good a duchess as any other, so why not end my search here? She believes I am only minor gentry and will hardly give me the time of day, but I—"

Logan frowned as Opal interrupted him with an excited clap of her hands. "You mean she still is unaware that you are a duke?"

With anyone else, Logan would have rebuked her for the interruption, but he had a soft spot for Opal. "Yes, which is why I have an unusual request. At the gathering, we must hide my title from Miss Ashford. I have the chance to woo her as someone other than a duke, and I will not allow this opportunity to pass me by."

Reuben exhaled. "I just wish you would choose any other lady. I thought I told you enough of her character to dissuade you from pursuing her. Poor Opal almost has a fit of the vapors every time they are together."

Logan sent Opal a skeptical look and was relieved to see a twinkle in her eye as she shook her head no. Reuben had a way of exaggerating the situation and had done so once more. Logan coughed and took a sip of his tea. "Be that as it may, she is overall a good person. One that I find appealing."

Reuben nodded as he picked up his water goblet. "That may be true, but you are playing with fire. For all we know, Miss Ashford already knows you are a duke and is just waiting for the perfect moment to claim you ruined her."

"Oh, believe me, she does not know. Honestly, I believe Miss Ashford is just a lonely woman, and once she realizes she is in love with me, will forget all about titles and beg to be mine. As a baronet or knight, of course."

Opal scoffed. "Sure she will. That outcome seems as likely as her remaining unmarried and ending up a spinster. I wish you luck."

"Laugh all you want," Logan said, "but I play to win. When I say Miss Ashford will agree to marry me without the knowledge that I am a duke, I guarantee it will happen, contingent on your cooperation, of course. Now, here is the plan." Logan informed them of his strategy for the party and reveled in the challenge it presented. The mere thought of acting as someone other than a duke was exhilarating. This soiree would be most promising, indeed.

Chapter 3

The night of the ball was upon them, much to Eleanor's dismay. While she was not one to miss a ball in London, these country dances did not compare. Overall, they were a tremendous waste of energy. Of course, her mother disagreed. As a result, Eleanor sat in her room as her new lady's maid worked on her hair.

"It needs to be curlier, Olive," Eleanor said, growing more and more frustrated with her maid. Ever since her cousin Laura had married and lured away their shared maid, Eleanor had worked hard to train a new one to see to her needs. This one showed promise but was not yet proficient.

"It's Olivia, my lady," the maid corrected, as she tugged a little too hard on a section of Eleanor's hair.

"Ouch." Eleanor winced, feeling a headache creeping in at the base of her skull.

The maid looked frightened but continued with her work. Eleanor was not worried about her hair for this night's events, but when the season was back in full swing she would care a great deal. On second thought, perhaps it did matter how she looked tonight. There was one certain gentleman who had never seen her looking her best. She swore she did not seek to impress him. Rather, she wanted him to be as attracted to her as she was to him. It was only fair.

Her thoughts drifted to their ride a couple of days

past. He had a knack for infiltrating her defenses and forcing her to share a part of her she had never shared with anyone. Feeling vulnerable around a man was not ideal, but somehow he had made it seem normal. And then there was that kiss. Eleanor knew she would never forget the moment their lips met under her weeping willow. The passion his kiss ignited within her had been intense and left her reeling.

Eleanor sighed. If only Logan was in possession of a title. She glanced at her reflection in the mirror and was pleased by what she saw. The maid had ended up doing a fine job on her hair and even allowed a spare strand to escape along the side of her neck, just as Eleanor liked.

As she rose from her seat, she noted with pleasure how her gown did not detract from her beauty. She had chosen a plain white gown, in the latest fashion that emphasized her impeccable figure. She exited her room and drifted down to the foyer. After a couple of minutes, her mother and father arrived, and they made their way into the carriage.

"Eleanor, dear, where is your jewelry?" her mother asked. Lady Ashford looked lovely in this season's latest fashion, complete with large sapphires on her ears and around her neck. Eleanor had seen her mother wear less finery to a ball in London the previous year.

"Jewelry would not have looked right with this gown. I could remain here at home if it is too embarrassing for you," she said, hoping her mother might change her mind and allow Eleanor to avoid the ball.

"Do not be ridiculous." Her voice was reproachful, although no emotion showed on her perfect face. At a young age, Eleanor had found it fascinating how her mother never showed expressions. Now, she understood it was to deter any wrinkles or lines from forming.

The rest of the short carriage ride was silent, with only Lord Ashford's declaration of disgust with how late they were when he glanced at the carriage clock. He would spend the evening in the cardroom until he was summoned by the ladies to return home, just as he did at every event.

The Gammon manse loomed before them, well-lit and inviting. Eleanor was surprised to see the number in attendance as they entered the house. She had not realized there were this many people of acceptable status in the area. Lord and Lady Gammon greeted them, and Eleanor made her way to the refreshments, in dire need of some champagne to soften the evening.

Having downed a glass, Eleanor felt much better until she heard the annoying voice of the vicar's daughter, Beatrice. She turned to face the girl and surveyed her with a cool look of disdain. Beatrice was a trifle shorter than Eleanor, with dark brown hair and brown eyes. She was pretty enough, but the calculating look in her eye detracted from her looks and made her appear almost catlike.

Beatrice smirked as she said, "How is it you're here? I had heard you were not allowed at public functions anymore."

The gossips had not been kind to Eleanor when she left at the beginning of the current season. Certain rumors had been bandied about, and all were untrue. Some people thought she was enceinte, while others claimed she was ruined or a shame to her family. What else should one expect when a lady abruptly departs

London after a lengthy courtship with an earl? People were wont to talk.

And now that gossip had followed her, even here. "I was invited." Eleanor's lips curled into a sneer as her eyes roved over Beatrice's gown. "Pray don't tell me that is your *best* dress. Why, it looks like something a milkmaid would wear." She made sure to follow that statement with a look of pity.

An intense flash of hatred appeared in Beatrice's eyes. "Of course I have better dresses." Eleanor quirked an eyebrow in disbelief as Beatrice dropped her gaze under a false pretense of modesty. "But I chose to wear a less showy dress so I would not outshine those less fortunate than I. You should have shown consideration and done the same."

A general hush had fallen amongst the crowd around them. Beatrice continued on her bitter tirade despite the fact that they caused a scene. "I hear there are a lot of things you should have done differently, such as avoiding casting aspersions on your own cousin's parentage and insulting an earl by thinking him a servant."

Eleanor's ears burned at this point. She should not have responded to Beatrice's comment, but she was not about to turn the other cheek rather than stand up for herself. She opened her mouth to impart a scathing retort when Logan broke through the crowd. He hurried to her side and whispered, "Ah, Miss Ashford. I believe you promised to stroll with me." His strong hand took hold of her elbow, and he guided her away.

"Thank you," Eleanor whispered, blindly allowing him to guide her to the balcony. She was enraged and disappointed in herself. She should not have allowed her temper to rule her tongue as she had. She had sworn she would rein in her temper ever since her debacle in London, but she had failed.

They entered the balcony, stopping in front of the open doors so curious onlookers could still see them. She did not need to be compromised tonight. She exhaled a sigh of relief at escaping the confines of the ballroom. The moon hung low, which gave them plenty of light to see each other with. She turned to the railing and allowed her frustration to show as she said, "I should not have said those things."

"Which ones?" he asked mockingly as he joined her next to the railing.

She glared at him. "Truth be told, all those things, even the ones she accused me of." She laughed as she turned to look at the gardens spread out below them and said, "The earl incident was an accident though. I had drunk a bit too much sherry, and the earl was wearing the exact same shade of red as the footmen. I swear they looked identical." She shook her head and smiled. "It was an honest mistake that I took him for a footman, but Mother decided that was the last straw and made me take a break from the season by adjourning to the country."

"I see. What about the other accusation? I thought you were friends with your cousin."

Eleanor sighed and allowed her shoulders to droop. She was not sure why she answered his questions, other than he had a way of putting her at ease. She felt she could trust him. "That is a bit of a longer story, but I will try to sum it up for you. I had been interested in an earl but realized he was enamored with a different lady. I concocted a plan to separate the two but decided against going through with my plan. Then, in a fit of temper, I cast doubts on the other lady's lineage. It was shameful, and I regretted my words immediately. My cousin was at the scene and intervened, making it appear that my accusation was preposterous and making it unclear who I even spoke of." Eleanor smiled in certainty that he would condemn her for her actions and said, "Now, my cousin is married to the lady's brother. Laura refuses to speak to me, and I have been sentenced to time in the country."

His gaze bore into hers, and she trembled at the intensity in his smoldering eyes. "But you planned on telling the world of this lady's secret?"

"Originally, yes." She stared down at her gloved hand which gripped the rail. "I changed my mind and decided not to say anything. Unfortunately, I spoke about it anyway." For some reason, it was important to her that he hold a positive view of her, so she added, "I wish I could go back and change what I have done. I make that wish every day, and every week I write a letter of apology to Laura."

"I see." He regarded her and Eleanor fought the urge to squirm. "What about the girl whose name you sullied?"

She had spent a good amount of time dwelling on the wrong she committed against Miss Farris, and if anyone else had asked her the question Logan asked, she would have laughed in his face. Logan was different though. He did not circulate in her regular set, but it was more than that. She could trust him to not spread gossip about her, and if she never saw him again, so be it. "I fully intend to make whatever reparations I can when I return to London."

He continued to assess her until he nodded his head. "Very well."

"Very well what?" She did not appreciate the fact that she had poured her heart out to him and all he did was ask a few questions and end the discussion. He could respond with more than that.

He raised an eyebrow at her. "Very well, I believe you wish to make amends. Is there something else I should have said?"

No exact words came to mind, so she shook her head. Infernal man.

"Well, if it helps, you look ravishing."

Her heart began to beat a loud cadence, and she smiled at him. Was this how other women felt when they spoke to gentlemen? If so, she could now sympathize with them. "Thank you, and thank you again for rescuing me from that scene." His very masculine scent wafted to her, and she inhaled the aroma. There was much to like about Logan, from his picturesque good looks, to his personality, and evidently his scent, as well. Why couldn't the titled, available gentlemen possess the same qualities?

She ought not feel this level of attraction for someone so far beneath her standards. Yet here she stood, wanting nothing more than to be swept off her feet by him. Even if she had wanted to make an exception for him and consider him a viable marriage candidate, her mother would never allow it.

Lady Ashford had held high marriage aspirations for Eleanor since Eleanor could remember. Every dance class and deportment lesson had been tailored to prepare her for a successful marriage. As a result, Eleanor knew she would marry well. She had to.

Such a notion had been simple and uncomplicated, until now. No gentleman had managed to elicit any feelings of attraction from her, except for this man before her, and what a difference attraction could make on one's resolve. She almost scowled but caught herself in time. He had not proposed marriage to her, only flirted with her on occasion. There was nothing to worry about.

She focused her attention back on Logan and asked, "So, why are you being so nice to me?"

Logan leveled his gaze at her and, without batting an eye, said, "I plan to marry you."

Eleanor froze as the words hit her. He couldn't mean that. She began to laugh when the knowledge sank in that he was, in fact, serious. His attentions would never do, and he needed to realize it. Yes, he could not be hers, even if her heart sank at the thought.

She shook her head and averted her gaze. "You know I will only marry a man with a title."

"You say that now, but after I make you fall in love with me, you will change your mind."

Her gaze swung back to him. He was so conceited. "I do not believe in love."

Undeterred, he leaned in and tilted her face so their lips were mere inches apart. His green eyes transfixed her, and she almost leaned into him but caught herself in time. He chuckled and released her. "I do believe you are halfway in love with me already."

Eleanor swayed as he pulled away and managed to tear her gaze from his. The green of his eyes was unusual and appeared almost like grass after a rain. They were bright but contained specks of something darker. Dangerous. She was drawn to him, despite her best efforts, and would have remained immobile except a small breeze blew a strand of hair across her face. She blinked and became aware of the sound of ballroom music playing.

His hand caught hers, and she returned her attention to him as he said, "I will make you admit your love for me. Just wait."

The magic of the moment was gone, and a tide of annoyance overtook her. As she took a step away from him, a flicker of movement caught her eye. A couple glided forward but stopped when they caught sight of her and Logan; then they retreated back to the ballroom.

She was unsure of why the couple left but chose to focus on her rant against Logan. "Your ego knows no bounds. You may be possessed of incredibly good looks, but I can assure you, a titled plain man will make you appear ugly in comparison."

He offered her a lazy smile. "Even the earl dressed like a footman? Somehow, I think not."

"I told you that was an accident." She tapped her foot and asked, "Why in heaven's name should I want to marry you out of all the potential good matches? Are you outlandishly rich or something?"

His lips twitched, and he said, "You will want to marry me because you will fall in love with me. You may not believe me now, but you shall see."

He had a way of charming her, but Eleanor knew he was wrong. She would not be swayed, no matter what. "I will love you the same day I love horses."

He laughed in response and allowed his gaze to drift over her. "Would you care to place a wager?"

"Of course I would."

He smiled as a predatory gleam entered his eyes.

"We shall agree that if you fall in love with me, you will marry me and live in the far corners of England."

She raised an eyebrow and met his challenge without flinching. "And when I do not fall for you?"

"Then you may have a favor of your choosing."

With a nod, she held out her hand. "Very well, I accept your wager."

He took her hand in his and smiled. "Well then, my water nymph, will you be in residence at the Ashford estate for the foreseeable future?"

She extricated her hand from his, despite her desire to keep touching him, and asked with a laugh, "Why do you keep calling me a water nymph? It is unusual."

"When I first met you, you emerged from the water to lure me in with your enchanting, surreal ways. Only a creature from legend would be able to do that, and you, my dear, are that creature."

"Hmm." As far as compliments went, this one was unique. She turned away from him and placed a hand on the cold stone wall. The granite was cooling to her overly hot skin. Strange, she had not been warm when they first ventured outside into the chilly evening air.

She avoided his comment by returning to his previous question. "I cannot say how long I will stay at the estate. Mother wants me to run into this mysterious Duke of Waking. If we hear he is in London, then we may return much sooner than expected. I had heard he was supposed to be here tonight but so far have not seen him."

"Hmm. I do believe chasing after this duke would be rather futile."

Eleanor turned to him and asked, "What do you mean by that? You should know very few ladies can compete with me in most things."

"Oh, I do not doubt that, but I happen to be a very close friend to His Grace and know he does not like to be chased by women."

"Well, I never!" Eleanor exclaimed, annoyed at his insinuation that she would be so common. "I will have you know that I do not chase men, at least not in a way that they would notice. Besides, I do not believe you are friends with him. Why would a duke be friends with you? What are you, anyway? A knight? A baronet?"

"I am many things, but a baronet is one of them." He smiled and said, "His Grace, Lord Gammon, and I are all very close friends. In fact, we are going to visit him at his seat, Waking Hall, in two weeks. I am sure I could conjure up an invitation for you. Lady Gammon shall join us, so you would be chaperoned."

"Maybe you do have your uses." She smiled up at him through her lashes. "Tell me about the duke then. What does he look like?" Her curiosity was aroused. The most she had heard was the duke was handsome and rich.

His eyes twinkled as he said, "Well, he is similar in build to me, and his hair is almost the same color. In fact, many people confuse the two of us. You would not believe the number of people that have called me Your Grace tonight."

That explained why the couple had left the balcony. If the duke was even half as handsome as Logan, then she would be very lucky as she was having a hard time dragging her eyes away from him. "I will bring my own chaperone to this gathering, if, in fact, you can secure an invitation."

Logan shrugged his shoulder. "Very well, meet me

at your willow at noon in two days, and I will give you the details."

Eleanor nodded. She was ready to return to the ballroom. Logan acted the consummate gentleman as he escorted her back to her previous position at the refreshment table and then left to engage in a bit of cards.

Once again available, Eleanor was set upon by several young men. None were appropriate suitors for her, but she would not begrudge them her dazzling smile or charming wit simply because of their unfortunate circumstances. The dances were all country reels, but everyone at the assembly seemed to enjoy themselves, and even Eleanor appreciated the exercise.

Logan never returned to the ballroom, although Eleanor swore to herself she did not watch for him. She also would never admit that she longed for her ride with him in two days. That, in itself, was unusual. She never desired to ride a horse.

As Eleanor began to tire, she took a break near the refreshment table. Beatrice was once again shooting Eleanor reproving glances as she had done throughout the evening. Eleanor snubbed Beatrice by turning her back on the girl and considered what Logan had said about her lack of friends. If all women were like Beatrice, then Eleanor would be much happier friendless.

"Are you enjoying yourself?"

Eleanor turned to see Lady Gammon standing next to her with a pleasant smile. Eleanor had always thought Lady Gammon was quite a beauty but in a rather exotic way. If the gossips were to be believed, Lady Gammon had some Spanish blood in her, which would explain the dark complexion and hair. Eleanor dipped a perfect curtsy and said, "Why yes, Lady Gammon. Your event has turned out to be quite charming."

Lady Gammon watched the dancers float by and chuckled. "Ah. I imagine you would never call a ball in London charming, but in the country, it is perfectly acceptable."

Eleanor's cheeks heated, and she tried to remedy her error by saying, "I meant that as a compliment. I have enjoyed myself, you know."

"Of course, I knew you had meant to compliment my little party, but I could not resist teasing you a bit. Tell me, is your enjoyment due to a certain gentleman?"

"Of course not," Eleanor responded a little too quickly.

"Logan apprised me of his interest in you, so you needn't act so shy about it."

"I am not acting at all, my lady. I view him as a friend and nothing more. I would say I am interested in a different friend of yours."

"Who I imagine is the Duke of Waking." Lady Gammon paused to snatch a glass of lemonade from a passing footman. She sipped her drink as she surveyed the crowd before her and said, "Aside from the title, what sets the duke above Logan?"

Eleanor also took a sip of her beverage. "Truthfully, I have not met the duke." She giggled at how absurd she must sound. Most women did not plan to marry a man they had not met. "I do think it is amusing how similar the two are in looks though. Logan warned me about that, and sure enough, one gentleman commented on the duke's attention toward me. Of course, I corrected his erroneous identification."

The revelation brought a soft laugh from Lady Gammon. "How extraordinary. Somehow, everyone in attendance tonight is under the impression this ball was thrown for the Duke of Waking, and he is not even here. Logan's presence has everyone confused." She paused to smile at a passing guest before returning her attention back to Eleanor. "What are you doing tomorrow afternoon? I insist you visit me for some tea. Unless, of course, you are otherwise engaged."

"That would be lovely." Eleanor smiled, unused to such invitations from ladies without a hidden motive. She imagined Lady Gammon had some secret reason to invite her, but she would keep an open mind in hopes of purer motives.

Having bade each other a pleasant evening, the two ladies parted ways, and soon Eleanor was gathering her shawl around her in preparation to depart. The night had turned out to be rather enjoyable, and she was excited for her outing to visit Lady Gammon. Naturally, her mother would encourage the visit. Friendship with a countess was never bad for one's social standing.

Eleanor and her mother entered the carriage as the orchestra concluded a reel. Her father would return later, when all the card games ceased for the evening. The footman closed the door, and Eleanor settled into her soft cushioned seat.

"What a marvelous night!"

Eleanor's spine went rigid as she sat up with a start. "You think so?"

"Of course." Her mother *tsk*ed and speared her with a look of disapproval. "The duke spoke with you, at length, on the balcony."

"That was not the duke, Mother." Eleanor held her breath, waiting for the stern upbraiding she would receive.

Lady Ashford's brows drew together in confusion. "Then who was that gentleman?"

"No one." Eleanor exhaled the words even as a sense of wrongness froze her heart. He was more than no one, even if he was not the duke.

"You mean to tell me you spared that insignificant cretin your undivided attention?"

Her mother's eyes turned glacial, and Eleanor pulled her mask of indifference over her face. She had learned long ago to numb herself to her mother's words.

"What if the duke had seen you with him and received the wrong impression? No member of the peerage will wed a lady who might make him a cuckold, and he might have concluded you would."

Eleanor knew all of this and did not need to hear it again. She turned her gaze to the window, even though the moonlight lit very little. When her mother paused to draw breath, she whispered, "I understand. I will not misbehave again."

"See that you do not. I should hate to completely remove you from society."

Eleanor could not marry well if that happened, and Eleanor ignored the threat. Her family would stop at nothing to marry her off. She swung her gaze back to her mother and smiled. "Lady Gammon has invited me for tea tomorrow."

"Oh?" Her mother's voice still held a cool note but would warm with the turn in conversation.

"Yes. I shall take tea with a countess, so my trip to the balcony must not have done too much damage."

Slowly, Eleanor's mother nodded her head. "Yes. That will do nicely."

Of course it would. Friendship with a countess never harmed one's social standing. Her mother's disapproval was stymied, which allowed Eleanor to settle back into the cushions for the remainder of the trip home. Someday, she would depart all of this and be mistress to her own home. She could ignore her mother and all the expectations placed on her and just be.

Chapter 4

Eleanor once again found herself in her carriage, riding the short distance to the Gammon estate. Her stomach was a bit off, and the motion of the carriage did not help. She might see Logan today, whether she wished to or not.

She should not desire to see him, though. Although judging by her queasy abdomen, she did. For the feeling in her belly was one of excitement rather than abhorrence. Matters would be simpler if she did not want to see him, though.

Imagine if she married Logan. She scowled at the thought. A lack of title would cause many doors in society to close to her, and she would be forced to circulate in a lesser tier. If Eleanor wanted to remain in the upper echelons of the *ton*, then she had to marry well, and a baronet did not qualify as such.

The carriage pulled to a halt, and Eleanor emerged to the welcoming sight of the large manor. Such a house was what she desired, or perhaps several. A duke would have many houses far grander than this.

She entered and was directed to a small sitting room, located just off the foyer, where Lady Gammon sat waiting. "Good afternoon, my lady," Eleanor said with a polite smile and curtsy.

"Miss Ashford, how good of you to join me." She indicated a nearby chair with a gentle wave of her hand.

Eleanor took a seat in the indicated chair and examined her surroundings. The room was richly decorated in cream and burgundy. Very tastefully done, while not too feminine. "I love the room," Eleanor said, although if this was her sitting room there would be more pink.

"Why, thank you. I cannot abide rooms done in pink. Just because I am a woman does not mean I have to love the color. Also, if I ever want my husband to join me for tea, I must have a room he can feel comfortable in."

Eleanor's hand twitched at Lady Gammon's words. "You mean you actually spend time with Lord Gammon?" Such behavior was most unusual in the *ton*.

Lady Gammon took a sip of her tea and nodded. "Of course. I know it is not fashionable, but I like my husband."

"How fortunate for you. I imagine most ladies either get companionship or status through marriage, not both."

"That is possible, but I never was concerned about titles. I fell in love with Reuben for himself. The title was just a bonus."

Eleanor leaned forward, trying to hide the disbelief from her voice as she said, "You mean to tell me his title had no effect on you? If he had been a mere mister, I am sure things would be different, and you would not have married him."

"Actually, this may come as a surprise to you, but his title was a bit of a deterrent to me. You know I am the granddaughter of a duke, but did you know my father is a simple vicar?" She laughed as her comment elicited a small gasp from Eleanor. "When my grandfather gave me a season, I vowed to marry for love. My preference was to find a man to make me happy. One with a house in the country. I did not want to marry a peer, as that would only complicate my life. Unfortunately, I fell for Reuben and have been defying societal conventions ever since." She smiled and indicated her outdated dress. "I used to be concerned with fashion and appearing just so, but I realized no one important to me cares about my clothing. Yes, people may think I am odd, but I do and wear what makes me happy."

Lady Gammon was known for her eccentric ways, but Eleanor had never expected to hear an explanation for why. "But what does Lord Gammon think? You are a reflection of him, so does he not prefer you to dress fashionably?"

Lady Gammon cocked her head and surveyed Eleanor with a puzzled look. "What sort of gentleman are you trying to marry? To me, the worthwhile ones do not keep up with ladies' fashions. Reuben thinks I look good in the dresses I wear, and that is what matters to him."

"There are plenty of gentlemen that care about fashion."

"Yes, but are they gentlemen that actually interest you?"

Eleanor nodded. The lady had a point. It was one thing to care if a lady looked attractive, it was quite another to say whether she was in the height of fashion or not. "So, what is your purpose in telling me this?"

The countess contemplated the liquid in her teacup before saying, "I know your mother. Not saying there is anything wrong with her, but her priorities have always been superficial, at best. My guess is you have never heard a lady can be desirous of other things than wealth or status."

Eleanor plastered a smile on her face and tried to hide her annoyance that Lady Gammon assumed such things about her mother, no matter how true. Lady Ashford had always had the best of intentions for her daughter. Marriage was, after all, essential to a lady's well-being, and if Eleanor ever questioned that notion, she only had to look at her aunt. Mrs. Westfield had been widowed at a young age. She was left with nothing and had to rely on family to support her.

Lady Gammon spoke before Eleanor could form a reply. "Oh, you needn't appear so affronted. I am not intending to insult you or your mother. I am simply trying to explain why Logan is an acceptable suitor for you." She laughed and settled her teacup on the table in front of her.

Eleanor's eyes narrowed at the countess's laugh. The lady did seem to behave unpredictably at times. "What you say might be true for you, but I doubt I could be happy without a titled gentleman."

"That may be," Lady Gammon said as she glanced at a clock on the mantel and rose from her chair. "Please join me on a stroll, Miss Ashford."

Eleanor followed her out the door and was unsurprised when their short walk down the main hallway ended in the library where Lord Gammon and Logan happened to be. Lady Gammon's eyes twinkled as she feigned surprise. "How fortuitous to find you both here."

"Where else would you find us at this time of day, my dear?" Lord Gammon asked as he smiled at his wife.

Eleanor could only shake her head. Lady Gammon's attempt at matchmaking was transparent, at best.

Lady Gammon went to her husband's side and whispered something in his ear. He grinned and pointedly looked to Logan. "Opal desires to take a stroll. Would you two care to join us?"

Logan turned his gaze on Eleanor and quirked his brow. "Well, my lady?"

"I would love to…" She paused midsentence and tried to make it seem as though a random thought popped into her mind. "Oh! I just remembered I must hurry home for something." She turned to Lady Gammon and thanked her for her hospitality. Then, she departed the room.

She hurried down the hall, her feet making the softest of whispers on the fine damask rugs. She could feel him draw nearer, the anticipation building within her to the point she almost whirled around to check his location. The foyer lay just beyond the next hall, and an indubitable knowledge encompassed her. She would never reach it in time, not before he caught her. She rounded a corner, and the entryway, preceded by a lengthy hall, came into view.

"Now what could possibly be so important at home?"

She groaned as he seized her elbow and nestled her hand in the crook of his arm. Eleanor shot him a glare. He must know she sought to avoid him, yet he acted oblivious. "A gentleman does not ask what matters a lady must tend to."

"Or you have nothing pressing at home and seek to

avoid me." He smirked, his eyes narrowing on her cheeks as they heated.

He was much too astute. She would see him tomorrow, assuming she wished to, but more importantly, she needed to avoid spending so much time with him. His personality appealed to her more than she cared to admit, not to mention those dark green eyes, which pulled her in and made her forget herself.

She would not forget herself now, however. She scoffed at his oh-so-accurate statement. "Don't be absurd. I am to ride with you tomorrow, remember?"

The promise of freedom lay just down the hall, away from him and from the unwanted emotions he stirred within her. She increased her pace to a brisk walk, shoving aside all unbidden thoughts of her emotions in the process. "You know," she said with a smug smile, "I decided something about our bet. Should I win, I believe I will require your absolute silence whenever I ask for it."

"And when I disobey? I hope my punishment gives you some pleasure."

His sensuous look caused Eleanor to gulp as she, once more, increased her pace. Logan kept up with her, his long legs eating the distance with ease while her shorter ones struggled. No longer did her feet tread in silence. Instead the two raised a din to echo through the halls.

The hall ended as they reached the foyer. She was so near to the door. Only five more steps and she would reach her freedom. "There will be no pleasure between us. Ever." She kept her gaze planted on the ground, focused on the remaining distance to the door.

"Why don't we put that ridiculous notion to rest

right now?" He dropped her hand, instead reaching out to her shoulder and whirling her to him.

"Wha—" Her question was cut off by the assault. All of her person spun into him, all but her foot, which caught on the damask rug. She cried out as pain lanced her ankle. Her slippered foot wrenched out of the rug, and she fell into Logan with a thud. He grunted at the impact, grabbing hold of her as he too fell. A loud crash of glass breaking resounded through the house as they came to rest on the floor.

As Eleanor lay on Logan once again, her mind was filled by a dull haze of pain from her ankle and the exhilarating feeling of being close to him once more. Her pulse raced, and her stomach tensed in an unusual manner that was not exactly painful, but mortifying, nonetheless.

She lifted her head and took in the scene before her. A small mahogany table lay upended with the remains of blue and white pottery strewn out before it. She laid her head back on Logan's chest. Could this day get any worse?

In mere moments, several servants appeared, along with Lord and Lady Gammon. "Oh dear," Lady Gammon murmured with a gleeful gleam to her gaze as she took in their appearance. She stepped forward and offered her hand to Eleanor. Eleanor grasped Lady Gammon's hand, putting weight on her foot but fell back when a searing pain shot up her leg. Her worst fears were confirmed. She had suffered an injury.

"Ooomph." Logan groaned as she fell into him once more. As Eleanor continued to lie on him, he asked, "Are you going to move?"

Eleanor shifted and managed to thrust her elbow

into his ribs. She grinned when he emitted a muffled curse. A gentleman shouldn't be allowed to behave so barbarically and not receive some form of retribution in return.

Lady Gammon turned to give directions to the servants. "Send for the doctor. It appears Miss Ashford has hurt her ankle." She then directed another one to prepare a bedchamber for Eleanor's use. As she turned back to Logan and Eleanor, she placed her hand on her hip in annoyance and said, "Logan, stop lying around, and carry Miss Ashford to the Blue Room."

Logan glared up at Lady Gammon. "Who says I am not injured, as well?"

Lady Gammon made a dismissive gesture and laughed. "You would not look quite so pleased with yourself if you were injured."

Eleanor's eyes met Logan's, which was a mistake, as they were mere inches from her own. She ducked her head down and breathed in the scent of him. She really needed distance from this man.

Logan disentangled himself from Eleanor, before lifting her in his arms. "Shall we, my dear?"

She shook her head. "This is all so very unnecessary."

"Be that as it may, you have no choice but to do as bidden." He strode out of the foyer and down the hall, carrying her away from freedom as Lady Gammon followed behind them.

She had been so close to the front door when it was painfully ripped from her grasp. "I am more than capable of riding in a carriage with a hurt leg." Everyone ignored her, and she was soon deposited in a large bed in the Blue Room.

"Exactly how did you end up on the floor?" Lady Gammon asked as she propped a pristine white pillow under Eleanor's head.

"Such is the natural conclusion when one is manhandled," Eleanor said with her eyes planted on Logan.

Sheer joy erupted within her when Logan's head reared up with a shocked look in his eyes. "Are you implying I manhandled you?"

"I do not imply anything. Why imply when I can state that you, Logan, manhandled me?"

Lady Gammon laughed. "She has you there. Now, then…" She coughed. "Logan, would you please excuse us? The doctor should arrive shortly."

Logan swept a low bow to the ladies and retreated, pulling the door shut with a gentle click. Several minutes of silence passed as the two ladies waited for the doctor.

The doctor arrived with an air of grandeur, bowing low and then depositing his satchel on a side table. He removed her stocking and conducted his examination. Eleanor had a minor sprained ankle, and he suggested she stay in bed until the swelling went down to avoid complications.

"I think it safe to say you will spend the night here," Lady Gammon said to Eleanor once the doctor departed.

"I suspected as much." Her heart sank. "I am sure I will be better by morning."

"Hopefully." Lady Gammon blanched. "Not that I want you to leave. You are more than welcome to stay indefinitely, you know."

Eleanor nodded and smiled. "Of course." Granted,

she did not quite believe Lady Gammon, but the sentiment was thoughtful nonetheless. "Thank you for your hospitality, and please forgive me for the vase. I am sure it was quite dear."

"Oh shush, you do not need to thank me for acting as any good hostess would. As for the vase, I could never hold you responsible for its demise when it was Logan's graceless actions that engineered its untimely finish."

Eleanor relaxed a little against the soft pillows that propped her up. Guilt gnawed at her stomach whenever she thought of the broken vase, and she was happy to see Lady Gammon unfazed by the whole ordeal. As for Logan being held accountable, well that was another matter. "I cannot imagine what good it would do to hold Logan responsible. It is not as if he could afford to replace such a priceless heirloom."

Lady Gammon's delighted laugh filled the room. "I would never be so crass as to make a guest pay for something broken in accident, but if I did, Logan would certainly be able to afford it." She turned to depart and stopped at the doorway. Traces of laughter lingered in her voice as she said, "I will leave you to rest. I already sent a message to your family, but if there is anything else you require, please let me know."

The door closed without a sound, and Eleanor was left with one major question. Just how wealthy was Logan? Common sense suggested Lady Gammon exaggerated the size of Logan's pocket book. Landed gentry tended to be comfortably situated, not rich.

No matter how much wealth he possessed, she would not be swayed. She was still resolved to marry a member of the peerage, not a baronet who did her bodily harm. After his behavior this afternoon, she would have to be unhinged to think him a catch. Aside from the sparks that had flown from crashing into him, his actions had been quite intolerable.

****

"The doctor has seen her, Your Grace."

Logan turned from the window as Opal entered the library. "And?"

"And she has a swollen ankle and will be unable to travel tonight."

A pang of guilt hit him at her words. He should have been more careful with her, not throwing her about like a piece of baggage. He did not dislike the fact that she would spend the night here. He grinned at the thought. Of course, he would do nothing improper, but he could advance his suit.

A dying fire smoldered in the hearth and cast a soft glow in the room. The day had been chilly for spring, and a fire was necessary to ward away that chill. Opal sat in one of the well-padded chairs and leaned her head back to look at him. "Are you sure you didn't plan this? Otherwise, how on earth did you break my vase? Reuben tells me the thing had been in the family for generations."

"Did someone say my name?" Reuben asked as he entered the library.

Opal smiled up at him and imparted the news of Eleanor's injury. "I see," he said as he took a seat in a chair next to his wife. "Is that why Logan has such a disturbing smile on his face?"

Logan immediately counseled his features, and Opal laughed. He glowered and said, "I wish to invite you both to a house party of sorts. I cannot call it a true house party, because the only people that will attend are myself, Miss Ashford, her chaperone, and you two. Oh, and the duke, of course."

Opal's dark eyes grew round, and she straightened. "How will you and the duke attend the same gathering?"

"Something will have to delay the duke's arrival." He waved his hand and smiled. "I will figure that part out later, but the party is in two weeks."

Reuben pulled out his snuff box and took a pinch before he regarded Logan with a somber expression. "You know we will support you, but I still don't like her. Everything I hear about her indicates she is a—" He coughed and looked guiltily at his wife. "Well, you know. She is not nice."

"The reports I received said the same thing," Logan said, not bothered by her reputation. He understood Ellie had done some undesirable things, but he had a feeling about her. With the proper encouragement, she very well could surprise everyone by being likeable.

"Wait…" Opal stared at him wide-eyed and asked, "You had her investigated?"

"Of course I did," he said as he crossed to a bookshelf. "I will not marry any woman without knowing everything about her."

"And the report didn't change your mind?" an astounded Reuben asked.

"No." Logan exhaled and scowled. He selected a book and tucked it under his arm. "When I was young, everyone treated me as if I could do no wrong. When I entered society, I acted badly, treating everyone as if they were beneath me. I am sure Miss Ashford suffers from the same misguided notions I did, except she also has a ruthless mother to sway her."

The fire crackled, and Opal leaned her head back against the chair. "I hope you're right. I heard she fought with the vicar's daughter at my soiree. That does not do much to recommend her."

"From what I heard, the vicar's daughter started the fight." Logan scowled and stepped to the doorway. "You don't have to believe me, but I see good in her. If she were humbled, even a little, she would be a completely different person."

"Oh?" Reuben asked as his mouth dipped down in a frown.

Logan stopped before he left the room. He looked over his shoulder at them and raised his brow. "Yes, and I believe her falling for a baronet would be just the thing. Her worldview would change if she believed she were to marry landed gentry."

He hurried down the hall before he could hear any more of their negative words. Reuben and Opal meant well, but they did not understand what brewed between Ellie and himself. In fact, he wasn't sure if he understood, either. All he knew was, on the balcony the previous night, she had spoken with such a vulnerable look on her face, and he had believed her. She had made some poor decisions, but she regretted them.

He rounded a corner and caught sight of the door to her room. His steps were purposeful. He would see her and remind himself once more why he wanted her. As he reached her door, he paused and studied the handle.

If he were honest with himself, he might not have liked Ellie if she had met him as the duke. She would have been yet another cloying female, desperate to gain the title of duchess. The fact that she did not know his title allowed her to drop her guard around him and show her personality, one that he could only assume no one else saw. Yes, he liked the lady, barbs and all.

There was something special about her, aside from her beauty. Her sapphire eyes bespoke honesty and intelligence—two qualities rare in ladies of his acquaintance—and those moments when she allowed her true self to shine forth were like rain to parched soil. While he understood she might be duplicitous if she knew who he was, he also understood all her mercenary actions were to gain a mate, and that he could forgive.

He turned the knob and opened the door. Of course, he really needed to stop falling when she stumbled against him. It was not very ducal. Next time, he would catch her rather than allow either to tumble to the ground.

His breath caught at the sight of her. The afternoon sun streamed through the window and lit up the blue room. She reclined on her periwinkle bed with pillows piled behind her and a book in hand. As he entered, she marked her place and smiled at him.

He could get used to such a welcoming smile. "Ellie." Logan sat in a chair next to the bed and performed a haphazard bow. "Your knight in shining armor arrives, bearing all manner of entertainment for you."

She raised an eyebrow at the novel he held in his hands. "I see one thing, not 'all manner' as you so optimistically stated."

She fought so hard to dissuade him. He shook his head and smiled at her. "You discounted me. I happen to be quite skilled at entertaining ladies, in more ways than one. I shall demonstrate if you like."

"That is quite all right. Leave the book on the night table, and kindly depart."

Instead of heeding her wishes, Logan settled further into his chair. The blasted thing creaked, and he shifted forward again. Once more, it creaked. He would have to get the thing replaced.

"What are you doing?"

He looked up and appreciated the spirited look on her face. Even in distemper, she entertained him. He propped his foot up on his knee and said, "You really need to learn to control yourself. This time when you threw yourself at me you ended up here. What will happen the next time?"

She had the audacity to roll her eyes at him and laugh. "Oh, do be quiet." She tilted her head to the side. "You know, I believe you owe me an apology."

"Well, Ellie, let me apologize then. I am deeply sorry for the harm that has befallen you." Her eyes widened when he said her name again, and he almost chuckled out loud. She was so enjoyable to tease.

"And for manhandling me?" she asked and waited with arms crossed over her delectable bosom.

"I am afraid I cannot apologize for that. Your terms for our bet mandate silence when you will it. I had to show you I do not require words to convey my meanings, and I would do it again given the chance."

"What meaning did you attempt to convey? That you wished to injure me?"

He leaned forward, and the chair creaked once more. He ignored the sound as his eyes settled on her plump lips. "You know very well that I wished to kiss you."

She uncrossed her arms and gave a half-hearted

sigh as she settled into the pillows further. "I suppose I shall have to change my terms then. You are terrible at conveying your intentions without words." When he nodded in agreement, she laughed. She closed her eyes and said, "Since you are here, please make yourself useful and tell me of your home."

Logan enjoyed the uninterrupted view of her as she reclined on the bed. He launched into a description of his childhood home, Briarthorn, telling her of the main house, which was actually a small castle used in ancient battles against the Scottish. He spoke of the small cold river that ran through his property and the lake located near the castle. Trees abounded on the estate, and he assured her how much she would enjoy living there in the future. Lastly, he spoke of the small town, Corningwall, which was roughly the same size as the little town located near to them now. He finished his description by adding, "I will be sure to add weeping willows by the river so you can always have your perfect little spot." While he enjoyed the sound of that, he was surprised to see she had fallen asleep without hearing his little promise to her.

He sat at her bedside for a few additional moments and savored the lovely view. She looked angelic in sleep. Invitingly perfect. He soon rose, pressed a soft kiss to her hand, and departed the room. He would return later in the evening to check on her once more.

****

The supper hour was long past, and Logan longed to return to Ellie's side. Before he could visit her, however, he had to meet with Reuben for a nightcap. As Logan entered the library, he was delighted to see Reuben already waiting for him. Reuben poured scotch into two glasses and extended one to Logan. "Your Grace, you look troubled."

He accepted the proffered beverage and erased all traces of emotion from his face. "I received a letter today from my cousin, Lord Edwin."

Reuben sipped his scotch and asked, "Oh? What has Edwin been up to?"

Logan's uncle had two sons. The eldest was a degenerate, and the youngest lived to please his father. Edwin was the youngest. "From what I have read, cousin Edwin has decided to take a wife. When he went to London, Charles tried to show him a good time by escorting him to his favorite haunts."

Reuben's eyes twinkled and he leaned forward. "I bet Edwin did not take well to that."

"Not if the page and a half pertaining to the matter is to be believed." He chuckled and sipped his scotch. He turned to the fireplace and smiled as he reminisced. "The two have always been polar opposites. I am sure the night did not last long, and I am doubly sure the two have not met since."

"Why would Edwin take a wife now?" Reuben walked back to the decanter to pour himself some more scotch, not bothering to look at Logan as he did so.

"I am sure his father recommended it. Edwin does nothing without his daddy's approval."

"Which truly is the exact opposite of Charles." Reuben took a sip and turned to Logan with a look of innocence. "How does Miss Ashford fare?"

Logan did not betray any emotion at Reuben's question, although he would not be surprised if Reuben could sense his anxious desire to return to her side. He lifted his glass and took another, longer swig, welcoming the numbing warmth of his scotch as he turned to inspect a painting of a hunting dog. "As far as I can ascertain, she will recover without mishap."

"Did you ask her when you stopped by her room? You know Opal would not approve of your little visit."

"As if that would stop me." He smirked. "I love Opal, but propriety can be damned when it comes to Miss Ashford."

Reuben eyed Logan, as if he was meeting him for the first time. "Well, well. It appears Opal was correct. Have you made much progress with her? Or is this a one-sided love affair?" He laughed at Logan's dour expression. "To think, the lofty Duke of Waking has fallen for a woman who wants nothing to do with him in return."

"I have not fallen for her," Logan said, annoyed. "We both know I will win her in the end. She just needs a smidgen more time before she understands her feelings for me."

"Is that right?" Reuben laughed again. "Luckily, out here in the country, you have no competition. That should help your odds."

Logan was irritated at this point, even though he knew his friend jested. He threw back the rest of his drink and said, "It appears the duke wishes to have his house party next week instead of the following week. Make sure your schedule is cleared."

Logan left the warm library to return to Eleanor's side. He did not wish to waste a perfectly good evening on Reuben when he could be with her. As he drew away from the library, he could hear Reuben's mocking laughter reverberate through the dimly lit hallway. Reuben enjoyed Logan's predicament, especially when that enjoyment irritated Logan to no end.

****

Having napped the evening away, Eleanor was now having trouble returning to her blissful slumber. After Logan left her with his endearing promise to create her very own special place, she had dreamt of his green eyes and charming smile. No one had ever expressed a desire to give her something as special as Logan had. In fact, no one had offered to give her more than flowers or some insignificant trinket.

His offer had been magical, which was why she had feigned sleep. She did not know how to respond to him, so no response was much simpler. When she did fall into slumber, she dreamt of a willow tree by a stream, just as he described.

There had been trees around them and green grass as far as the eye could see. A castle rose high on the hillside next to her, and Logan knelt in front of her, placing soft kisses on her lips. His presence in her dream had seemed so real she had almost expected to find him upon waking.

She shook her head and stretched. What was the magic in a dream if it never could be real? Her ankle no longer throbbed, and she decided to test it by taking a few steps to the chamber pot. She concluded her personal business and hobbled back to the bed until a sudden sharp, stabbing pain caused her to cry out. She hopped the remainder of the distance back to her bed and managed to lie down before the door opened.

Eleanor groaned as Logan closed the door behind him. The air shifted with his entrance, sending the few candles dancing and the shadows rioting around them. "Oh, go away." She was in too much pain to deal with him now.

Logan stopped and surveyed her. He appeared restless, and suddenly he smiled. He strode to her side and said, "Really, Ellie, you should drop the act already. Our shared attraction is much too strong for you to speak so shrewishly toward me."

The words he spoke were true, but she would not allow him to say such things to her. She raised herself so she could sit upright and said, "Why I never!"

He cocked his head to the side. "Really? I find it hard to believe you have not been called worse." He sat in the new chair next to her bed, which the servants must have exchanged earlier in the evening, and caught her hand in his.

She pulled her hand away. "I should think your words have ruined any chance for polite conversation tonight." Her dreams about him were cruelly false. There was no magic here.

He smirked and spoke in velvet tones. "Who said I came here to talk?"

Eleanor picked up her book and said, "Then watch as I read in silence. That is almost as good as your absence."

She feigned reading her novel and tried to appear indifferent to his presence, even though internally, she quivered from excitement. He tended to say rather forward things to her, and she quite liked them.

He rose with a growl of frustration, ripped the book from her hands, and threw it aside. "You may appear unaffected, but we both know it is a lie." With a fierce growl, he leaned in and captured her lips with his.

Shocked by the sudden onslaught, Eleanor was frozen in place. Logan seemed like a different man tonight, but as he kissed her, she forgot his strange actions. Instead, she remembered the Logan from her dreams. The one with enough consideration to make her feel at-home in a foreign place. The one that could care for her without her worrying his devotion would lessen as her beauty faded.

She intertwined her hands in his hair, forgetting herself in this strange dream. She pulled him closer and allowed the wicked rush of abandonment to fill her. For one unthinkable moment, she allowed herself to consider the idea he was worthy.

Without warning, he broke off the kiss, keeping his mouth mere inches from her own. "Remember this when you try to tell me you want nothing to do with me."

With those words, he was gone, striding from the room as if he had not kissed her senseless. She picked up a light decorative pillow and hurled it at the wall. Her emotions were a tangled, keyed-up mess. She should never have succumbed to him, but she found it almost impossible not to. How could she, when her every secret, forbidden fantasy included him?

Chapter 5

The following morning, Eleanor awoke to the sight of the maid opening the curtains to let in an excessive amount of sunlight. Eleanor squinted as her eyes adjusted to the light and recalled too late that squinting led to wrinkles. "Must you do that?" she growled, which caused the maid to jump in surprise.

The maid dipped a hasty curtsy and said, "My apologies, my lady. I thought the sun might do you good."

"Well, that should teach you to think," she muttered, pulling herself to a seated position. "Go fetch me my breakfast."

The maid nodded as tears pooled in her eyes. She hurried to do Eleanor's bidding. At the sight of the maid's tears, Eleanor's heart gave a twinge of guilt as she realized she had been harsh. She settled back into bed and tried to doze a little. Sleep had proven elusive in this foreign house. She would have preferred to sleep in, but that would not be possible in such a bright room.

Her book beckoned, and she opened to her previous chapter. The words on the page could not hold her attention though, so she put it back on the nightstand and sighed. A knock sounded on the door, and Lady Gammon entered the room. She was a morning person, as her cheerful mien suggested. "Good morning, Miss Ashford." She smiled and asked, "Why on earth was Josephine crying?"

"Good morning," Eleanor grumbled. "Who exactly is Josephine?"

"Why, the maid, of course. Did she not stop by this morning?" Lady Gammon looked at Eleanor with a touch of concern on her youthful, unlined face.

"Oh, is Josephine her name? How very French of her. I fear my temperament is not in its best form in the morning."

Lady Gammon gave Eleanor another concerned look as she asked, "Is your ankle troubling you? I can send for the doctor again."

"Oh no, that is entirely unnecessary. In fact, after some tea, I would like to go home."

The countess looked even more downcast at Eleanor's suggestion of leaving. "Was it the room, then? I cannot abide the notion that my house is uncomfortable for guests."

Eleanor shook her head. "Your house is more than accommodating. My poor mood is due to Logan."

Renewed alarm surfaced on Lady Gammon's face. "He didn't do anything improper, did he?"

"Of course not!" The last thing Eleanor needed was to end up in a scandalous marriage of shame to him. She breathed in a sigh of relief when Lady Gammon relaxed. "I was just upset by his brutish behavior." That was certainly the truth, but Eleanor did not have to specify when or how he acted brutishly.

"Oh yes, Logan does have his moments. Although he should know better than to behave that way with you."

Eleanor nodded. She was in complete agreement with the countess. "He certainly knows how to upset me." She paused as the maid entered with her breakfast. After setting the tray down, the maid turned and left, and Eleanor helped herself to some tea. She poured sugar and cream into her cup as she asked, "Do you happen to know what Logan's surname is?"

Lady Gammon coughed and appeared frozen for a moment before answering, "Of course I do. He is Sir Logan—" Her eyes settled on a teacup and she finished, "—Tea."

Eleanor's eyed rounded in disbelief. "Did you say Sir Logan Tea?"

"Oh, I am sorry, you must have misunderstood. It is Sir Logan Teak." She exhaled and said in a rush, "Now please excuse me as I must alert the servants of your desire to leave."

Lady Gammon hurried from the room as Eleanor took another sip while savoring the pleasant aroma. She inhaled the first cup and then a second. Hopefully, it would provide her with the fortitude required to escape this house. She readied herself to leave, and just as she was preparing to depart her room, Logan once again entered unbidden.

"You are a vision, as usual." Logan smiled as his eyes roved over her.

He looked handsome as well and well-rested. "And you, Sir Logan Teak, are here again." She made sure to emphasize his surname as she glowered at him.

Logan stopped his advance as a confused expression flitted over his features. "Who told you my name?"

"Why, was it a secret?" she asked, knowing she was belligerent. He had that effect on her, yet she could not bring herself to be outright mean to him. Something in her could not hurt this man. While she wished to deter his advances, she could not bring herself to say the necessary words that would send him away.

"Of course not, Ellie." He smiled once more. "You had never seemed interested in my name before so I never told you. What do you think of your future surname?"

She ignored him and took several cautious steps. Her ankle did not give any hint of pain, so she increased her pace out of the room and down the long hall.

"I see you have decided to hold a grudge about last night," he said as if he spoke of the weather. "Before you depart, I thought to formally invite you to a house party, hosted by none other than the Duke of Waking."

That stopped Eleanor's progress and forced her to face Logan. "Oh?"

He smiled with a triumphant gleam in his eyes. "It is to be an intimate event, but you are invited. The little party is to commence next week."

"Hmm. I suppose I can be prevailed upon to attend, with my chaperone, naturally."

"I expected no less, Ellie."

She leveled her best affronted stare at him and placed a hand on her hip. "You really ought to stop calling me that. My name is Eleanor, although you may call me Miss Ashford."

"How benevolent of you," he said and then acted as though he considered her statement. He shrugged as he drew his conclusion. "I like Ellie so much more, though."

"I don't particularly care what you like or dislike, Sir Logan."

His eyes went to her lips. Her pulse quickened, but

her excitement was dashed when he smirked. "Yes, you do, Ellie."

He desperately needed to be put in his place. She stepped up to him and offered her most seductive smile, the one where she peeked through her eyelashes, and the same one all gentlemen succumbed to. His eyes narrowed, and she purred, "Maybe that will have to be the new terms of our bet. If I win, you cannot address me in such a foolish manner, and if you win, I will live near Scotland." She brought her hand to her cheek and pondered her statement. "On second thought, the two are hardly equal. I will have to think on an additional boon for you to bestow upon me."

All her feminine wiles were at work as she batted her eyes at him, but he seemed unfazed. "You can name whatever you wish, Ellie. I am that certain of victory."

She schooled her features and stepped back. Something as simple as his touch could send her world spinning, but he reacted indifferently to her flirtations. What good were her looks if she could not manage to distract him with them?

"I hope the rest of your week goes by without hindrance." He bowed over her hand and kissed it. "Don't get stuck in the mud on your way home."

She jerked her hand away at his sizzling touch. "Thank you." She turned from him and hurried out the front door. Relief washed over her at the sight of her carriage in the drive and not a raincloud in sight.

****

Logan chuckled as she left. He hated to see her leave. Her extended visit had been enlivening, and he anticipated the visit to Waking Hall, which would give him almost unfettered access to her. He turned and walked to the dining room for some breakfast, and Lady Gammon emerged from a nearby room.

"Oh, hello, Your Grace. Has our visitor departed?" she asked with a cheerful smile.

"Don't you mean to address me as Sir Logan *Teak*?" He grinned when she blanched. "Couldn't you have produced a better surname than that?"

"Couldn't you have straightened these details out earlier?" she quipped. "Besides, you should thank me. Your last name was nearly Tea."

He laughed at her admission. "Then I thank you. I suppose Teak is not so bad."

Opal smiled and nodded. "How did she decide you were a baronet?"

"I told her." He shrugged when her eyebrows rose. "I do hold the title of baronet, so it is not a lie."

"Ah."

He ran a hand through his hair. He did not wish to lie to Ellie, but this time it was necessary. "Yes. Convincing Miss Ashford is one thing, but convincing my servants will be an undertaking. I cannot imagine how they will react to our plan. I suppose I will be giving them a May Day bonus or some other form of nonsense."

"Yes, that might help them remember to treat you as a guest. Good luck though."

He thanked her and escorted her into the dining room where Reuben sat eating his breakfast. It was one thing to convince his friends to play a part for him, but quite another to convince his loyal and trusted servants to treat him as a guest. Not that his servants would mind; his rank just might be too ingrained in them to address him as anything other than Your Grace.

Chapter 6

The carriage ride to the ducal estate seemed to stretch on forever. Eleanor had not been able to occupy herself with her reading as her stomach was too jumbled with anticipation to focus.

She could feel the pull of this visit as if it were a cord pulling her to her destiny. She felt a strange, calm certainty that her life would change in the next week, but in which direction she did not know. Meeting the duke would help lessen some of her anxiety and would hopefully sever this budding infatuation with Logan. He irritated her, and she could not get him off her mind no matter how hard she tried.

"Oomph." Eleanor's musings were broken by her aunt's fitful utterance.

Mrs. Westfield drifted back to sleep, and Eleanor's gaze settled on her maid who intently watched the landscape fly by. The maid appeared awed to see so much outside of her little village. The girl's expression shifted as new sights unfolded, and Eleanor softened toward the girl. How wonderful it must be to feel excitement over such mundane matters. Eleanor could not remember the last time she felt excited about anything.

She sighed and let her eyes drift shut. If only she could experience something half as magical as what her maid felt. As her thoughts wandered inward once more, she came to the sudden realization that she potentially denied herself such joys by searching for an advantageous marriage. In her quest to find a suitable husband, she had never taken into account the possibility of feelings and her own happiness outside of social standing. If she relaxed her requirements for a husband, could she find the exquisite feeling of bliss in marriage?

A title brought good standing amongst society, but would a happy marriage be better than a title? Her mind instantly turned to Logan. In all honesty, she had to admit his very presence filled her with a liveliness she had never experienced before. Her true inner self wanted nothing more than to throw everything aside for the chance of something more with Logan, but could she truly do something so daring?

The way he treated her suggested she should consider such a rash act. She had never met a gentleman so thoughtful. Yes, his behavior was a bit brutish, but his promise to create a magical place at Briarthorn seemed so honest. He wanted to make her happy. She was not to be his pretty bauble, led about to impress his friends. No, he wanted her for her, and how could she resist that?

Once more she uttered a sigh. She may wish to pursue something with Logan, but it would never happen. Her mother would not allow it, and Eleanor would not fight her. No, a duke was much better as a marriage candidate than a baronet, and Eleanor knew which one she would marry, no matter how much she might desire the other outcome. Besides, if she did wed a mere baronet, she might not be able to support her aunt in the style Eleanor dreamed of.

She finally managed to drift into a fitful slumber. When she woke, the skies had darkened, signaling they neared their destination.

"Are you excited to meet your duke?" Mrs. Westfield surprised Eleanor by asking.

"Of course." Eleanor smiled, hoping her inner turmoil was not evident.

Mrs. Westfield smiled. "We are all so very excited for this, you know."

Eleanor was very much aware of her family's aspirations for her, and she hid her annoyance by looking out the window. Her family held lofty dreams for her, or rather, her marriage prospects. She rather doubted they cared what became of her after she secured a titled husband, aside from Mrs. Westfield, that is. Her aunt would still care.

The carriage continued to fly down the road. Her eyes were unfocused until the outline of an enormous mansion came within sight. There were enough trees surrounding the house that Eleanor could not see it in its entirety, but she could make out enough of it to realize it was the largest house she had ever encountered.

A shiver ran through her as the carriage turned to go up the drive. A light flickered in the window, and despite all rational thought, she knew it was Logan awaiting their arrival. The carriage came to a halt in the courtyard, and the door swung open to reveal a liveried footman. He helped Eleanor down from the carriage, and she approached an intimidating set of double doors.

She could make out a few gargoyles perched high upon the walls, and a chill of foreboding crawled down her spine. Maybe by day the gargoyles would look friendlier, as they could not look any less approachable than they did now. One of the heavy oak doors swung open with a groan, and the light from within beckoned Eleanor to enter while also chasing away some of the chills of the night.

"My lady." An aging butler greeted Eleanor with a bow and indicated she should enter. She stepped in and was greeted by the musty smell of an old house. "His Grace is most pleased to have you as a guest. He has instructed me to place you in the Gray Room as it has the best view aside from his own chambers."

"Thank you. That sounds delightful." Eleanor smiled and was led to her room. Mrs. Westfield and her maid trailed behind, all looking in awe at the rich décor around them. Eleanor was used to living in luxury, but nothing she had experienced could compare to the ducal mansion. Even the marble her feet currently trod spoke of riches. It must have been imported from Italy or some other exotic location.

Mrs. Westfield went to a nearby chamber, and Eleanor entered her own. A footman carried in her luggage, and the butler informed her a light supper was to be served in the dining room in one hour.

Despite her exhaustion from the trip, Eleanor was pleased by the news. She would finally meet His Grace. The sooner the better. "Olive," she said as the door swung shut. "We don't have much time. You must pull out a dress and do something to my hair."

Her maid rushed to do Eleanor's bidding and chuckled as she said, "Someday, my lady, you will get my name right."

Eleanor was too focused on her upcoming meeting to register her error. Her nervousness increased with each tick of the clock on the mantel. She inhaled and tried to calm herself. She focused on the interior of her room to distract herself, placing her hands in her lap to hide their shakiness.

The duke did not lack in funds, as evidenced by the richness of the fabrics and intricacy of the furnishings. Her large canopied bed was a dark gray and would keep her quite warm no matter what chill prevailed in the air. The colors in the room, which were various shades of gray, soothed her, and Eleanor allowed herself to relax into her maid's increasingly capable hands.

After a short period of time, Eleanor's hair was swept into a simple but charming chignon, and she was dressed in a tasteful powder blue gown that brought out the vivid hue of her eyes. She would make a positive impression on the duke tonight. She floated to Mrs. Westfield's chambers and rapped on the wooden door.

Mrs. Westfield opened the door and smiled when she saw Eleanor. "You look lovely, my dear. I daresay I have never seen a more ideal duchess."

"Thank you, Aunt. Shall we?" she asked and moved aside so her aunt could exit the room.

Mrs. Westfield smiled, and the two returned to the foyer. There, a footman directed them to the dining room. As they entered, Eleanor's gaze landed on Logan's and seemed glued to him until she tore her eyes from his. His heated gaze followed her to her seat, where she gained enough control of herself to look around at the others in attendance. Much to her surprise, only Logan and Lord Gammon were seated at the massive dining room table.

"Where are His Grace and the countess?" she asked.

Logan smirked at her and said, "Good evening to you, too. Lord Gammon and myself are well, thank you for asking. Lady Gammon and His Grace are indisposed. The duke has a cold or something of the sort."

"Oh, how dreadful. I hope Lady Gammon has not also caught the cold," Mrs. Westfield said with a touch of concern.

Lord Gammon chuckled as his chest puffed out in a self-satisfied manner. "Oh no, my countess suffers from a different ailment entirely. One that cannot be caught."

Eleanor had no notion what he spoke of but was more concerned with the duke's health. "What ails him? Has the doctor been called?"

Logan's dark brown eyebrow lifted in reproach. "Oh, the duke's needs have all been seen to, fear not."

Eleanor eyed him, unsure why he had used such a cryptic tone. He stared back at her until the silence was broken by the meal's arrival. The butler and the same footman from earlier carried in food trays and deposited them on the table. Eleanor stared in wonderment at the two. In an estate this size, there should have been a staggering amount of servants, yet so far she had only seen two.

"How far along is the countess?" Mrs. Westfield asked.

Lord Gammon beamed with pride. "We believe the child shall arrive mid-October. Do you have any children of your own, Mrs. Westfield?"

Mrs. Westfield shook her head as sorrow filled her eyes, and she began to tell the tale of her marriage. She had married the man she loved, only to find out he was a degenerate wastrel. After a short period of time, Mr.

Westfield had succumbed to his poor choices and left his wife a widow at a young age. Eleanor had heard the sad tale many times and felt sorry for her aunt. She did not, however, wish to hear the story again.

She took a sip of her wine and eyed her food. The fare was simple. Not the sort she would expect from a wealthy household, much less that of a duke. She took a dainty bite of her shepherd's pie and changed her mind. This was just the sort of food a duke would offer. It was delicious.

Mrs. Westfield continued to speak, and Eleanor entertained herself by toying with her food. When she finished, she sat back and observed the room. The walls were burgundy, and a massive chandelier hung in the center of the room. The ceilings were vaulted, and an extremely large fireplace took over much of the opposite wall. If she were to hazard a guess, she would say this dining room was very old. Most likely, in the past, this was the place where everyone gathered to feast every day and to be kept warm by the fire.

The meal came to an end, and Eleanor poured herself a touch more wine. She hated sleeping in unknown places, and wine always helped her. Mrs. Westfield was the first to stand. "I think I will see myself to bed. Are you ready, Eleanor?"

Eleanor shook her head and indicated her wine. "I will go upstairs soon."

Mrs. Westfield smiled, wished everyone a good night, and departed. Lord Gammon spoke when she disappeared from view. "I think I shall also depart for the night as Lady Gammon would be sorely disappointed if I remained. Good evening." He bowed, winked at Logan, and also left.

Silence filled the room, and Eleanor was acutely aware of how alone she was with Logan. She sent him a penetrating look and said, "You planned this, didn't you?"

He swirled the wine in his long-stemmed glass. "Hardly, my dear. You are the one with the absent chaperone."

"She is only absent because she knows you do not pose a threat to my virtue. If His Grace were here, no force on earth would convince her to depart."

All traces of humor left Logan's face as he said, "Oh yes, the duke. You have yet to meet him, yet you are so set on marrying him." He downed the rest of his wine and stood with a reproachful frown. "I should hope tomorrow you can at least have the manners to acknowledge the others present in the room with you."

Eleanor also stood. She was annoyed that he would question her manners, although she supposed she had been remiss by not addressing those at the table. "It is not ill-mannered for me to show consideration for my host." She picked up her wine glass and also tossed back its contents. The warmth spread through her limbs, and she smirked.

"That may be," Logan said, his voice sounding unusually cold, "but ignoring everyone else is ill-mannered. You spent the majority of the dinner in a brooding silence, while your chaperone attempted to fill the gap."

Eleanor glared at him as he stood so elegantly across the table from her. She would not stand here to be lectured by him. "I do not need to answer to you." She spun on her heel and walked to the door. She paused under the doorframe to add, "Now, please excuse me. I wish to retire for the evening."

He stood in place and smiled a cold little smile. "Good night. Just remember your precious duke may sound ideal now, but in the light of day he could be the opposite of what you think."

He would say something aggravating before she left. She slammed the door shut that she had just opened and turned once more to Logan. Eleanor marched up to him and scanned his face. "Are you jealous?"

A wicked light appeared in his eyes, and Eleanor swallowed. She always liked to get the last word, although now she worried that was not the most intelligent decision tonight. A small part of her thrilled at the idea that he could be jealous, and she waited with anticipation for what he would say.

"Do you want me to be jealous?" His finger came up to trace the outline of her rosebud lips, and her mouth went bone dry.

She swatted his hand away and tore her eyes from his. "Of course I do not want that. I gain nothing from your jealousy."

Logan ignored her wishes and turned her face toward his until she met his gaze. His green eyes searched hers until he found the hidden answer he looked for. Then, he dropped his hand from her face and stepped away.

Surprised by his sudden departure, Eleanor stood dumbfounded for a moment. "Do you have no response?"

"None whatsoever."

When Logan had grasped her chin in his large, masculine hand, she had thought they were on the precipice of a kiss. The moment he stepped away without quelling the building tension, she felt robbed of something. Now his complete disengagement from their altercation left her beyond confused. With a disgruntled cry at the myriad of emotions he forced her to feel, Eleanor spun around and exited the dining room. She would go to bed and not give one more thought to the infuriating man.

Upon entering her room, she flung herself under the canopy on her mattress. His smug face came to mind, and she threw a ferocious and unladylike punch at her pillow. She closed her eyes, shutting out his infuriating touch. The only thing she saw was Logan's green eyes and sensuous smile. Tonight would be a long one for her, of that she was certain.

****

Logan spent the morning taking a long, vigorous ride through his estate. He hated to admit to himself how possessive he felt of Ellie, and he definitely did not want to admit the strong feelings of jealousy that had overtaken him the previous night.

He chuckled as he remembered their encounter. Ellie had a temper and a need to win that bespoke her passionate nature. He was looking forward to their interactions today.

Once his ride was complete, Logan entered the stables, dismounted, and handed off Raphael to the sole groom. He had sent almost all the servants on a holiday, so he would not worry about one of them calling him "His Grace" around Ellie.

His butler had not taken the news of his plan well, and Logan had worried the poor fellow would have an apoplectic fit from the very idea. Fortunately, his loyal butler had gained control of himself and agreed to act as an accomplice. Logan had let him choose which servants remained, and he had sent away all but a select few. Evidently, only one groom was deemed necessary to keep the stables running.

Once his task was complete, Logan entered his house where he happened upon Reuben. "Good morning, how does Opal fare this morning?"

"Not too well," Reuben said with a dour shake of his head. "She cannot keep anything down and lies about moaning and cursing at me. I needed a break from the abuse."

Logan inclined his head in sympathy. His friend had looked so happy at the promise of an addition to his family but now was forced to deal with some of the less pleasurable aspects. "I am sure she is very understanding of your plight."

Unable to hide a grin at his next statement, Reuben said, "Unfortunately, no. She acts as though she is the only one in pain, not realizing I feel a great deal for her predicament."

Logan scoffed. "I cannot imagine why she is not more empathetic."

The pair laughed at the exchange and walked to the dining room for an early lunch. After a short while, the butler came to Logan's elbow and whispered, "She is taking a stroll in the South Gardens, Your Grace."

Reuben burst into laughter. "You mean to tell me your servants are spying on her for you?"

Logan scowled and stood. "Of course they are. I am not going to spy on her, so who else would?"

"You could try bumping into her and allowing love to find its way," Reuben said as he speared a sausage with his fork.

"Nobody has time for that."

****

Eleanor slept the morning away and woke to the intense feeling of hunger gnawing at her stomach. She had not eaten much the night before due to a certain someone's annoying presence. She rang for the maid and crossed to the vanity. Today could very well be the day she met the duke, and she needed to be ready.

"Good morning, my lady." Her maid dipped a brief curtsy as she entered the room. "I took the liberty of calling for a tray. It should be here shortly."

Eleanor smiled back at the girl and said, "That is perfect, Olive. Now we must do something to my hair. Something refined, but not too overdone. I don't want anyone to think I tried too hard."

Her maid frowned and shook her head. "You still are not getting my name right, my lady."

Eleanor inclined her head and regarded the maid. She had thought she was doing so well, but evidently she was not. "I do apologize. If not Olive, then what is it?"

"It's Olivia, my lady."

Eleanor nodded. She was a bit miffed with herself for her lack of attentiveness. Yes, maids were servants, but Eleanor wished to form a loyal relationship with her maid, just like the one Laura had with hers. "Olivia it is, then."

She was interrupted as a knock sounded on the door. Olivia crossed over and accepted a tray of food from the butler, thanked him, and closed the door.

"Olivia, do you not think it strange there are only two servants here?" Normally a butler did not perform such mundane tasks as delivering food to guests.

"I thought the same thing," Olivia said as she leaned toward Eleanor and then whispered, "The cook was the only person below stairs this morning. I have not seen a single maid this entire time."

"How can a duke lack servants at his primary estate? It almost seems as if he is not in residence." That would explain the absence of servants at least. She shoved the idea aside. The duke was in his sick bed, and there must be an excellent reason for the absence of servants.

Once she finished dressing and eating, Eleanor left the room. Her dress was light green and spring-like and was inspired by the view from her window. Exquisite gardens lay just beyond her bedroom and were showcased by a sunny, warm day. She would go for a walk and find something interesting to paint later, and maybe the duke would make his appearance.

Eleanor trod amidst the newly budding foliage, her slippers making the barest of whispers against the pebbled path. Her mind was preoccupied with ever-present thoughts of Logan. She had hoped the garden teeming with all manner of flowers would be distraction enough, but she could have been in an empty room for all the attention she gave it.

A bright yellow tulip caught her eye, and she made a desperate attempt to focus on its beauty. Logan drifted from her thoughts as she seared the details into memory. She could paint a scene of tulips which surrounded a wrought-iron trellis. Or maybe a bench. Yes, a bench would be just the thing, and then she could add some sort of creature on the bench.

The snap of a twig interrupted her, and she glanced

up. Logan strode toward her while looking much too handsome in his riding gear and not at all apologetic for interrupting her walk.

"My lady." He smiled at her and extended his hand to help her up from her crouched position.

"I wondered how long it would take for you to find me." She accepted his hand and stood. An electric current of awareness shot between them, and she stifled a gasp. His touch had a drastic effect on her, no matter how slight. An annoying, smug look appeared on his face. She must not have done a very good job at hiding her attraction for him.

"Shouldn't you be more prepared if you expected me?"

"Whatever do you mean?"

He smirked. "I think you know. Or maybe I am just so irresistible you responded to me without thought."

He held much too high of an opinion of himself. "You are hardly irresistible."

"Then why did you gasp?" His green eyes gleamed with wicked enjoyment, and his lips curled into a smile.

Physical attraction meant very little, not when there was no chance of an actual relationship developing. She raised her eyes heavenward and sighed. "I am currently making physical contact with you, yet it has not affected me in the slightest."

"I beg to differ." Raising her hand, he pressed a fairy-light kiss to the back of it while keeping his eyes glued to hers. Heat suffused her cheeks, and she tugged at her hand. She did not like to be proven wrong, but the blush had risen unbidden and she could not deny its presence.

He raised a disbelieving brow and held onto her

hand. Despite her best ladylike efforts to dissuade him, he guided it to the crook of his arm. "I thought you might enjoy a tour of the manor you wish to be mistress of."

The extended contact with Logan destroyed her ability to employ reason. Instead of thinking on the matter at hand, she was forced to appreciate the little details about him. The ones she should forget. More importantly, the ones she *couldn't* forget. For twice now, she had betrayed her response to him, and twice, he had not teased her or made sport of her when he could have. Instead, he changed topics by offering to do something nice for her. The first was to invite her here, to meet His Grace, and the second, to tour the manor.

He guided her along, and her thoughts returned to the present. Even now, he opened the door which led to a foreign section of the impressive manor. An internal warning went off as she stepped in from the sunshine. This tour would lead to danger, but the rewards of Logan's touch far outweighed the risk.

She continued to follow without raising a single objection. She would go with him, but why not take this opportunity to see if his jealousy was an aberration last night? She gazed up at him and asked, "Wouldn't the duke be better suited to act as my tour guide?"

****

Logan almost laughed. His current predicament was his own making, but he was hard pressed to keep a straight face when she asked questions like that. He could not keep the grin from surfacing, however, and had to hide it behind a cough. "Do you truly believe he would do a better job? I will have you know I have spent almost as much time here as he has."

She scoffed in disbelief. "Now that I cannot believe." When he failed to respond, she slowed her steps and said, "I suppose you are just as familiar with Lord Gammon's estate."

He chuckled, checking his pace to match hers and guiding her past an alcove filled with suits of armor glinting almost black in the lackluster light. "If you recall, I ran into you while riding, not even aware I had left his estate."

She giggled as a splash of color appeared on her face. The way she laughed just then was carefree and unguarded and just how he wanted her. It was a thrilling feeling to find a woman who felt an honest attraction for him, without her awareness of his cumbersome title and deep pockets.

He felt so relaxed when she was with him, and he grew more confident of his success with each smile she offered. He would pay any amount of money to know what she was thinking behind those startling blue eyes, but he knew he needed more time before she ever admitted any desire for him.

They ambled down the long hallway, bypassing several unimportant rooms before he halted at their first destination. "After you, my lady," he said as he pulled the door open and offered her a slight bow. The room contained few articles of furniture, and every wall was filled with portraits. He swept his unhampered arm in a dramatic arch as her eyes rounded to take in the vast number of pictures on the walls. "The portrait room, my lady."

She disengaged from him and spun around in a slow circle. Nothing in the room could hold his attention as she did in that moment. Without bothering to mask her expression, she appeared enchanted and carefree, and he felt an almost physical shift in his heart.

She ceased her spinning and smiled up at him. "Oh! Maybe the duke has a portrait. What a grand idea to bring me here." She clasped her hands together in excitement. She started forward to the long row of paintings, and Logan rushed to intercept her. He had completely forgotten his father's portrait hung in the hall, and his father looked much too similar to Logan.

"What are you doing?" she asked as he stepped in front of her.

"He does not have a portrait. I do not want you to waste your time searching." He should have had the foresight to remove the blasted thing before she arrived at Waking Hall.

She jerked her arm away as all traces of excitement were replaced by annoyance. "Well, maybe he has acquired one since you were last here." She stepped around him and resumed her walk down the long line of portraits, glancing up at the noble faces of past dukes and duchesses.

Logan kept pace with her, hoping she would listen to reason but knowing she would not. After all, she had almost reached the end of the room where his father's portrait hung, and what could deter her? "I will give you one last warning to stop on your own before I make you."

"Oh, do be serious. This will take but a moment."

She showed no signs of complying, so Logan pulled her into his arms, stifling her feeble protests with his lips. The instant their lips connected, she ceased her struggles, properly entrancing him with her softness and willingness. Every time he touched her, a spark of magic erupted, and a kiss was like a little explosion, leaving him reeling and unable to function.

She moaned and held onto him in a tight embrace, her slim hands clutching his lapels. A tingle raced down his spine as she brought one hand to his hair, lacing it there and jerking him to her. He growled at the sensation her actions evoked. Her kissing lacked technique, but she more than made up for it in her eagerness.

Yes, she was a novice, and that knowledge, in that moment, astounded him. If possible, he would have pulled away then and whispered endearments in her ear, but alas, such a dream would never materialize. Instead, images of Ellie in dishabille flashed across his mind, and he deepened the kiss, unable to pull free.

In the past, there had been times where he longed for the comfort of a woman. Not necessarily in terms of bed sport, but to fill the void of loneliness he so often experienced. Today, with Ellie in his arms, his quest had reached its end. So long as she remained at his side, he would never feel that haunting feeling of loneliness again.

Whispering her name against her lips, Logan began to back her up against the wall when suddenly he heard a thud and the distinct sound of crockery breaking. He cursed as he broke off the kiss to find he had maneuvered Ellie into a very large, priceless Grecian urn. He couldn't care less about the ruined urn, but Ellie and the lost heated moment were another matter.

"Are you unharmed?" he asked as worry overtook his senses. She stepped away from him, running a hand down her skirt but failing to fix her off-kilter bodice and tousled hair. Her eyes held a look of dismay at the abrupt end of their kiss, which nearly caused him to pull her back into his arms and continue the embrace.

He stopped himself when the life sprang back to her eyes. "Of course I am, but look at this urn! His Grace will never understand what happened here, not that we can tell him the exact details." She wrung her hands and trembled from the shock of it all, continuing to speak and only pausing to draw breath.

Logan grinned as she rambled on about their predicament. They had a knack for breaking pottery, but at least this one was in his house. He took her hand in his and interrupted whatever bit of nonsense she imparted by saying, "Do not worry, it was an ugly thing to begin with. I cannot imagine it will be missed."

"Did you not see it? The thing was breathtaking." She groaned. She appeared distraught and very near to tears, which meant his grin was inappropriate.

He erased all signs of mirth and gave her a dour look, pulling her to him and stroking her back in a calming manner. "I would think it obvious I didn't see it; otherwise, we would not have stumbled into it in the first place." When she didn't respond to his joke, he tried another tactic. "His Grace will understand. There is no reason to get so upset." He placed a gentle kiss on the top of her head and savored the scent of the sunshine that still lingered from her time outdoors.

She stepped from his embrace and shook her head. Her eyes appeared almost frantic as she said, "Don't you understand? His Grace will never want to marry a clumsy lady who cannot navigate an empty portrait room. If men cannot make allowances for a lady who does not like horses, how could they possibly forgive this? My dowry may not even cover the cost of that urn." She groaned and shut her eyes.

"Who has filled your head with such ideas? We discussed this before. You should not worry so much about others' perceptions of you. If the duke does not wish to marry you because of this incident, then you are much better off without him."

Ellie thrust her hands on her hips and asked in a raised voice, "So your suggestion is I stop caring and end up alone? Maybe I can end up like Mrs. Westfield, always at the mercy of whatever kind relation decides to support me. I thought we decided you live in a dream world, because I must abide by certain rules of society in order to obtain a husband."

Logan ran a hand through his hair. She was so frustrating. "Obviously there are certain rules one must abide by, but perfection is not one of them." His expression softened as he said, "I, for one, would not care if you destroyed every priceless object in my house, provided it was unintentional."

Her breath hitched as she inhaled, and for one fleeting moment, a look of longing flickered in those eyes. She shook her head and whispered, "You do not mean that." She turned from him, still shaking her head as if she needed to convince herself of her words, not him. "I suppose you must. I am a good enough catch for you to make any number of sacrifices for."

"I mean precisely what I say, whether you are a good catch or not." Her jaw did not budge from its stubborn tilt, and he scowled as he turned from her. "You know how to ruin a moment." He extended his arm. "Shall we? The servants must be notified so they may clean up our mess before someone wanders down here and injures himself."

"I suppose." Ellie accepted his arm, although her body remained stiff. They departed the room and strolled along the dimly lit corridor in tense silence. After several moments, she sent him a wry smile and said, "You probably told me I could break every priceless thing in your house because you do not own any."

He quirked an eyebrow as he relished in the irony of the situation. "I have plenty of money, at least enough to own some precious items. Maybe not as many as your duke, but enough."

"Hmm."

"Yes, my lady?"

"Well, it appears you are rather jealous of His Grace. You tend to act barbarically when I speak of him, and you would not even allow me to look for his picture."

He tensed, and she smiled.

He continued to stroll without response. If she wished to believe he acted out of jealousy, then he would allow her to, although it irked him when she put the duke on a pedestal without having met the man. "I will admit I have a soft spot for you, although if you were to compare me to any other man than the duke I would not care."

"Hmm. He must be quite the specimen then." She arched an eyebrow and looked up at him, batting her lashes in a masterful example of coquetry.

Logan could see she teased and attempted to elicit his jealousy once more. Fortunately for her, he would play along. He tugged her to him and spoke in a low growl as he trailed kisses down her neck. "You play a dangerous game, my lady. Are you sure you wish to speak of him in my presence?"

She giggled, arching her spine to bring herself nearer to him. "I do not believe the duke would waste time talking right now."

Logan's eyes widened with surprised approval, and then he wisely chose to stop talking and kiss her. With a melting sigh, Eleanor's lips parted to allow Logan's entrance. He growled his desire. Her agile wit only heightened his desire for her. No matter what others said of her, she had many good qualities, and he enjoyed discovering each and every one of them.

And he would. After all, he had made startling progress with her, this lady that would be his wife. She may act as if she preferred some unknown duke, but she behaved much more welcoming toward him with each encounter.

His hand drifted to her hair and intertwined in its soft confines. He was enraptured by the spell she wove around him. No matter how hard she fought him, her kisses betrayed her feelings, and he himself grew more attached with every candid moment they shared. Logan began to back her up into the wall, wanting nothing more than to give her pleasure but realizing it was too soon to do anything drastic. He trailed hot kisses down her throat once more and paused to nip gently at her collarbone while his hands trailed down to her shapely bottom.

Eleanor arched her back in response to his touches, allowing him an appreciable view down her bodice. She grabbed a fistful of his hair and jerked his mouth back to hers. He smiled, pulling away despite her grumble of protest. The physical aspect of their relationship was progressing too quickly. He wanted her heart much more than he wanted a simple dalliance. After all, he could have her endlessly once she fell for him.

He smirked as he regarded her. "How does your duke compare in *that*?"

Ellie's dreamy expression vanished. "You ass. I would not know." She stomped past him and said in passing, "If you had half a brain, you would not have asked that."

"My lady."

She turned back to him and raised a haughty brow. "Yes?"

"Did you plan to repair your hair before or after everyone sees you so disheveled?"

Eleanor's hand flew to her coiffure as a blush suffused her face. She mumbled a polite, albeit reluctant, thank-you and set her hair to rights. Once she looked presentable again, she turned her attention back to Logan. "Oh, do not look so smug. You have proven nothing except you are an acceptable kisser. Besides, it is hardly commendable to lure me on this tour just to accost me."

"Now, now, my dear, do not turn spiteful after everything we shared together. Besides, I had wanted nothing more than to talk to you on our adventure."

Ellie threw her head back and laughed. "I doubt that."

He had hoped they might kiss but never dared dream of a kiss that left him reeling and in want of much, much more. "What must I do to prove myself to you?"

She considered him for a moment, and then a devious smile appeared on her face. "You may join my chaperone and me for afternoon tea." She did not bother to wait for a reply before she stomped away. Logan was left with a knowing smile and the view of her delectable backside.

Chapter 7

Eleanor and Mrs. Westfield chatted in the little parlor granted them for their afternoon tea. A tray laden with tea and biscuits awaited their attentions, but neither touched it. Instead, they focused on discussing the décor of the room. The green brocade upholstery and faded yellow walls left nothing to remark against. Even the seating offered substantial padding, but there was one thing Mrs. Westfield did not approve of, which was the addition of a third party.

"I cannot comprehend why he must take tea with us."

Eleanor exhaled a frustrated breath and leaned forward in her solitary chair toward Mrs. Westfield, who was seated on a couch. "Sir Logan has an agile mind, and you will enjoy discourse with him."

"You say that, but I am unconvinced."

Shaking her head, she sat back and crossed her arms over her chest. She could hardly disinvite the gentleman now, even though she wished she could do precisely that. Oh, why had she invited him for tea? At the time, it seemed a logical punishment, yet now, the retribution was not for him. Rather it was for her. With even the slightest mishap, Mrs. Westfield would see through her icy façade of indifference and realize Eleanor liked the gentleman. And that would not do.

The parlor door swung open, and Eleanor's mind

hastened to the present. Logan stood framed in the doorway, looking handsome and unfazed by the day's events. She sighed as she drank in his masculine physique, but when his eyes met hers, she snapped her mouth shut. Could she get any more obvious about her attraction for him? She darted a glance at Mrs. Westfield, who appeared to have missed Eleanor's slip. Exhaling her relief, she smiled a welcoming smile to Logan.

"Ladies." He bowed as he entered the room and took a seat across from Eleanor on a dainty chair.

Eleanor poured the tea into three porcelain cups as he said, "Have you broken anything else today, Miss Ashford?"

Eleanor set the teapot down with a loud clatter. Logan did not make her task of keeping Mrs. Westfield unaware any easier. If anything, his little question had the exact opposite effect, for such a direct inquiry was sure to raise suspicion.

She pasted a polite smile on her face and said, "Why no, Sir Logan."

"And you have not caused anyone else to break anything?"

Eleanor arched an eyebrow and shot a coy smile at him. "As if I would tell you if I had." Now that she had discovered his jealous side, she might as well use it to her advantage. His hooded eyes watched her and betrayed no trace of emotion, even though she could feel a hum of tension between them.

Mrs. Westfield appeared near to experiencing an apoplectic fit. "What manner of conversation is this? No one had better break anything of His Grace's."

Eleanor laughed and patted her aunt's hand. "Do

not worry, we jest." She turned her gaze to Logan and smiled. "I would never dream of breaking anything of His Grace's."

"That would be an unusual dream to have, my lady."

That was one thing about Logan that she appreciated. His humor. She quirked her eyebrow at him and smirked. "I would think most ladies dream of His Grace."

A spark leapt to his eyes, and he leaned forward. "Oh? Even when they have not met him? That seems a touch mercenary to me."

Mrs. Westfield frowned and glanced from Logan to Eleanor. "Well, my dear niece was raised to be ambitious. It's not as if she would dream of a baronet." She placed a hand over her mouth in mock chagrin. "Oh dear. I did not mean to offend, Sir Logan."

Eleanor scowled. Her behavior today was far from secretive, and her aunt must understand the cause of underlying tension between her and Logan. She would receive a stern lecture later, but such a reprimand meant little.

She coughed and changed topics. "Sir Logan, my dear aunt and I were just discussing what a mystery you are."

Logan quirked an eyebrow which indicated she should continue.

"It appears my aunt has never heard of you, which seems unlikely if you are as wealthy as you claim."

He shifted in his chair. "I had not realized I was to be interrogated this afternoon. All I can say is I have no way of knowing why you have never heard of me, Mrs. Westfield."

Mrs. Westfield nodded her agreement. "That is precisely what I told Eleanor. I am not so acquainted with the landowners so far north." At this point, she began to discuss her travels in her younger years. She focused on her trips to the northern regions of England. Logan raised a discreet brow at Eleanor, and she almost giggled out loud. Mrs. Westfield could talk at length given a chance.

When her tales slowed, Mrs. Westfield sighed and sat back in her chair with a dreamy expression in her eyes. Eleanor took advantage of the interlude and asked Logan, "So you have very few relations, but what else should we know about you?"

"Well, my favorite treat is apple tarts. They taste divine, especially served with clotted cream as dessert. I am not much of a drinker or gambler, and I would like to have a certain blonde, blue-eyed woman marry me someday."

Eleanor sent her eyes heavenward and groaned as Mrs. Westfield leaned in with eyes narrowed in hawk-like intensity. "Oh, is it someone we know?"

His eyes went to Mrs. Westfield's, and he shook his head. "I am afraid I cannot say. The lady does not return my feelings at present." He added extra emphasis on the word present, and Eleanor scowled at him.

"How terrible," Eleanor's aunt murmured. "I always hate to hear of unrequited love."

His feelings for her did not qualify as unrequited love. He certainly had not said anything to her about love, at least. The only thing he had done to convey his feelings was kiss her. No, she would not countenance the idea of love, not when it would end up disappointing her in the end.

She smiled and leaned toward Logan. She would play along with this game. "Oh yes, Sir Logan. Unrequited love is such a tragedy. You simply must tell us if there is anything we can do to help."

He took a final sip of his tea and stood. He trained his gaze on her and nodded. "I am afraid there is nothing anyone can do, except hope the lady comes to her senses before it's too late." He bowed. "I am afraid I must depart. Thank you for the delightful tea."

As the door shut behind him, Mrs. Westfield turned to eye Eleanor. "Why do I get the impression the certain blonde-haired, blue-eyed lady is you?"

Eleanor took a sip of her tea and tried to tamp down her annoyance at having orchestrated this entire event. "Does it matter if I am the lady? I already know whom I will marry, and it is not him."

"I would say he is a great catch for any lady, except yourself. You are wise to say no to him. With your beauty and dowry, you can do so much better." When Eleanor failed to respond to her aunt's unsolicited advice, her aunt asked, "Have you heard word of the duke's health? I do hope he improves."

With a start, Eleanor realized she had not truly thought of the duke all day. She had pestered Logan with mentions of His Grace to engender Logan's jealousy, but Logan had remained firmly planted in her mind. What a terrible realization, and what implications did that hold for her?

****

With the end of tea, Eleanor was left with some free time on her hands before dinner commenced. She contemplated taking a nap but quickly blotted out that idea in favor of painting. Normally, she would direct a lesser servant to carry her supplies, but since there was a severe lack of servants she would enlist Olivia's aid.

Olivia followed Eleanor down the stairs and to the gardens, where the sun beat down and warmed the spring air to a pleasant temperature. With the dazzling array of flowers set out before her, Eleanor settled onto the garden bench to work.

She soon lost herself in visions of purple azaleas and wrought-iron trellises. Without realizing the passage of time, the waning light signaled the end for Eleanor's session. She sat back and surveyed her work. Although incomplete, the painting showed promise. She would have to return outside once more on the morrow to finish it.

She stood and stretched to relieve the tension in her back. Olivia packed up the supplies while Eleanor secured her canvas. She was always shy about her work, never allowing others to see it until completed and then only if it met her standards. Most did not. After all, her skill was tolerable at best, but she received pleasure from the act of painting which was reward enough.

Upon returning to her room, Eleanor prepared for dinner. The evening air chilled her, especially as the sun dipped below the horizon, so she chose a heavier gown in a buttercream color to warm her. She wasn't hungry yet, as her home kept to city hours where everyone rose later in the day and consequently ate later. In a duke's house, however, one did as directed.

Eleanor once again knocked on Mrs. Westfield's door. Her aunt had a headache and preferred to stay in bed for the night. Eleanor wished her well, and then made her way down to the dining room.

The gentlemen rose as Eleanor entered, and she hurried to her seat across from a peaked Lady Gammon.

"My lady," Eleanor said with a warm smile before greeting the gentlemen. Taking in the countess's tired appearance, she asked, "Are you feeling quite all right?"

Lady Gammon shook her head. "They say my sickness might pass soon, but I am not so certain."

Lord Gammon patted his wife's hand, while Eleanor said, "I am sure they are right." Not having been around pregnant women, she hadn't the faintest idea, but it sounded nice.

Logan smiled at her as her eyes met his. "Will your aunt join us tonight?"

"No. She claims to have a headache and wishes to remain in her room."

Logan's brow furrowed. He leaned forward, his lips tensing in a grim line. "The duke's illness began with a headache. I hope she has not caught what ails him."

Lady Gammon coughed. "Oh dear. I cannot imagine how she could possibly catch that. The duke has been quarantined."

"I hope she has not caught anything. I am sure she will be fine, but imagine if you should fall ill!" It could not bode well for a pregnant woman to catch a serious illness.

Lady Gammon shook her head. "I am afraid this illness originated in our household, which is where His Grace caught it. I must be immune to it or something."

This must be quite the sickness. Eleanor began to connect the dots, and she leaned forward to ask, "Is that why there are no servants here? They are all ill?"

Lord Gammon spoke with a slight smile playing across his lips. "Goodness, no, Miss Ashford." His voice lowered in a conspiring manner. "His Grace behaves in a most unfortunate manner at times. This is just one of his strange starts, although certainly not his worst."

Eleanor raised an eyebrow. She knew of no rumors in regards to such odd behavior, but very little was known of His Grace. How curious.

Lady Gammon chuckled in agreement with her husband. "Yes, he has his quirks. Why, he may not be sick at all! For all we know, it's some fabricated illness all in his head."

Such a trait was not something Eleanor desired in a mate. She lifted her eyebrow and asked, "Why are you friends with him then?"

Logan coughed and frowned at Lord and Lady Gammon. "He is a very good sort of fellow with many redeeming qualities." His tone turned frosty as he reprimanded the couple. "You two should be ashamed of yourselves for speaking of him that way in his own home."

Lady Gammon's eyes twinkled, and she giggled. "We felt Miss Ashford deserved to know the truth about our host, Sir Logan. Do not sound so personally affronted."

The food was carried in, ending the conversation as everyone's attention turned to the meal. Eleanor appreciated any information about the duke she could glean, although she had not expected such strange faults. It struck her as odd that Logan would defend him after behaving so jealously, but she supposed they were still friends at the end of the day.

"So," Lady Gammon asked Eleanor, "did my eyes deceive me, or were you painting in the gardens this afternoon?"

"Why yes, my lady, I simply cannot resist the pull of such splendor." Although she supposed she might paint anything if she were bored enough.

With a nod of approval, Lady Gammon asked, "Will you be outside again tomorrow? Some fresh air might do me good."

Eleanor smiled and nodded. She had eaten her meal quickly and was left to nurse her glass of wine while sneaking surreptitious glances at Logan. He appeared engrossed in conversation with Lord Gammon, which left Eleanor to appreciate the view of his strong jaw and other handsome features.

Lady Gammon sipped on her water and then whispered, "You have fallen for him, haven't you?"

Eleanor's cheeks heated, and she tried to keep her expression serene. "Whatever do you mean?"

"Your feelings for Logan." The countess sighed. "Your love for him is written all over your face."

Eleanor froze as the words washed over her. The notion that she could fall in love was ridiculous, especially since she didn't believe in its existence. "I can assure you that is not the case, my lady. I do not believe in such nonsense."

Lady Gammon regarded her with a dubious frown and said, "I can tell you from personal experience that love exists. I am still in love with Reuben as much as the day we first met. You may be in denial, but your feelings are clear. You love Logan."

Eleanor's breath ceased as her body failed to work. She sat immobilized in a state of shock at the countess's suggestion. She sneaked another glance at Logan. Could there be some truth to Lady Gammon's words?

Logan knew how to make her feel special, but he irritated her to no end. His very presence in the same room as her made her body overheat, all while she wished he would smother her in kisses. If there were anyone she could love, it would be him. Shoving the thought away, she quelled the notion. She still did not believe, and she doubted her opinion would change.

Eleanor rose as a general weariness overcame her. "I think I shall retire for the evening. Good night." She curtsied and departed from the room while carrying her unfinished glass of wine with her. She entered her room and took a seat in front of the fireplace. As she stared numbly into the burning embers, she took another sip of her wine.

Her mother always swore love did not exist, but her aunt swore it did. Her cousin Laura had married for love, and now Lady Gammon claimed to do the same. Could Eleanor be wrong? If she married the duke and later found out love existed, she would have made an enormous mistake.

She inhaled sharply as the realization came to mind that she no longer valued status above all else. Before meeting Logan, she would never have entertained the idea that marriage to a duke could be wrong for her. What in heaven had happened to her? She closed her eyes. Logan was not good enough for her to consider, but she did not think she wanted to consider anyone else.

A knock sounded on the door, and she rose, crossed the room, and opened it. Shockingly enough, Logan stood in the hallway. Dizziness descended, and her vision blurred from the astonishment of his unbidden presence on her doorstep. She blinked, forcing herself to focus and not swoon. Her constitution was stout under normal circumstances, but these were not normal circumstances. Gentlemen did *not* show up at a young lady's chambers. Ever.

Eleanor brushed aside her maidenly sensibilities, leaning out of her doorway and glancing down the hallway. As far as she could tell, they were alone, but she had no way of knowing if someone would come walking by. She grabbed a fistful of his shirt and pulled him into her room while shutting the door as swiftly as she could without making a sound.

"What are you doing here?" she hissed as she glared at him for his audacity. "I would be ruined if someone saw you!"

"Relax, my dear. I just wanted to make sure you are well. You left so abruptly after dinner." His gaze drifted down to the hand still gripping his shirt. He grinned and said, "Judging by the way you pulled me in here, I believe you are rather happy to see me."

She jerked her hand away from him. He was exasperating and so, so right. She was happy to see him.

She dropped her hand to her side and turned from him as he said, "You needn't answer me now, Ellie. Not when I know the truth."

And there he was, using that infernal name again. She growled as she stomped her foot, turning back to him once more. "My name is not Ellie."

"I think you will always be Ellie to me."

"Of course I will," she muttered. "How did you know which room I was staying in?"

"I overheard the butler mention it before you arrived." He took a step toward her and turned her to him. He brought his hand to her face and skimmed her skin, which caused all manner of butterflies to dance in her stomach. "You look a bit pale. Are you sure you are fine?"

She knocked his hand aside. "I am only pale because you presumed to show up in my chamber. You really should leave." She inhaled a breath of anticipation as he moved closer yet.

"Just one good-night kiss to assure me you are indeed in good health." He lowered his lips to hers without giving her time to respond. Her eyes drifted shut, which effectively shut off the voices of propriety suggesting she stop. She did not care how much money he had or that he was a baronet. All she cared for was the way he made her feel, which was intoxicated. Intoxicated by his sweet promises and alluring temptations.

He parted her lips with his tongue, and she allowed him access, despite the knowledge that she shouldn't. Every time they touched, she found herself entirely at his mercy, wanting, no needing, whatever he would give her. This time was no different. His hand dipped past the small of her back, and she practically thanked him by intertwining her hand in his coarse hair.

Her lapse was broken as a knock rang out. Eleanor jumped away from him as if scalded and drew in a ragged breath. "Hide." Without a word, he glided into her bed and pulled the canopy shut behind him.

Eleanor took several deep, fortifying breaths before opening the door to find her maid, Olivia. Olivia curtseyed and stepped into the room. "I figured you would like to change, my lady."

Eleanor surveyed the bed. She did not think Logan was visible, and she nodded. Most of her gowns required assistance to get in and out of, and this one was no exception. "Let's make this quick." She moved to the opposite side of the bed where she was almost certain Logan could not see her. Olivia divested Eleanor of her gown, and then Eleanor turned to her, hoping her grateful smile was convincing enough. "I am tired, Olivia. Please just give me my nightgown."

Olivia quirked her head and pursed her lips but did as bidden. Once the nightgown was on, Olivia asked, "Can I help you with anything else, my lady?"

"That should be all." Eleanor thanked her and directed Olivia to find her pallet for the night. The door closed behind her, and Eleanor whirled to the bed, throwing aside the canopy to find Logan. "You see! I told you it was a bad idea to come here. What if she had seen you?"

"What indeed," he murmured. "What a tragedy if we were forced to wed."

She nodded in agreement as she waited for him to get out of her bed. When he failed to emerge, she tapped her foot. Removing oneself from another's bed should not pose this much difficulty. "What are you doing in there?"

"It appears I have caught my clothing on something," he said from inside the shadowy confines of the canopy.

Eleanor climbed onto the mattress and mumbled, "What could you have possibly been snared on?" She could make out the outline of his prone form in the far corner of her bed, but from what she could see, he did not appear to be stuck on anything. "Are you unhinged? You are not caught."

He laughed, which only confirmed her fears. "I am caught, my lady, caught by you." Then he pounced. He rolled her onto her back as he smothered her in his embrace. He laughed as he placed feather kisses on her face. She giggled and tried to roll away, but his arms imprisoned her and she couldn't escape.

Her eyes met his in the darkness, and she stilled. His dark green eyes held a gravity that belied his laughter, and her heart constricted as she understood that he might have said she had caught him in a jocular manner, but he meant his words with fervent intensity.

The fire crackled, and she placed her hand behind his head. She drew him to her, and he kissed her. Fully, with nothing held back. She abandoned herself to him, without worry of repercussions, just understanding he would always catch her if she should fall. How could she not trust him with every part of her, when he proved himself as the most honorable, thoughtful, and wonderful man she had ever met? No, she was safe with him, safe with this gentleman she had somehow believed beneath her. Safe with a man who set her on fire and burned her to a singed, unrecognizable version of herself. She was safe, yet was she? Her heart said no with every thump. She yearned for him, for nothing but him.

With a final nuzzle, he pulled away and grinned. "See, I told you I am caught. I cannot escape your hold if I tried."

Acute, brutal awareness of her arms, wrapped around him in a wanton manner, hit her. The magic of the moment died, and she actually groaned. She, the epitome of a lady, groaned. "You are ridiculous."

He affected a hurt look and said, "You are supposed to be swept away by my romantic sentiments."

She laughed and scurried out from under him, despite her strong urge to pull him back to her and ignore his levity. She managed to get off the bed before she turned to him and said, "You tricked me into that and do not deserve rewards for such behavior."

"Fair enough," he murmured as he joined her in standing. His eyes drifted over her, and her stomach clenched at the predatory look in his eyes. "You should wear nightgowns more often. You look enchanting in them."

"I wear them as often as I ought." She smiled despite her retort. She should feel embarrassment that he had seen her in such an improper manner, but all it did was embolden her. Heat threatened to rise to her face as it occurred to her she could seduce him. Right now. The knowledge had always been there with most gentlemen, but with him it was an actual possibility, and she was oh so wicked to consider it.

He bowed and placed a sizzling kiss on her hand. "I have determined you are in robust health. Good night, my lady. I wish you sweet dreams." With that, he departed, leaving Eleanor energized and far from tired. The audacity of the man was too much.

Yes, he should not have come to her, and now she would have no choice but to dwell on him until she succumbed to sleep, which would prove elusive. How could she sleep when a large chunk of her heart had been ripped from her chest and given to him?

Chapter 8

Having slept soundly once she fell asleep, Eleanor woke rested and ready to face the day. She ate her breakfast in bed, and then she and Olivia returned outside. The overcast sky did not hold as much promise as the previous day, but Eleanor would forget the weather once she started painting. She always did.

She worked for a short while but was interrupted when Lady Gammon stepped in front of her. Lady Gammon appeared tired again but still quite lovely with her pregnancy glow. "Good morning, Lady Gammon. I trust you slept well?" She smiled at the countess and indicated an open spot next to her on the bench.

"Tolerably," Lady Gammon said as she came to stand next to Eleanor, declining to take a seat. "Your painting is lovely. You have a gift."

Eleanor blushed at the compliment and took a moment to observe her work. An iron trellis was the focal point, with lush, green vines intertwining up and over the structure. She had decided against the use of tulips; rather, she used the half-opened buds of azaleas. She could not complain about her work. Not only had she captured its beauty, but she had enhanced it to the point one might expect a fairy to come prancing out.

Eleanor rose from her chair and stretched, enjoying the change of standing after a long period of sitting. "Thank you. My work should not blind someone from its ugliness." She gestured to a path which meandered alongside a nearby pond. "Would you care to join me for a stroll?"

"I had planned to watch you paint, but if you would prefer to walk, I can adjust."

Eleanor turned to Olivia and directed her to cover her paints. They strolled toward the shoreline. The water appeared like smooth glass in its stillness, unblemished by any wind or external factor. Yet another vista Eleanor could paint.

They walked through the picturesque landscape, and Eleanor was startled by Lady Gammon's question. "Are you and your cousin no longer on speaking terms?"

Eleanor's thoughts raced as she pieced together the clues. Most ladies felt threatened by her and did not befriend her without ulterior motives. Now the countess fished for information on a juicy topic which any gossip would enjoy hearing. It all made perfect sense.

Eleanor tensed and schooled her features. A little white lie was preferable to malicious gossip. "We correspond regularly. Why do you ask?"

Lady Gammon shrugged. "I always remembered seeing you two together. Is she enjoying marriage then?"

Eleanor closed her eyes and yearned for a breeze to cool her face. She had already spoken to Lady Gammon of love and Logan's potential feelings. That much would become fodder, but she could mitigate the rest. "Of course. Laura has never been happier."

"That is excellent news." The countess slowed their walk to pick up a stone to skip across the smooth surface of the lake. "Three times," she muttered.

"Reuben will not be impressed."

"I beg your pardon?" Eleanor asked, although the last thing she wished was polite conversation now that she had uncovered Lady Gammon's motives.

"Oh, it is just something my husband and I do when we are by bodies of water." She stepped away from the bank and placed a hand to her belly. "They say I should feel my little one move soon."

Not having been around a pregnant woman before, Eleanor was shocked by the statement. "You mean you will feel the baby move *inside* of you?"

Lady Gammon laughed and lowered herself to the lawn. "Of course, once the baby is big enough. Now I am afraid I must take a break. I am not supposed to push myself after my miscarriages."

Eleanor ignored the potential for grass stains and joined Lady Gammon on the ground. A flash of pain passed through Lady Gammon's eyes, and Eleanor asked, "How long have you tried to have a baby?"

"Several years now." Her look was bittersweet as she said, "I have suffered two miscarriages, but each one has drawn Reuben and me closer. I know this pregnancy will be successful, though. I feel it."

Eleanor propped herself up on one gloved hand and turned to regard Lady Gammon. Would a lady in search of gossip share such intimate details? She doubted it. Only a lackwit would confide in a person and then turn around to gossip about her.

"You truly wish to be friends?" Something caught in her throat, and she turned away.

Lady Gammon's nose crinkled, and her lips turned up in a wry grin. "Of course, dear. Whether you marry the duke or the baronet, we will see each other frequently."

No one ever wished to be friends with her. Most ladies were too intimidated by her fortunate looks and avoided her. Those that did not avoid her openly shunned her. Except for Laura. Laura had stood by her, until now.

A mischievous note entered Lady Gammon's voice as she said, "You know if you marry Logan, you will be the baby's godmother."

Eleanor straightened as panic set in. Logan and she would not wed, although the thought of leaving him left her quite empty inside. "I am afraid that will not happen. He is still of an unacceptable class."

Lady Gammon rose and shook her head. "How unfortunate you believe that. Shall we return then?"

Eleanor agreed, and they ambled back to the behemoth of a house via the pebbled path they had taken on the way down. The thought that the countess had confided such a personal secret whilst she lied about her own weighed heavily on her, so she said, "Lady Gammon, I am afraid I misspoke earlier. Laura and I are not on speaking terms. In fact, I have no idea how she is as she refuses to respond to my letters."

"I thought as much. I heard rumors of you casting some aspersion against her. Naturally I do not always believe the rumor mill, but this time it appears true."

"Yes, well, I apologize for it every time I write to her. She does not forgive me, not that I blame her," Eleanor said as a stray blonde hair fell across her face. She pushed it behind her ear and kicked her boot against a stone.

"Sometimes a letter does not suffice. I would bet your apology would be much more effective in person."

"Yes, well, I will try that strategy and hope her husband has not banned me from their household." She doubted her cousin would allow that to happen, but she had also expected Laura to respond by now, so she could be wrong.

Lady Gammon chuckled. "No man should be foolish enough as to come between two ladies like that." They arrived back at their starting point, and Lady Gammon patted Eleanor's hand. She turned to enter the house but looked over her shoulder to say, "I am sure things will work out. Matters such as these always do."

The countess walked up the path, and her hips swayed with each step. Her trim figure still did not show any sign of the child within. A spark of jealousy bloomed within Eleanor as she thought of how happy Lady Gammon was. Not only did she have a title and wealth, but she was in love and now expecting her first child. Eleanor had not even realized these were goals she wished to attain, but seeing someone so blissful had decided things for her. She wanted it all.

She resumed her work and added the finishing touches to the artwork she would allow the world to see. Later on, she would add some personal details that would remain forever locked away in secret. As she began to gather her things, a shiver ran down her spine.

"May I help you, Sir Logan?" How had she allowed him to sneak up on her without realizing it?

"Your work is that of a master," he said, still looking over her shoulder at her painting.

"Thank you." She softened at his comment and said, "If you seek Lady Gammon, she just returned to the house."

"I know." He smiled down at her, and his eyes betrayed his appreciation for the view of her bosom. "I ran into her as I came out."

Eleanor stood and narrowly missed bumping heads with him in her rush. His look made her pulse accelerate and her insides turn to mush. If only she could kiss him, but seeing as she tried to keep her reputation intact, she had best refrain from such scandalous behavior.

"I would say we are getting much better at avoiding disaster," he said as he held out his arm.

After rattling off a few instructions to Olivia, Eleanor accepted his arm. "Are you escorting me anywhere special?"

He sent her a heartwarming smile and led her to the manor. "Of course. We must finish our tour of the house."

"Ah," she muttered while attempting to focus on anything else around her but him. All she could think to ask was, "How is His Grace today?"

Logan's face darkened, and his mouth slanted to a grim line. "He is about the same." Silence prevailed until they neared the manor. "Now then, is there any room in particular you care to see?"

She raised an eyebrow. He had ruined her perusal of the picture gallery the previous day, and she wished to see what he hid from her. "The picture gallery should suffice, and this time you can allow me access to *all* the portraits."

He smirked. "Or do you hope I will kiss you as I did last time?"

"Of course not!" Eleanor said as her cheeks heated. While she did indeed long for his kisses, he did not need to know. Logan led her through a set of heavy wooden doors, down a hall, and into the familiar room. Eleanor wasted no time dallying, instead she directed her attention to the newest portraits.

Dismay swept over her when she found no new portraits had been hung, although she swore there was a slight fading of the wallpaper around a rectangular area. She quirked her eyebrow and asked Logan, "Where is the missing portrait?"

Logan shrugged. "You will have to ask His Grace."

"Hmm," she murmured as she turned back to him. His eyes held a mischievous glimmer, and in that moment, she decided she no longer cared to see a painting of His Grace. Not when Logan stood near her, holding her heart with his own special blend of intrigue. "You may continue our tour now."

The couple walked in companionable silence, meandering through several rooms that should have received mention on their tour but were neglected. As they exited an ornate, gilded chapel, Logan finally broke the silence. "I spoke the truth earlier when I said your painting is lovely. Given the chance, I would frame it and display it in my house."

Eleanor laughed while her heart thumped to hear his praise. She did not share her art with people, just as she did not share her inner thoughts. With him, she wished to change that. An uncharacteristic feeling of shyness arose, but she thrust it aside. "Thank you, but you haven't seen the finished product yet."

"Whatever do you mean?"

"Well," she said, stopping their stroll to muster her courage. "I always do this in secret, but I add mythical creatures to my art." She stopped breathing as she waited for his answer. No one knew her secret, and he very well could laugh at her and shatter her.

He paused to consider her admission before chuckling. "You are drawn to your kind, I see, although I cannot picture a water nymph in the gardens."

She swatted him as a weight fell from her. He had not laughed at her. "Don't be absurd. I would never paint a water nymph unless it was a scene with water."

His expression softened, and he murmured, "How very appropriate of you." He paused to consider her, his expression intently serious. "I do believe when we marry, I will commission a painting of you in all your watery glory."

Disconcerted by his serious façade, Eleanor proceeded to walk once more. He kept pace with her and asked, "Why the secrecy in your artwork, though?" Before she could respond, he tensed and said, "Oh right, you cannot allow gentlemen to think you have a thought of your own."

"That is not true. I always display my wit, just not my eccentricities."

"Forgive the misunderstanding, my lady."

Eleanor placed her hand on his arm as they resumed their farce of a tour. She eyed the place where her fingers grazed his suede jacket. Drawing her gaze up his arm and to his profile, she stared in wonderment at this unusual creature before her. How was it he could convince her to question every belief she held? How could such a man as he accept her for her foolish eccentricities, when she herself could not?

He tilted his head and smiled at her, waiting for her to say or do something. She scowled and asked, "What?"

He chuckled, and she blushed. Her tone had been rather gruff. "Every time we touch, you emit a small gasp." A hurried denial rose to her lips, but he spoke before she could say anything. "Just admit it. You find me attractive."

Her blush intensified at his bold statement. "I do not. Your accusation is most untrue."

"It is all right, my lady. I cannot keep my eyes off you either."

A sense of pride filled her. Of course she realized she was beautiful, but his attentions meant so much more to her. They crossed over the threshold to an exquisite ballroom. All the cornices were a dark bronze color with equally dark marble on the floor. The walls were white, and the ceiling…That was the true masterpiece. The ceiling held images of white, billowy clouds against a backdrop of aqua skies.

She stared at the splendor before her. This ballroom was by far the most luxurious one she had stepped foot in. A ballroom such as this justified why she did not waste herself on such a man as Logan. With him, she lost sight of her goals. Logan could never provide for her as a duke could, yet why did it hurt so much to think of cutting him from her life?

Tearing her gaze from the ceiling, she turned to Logan and said, "I fear you are mistaken, Sir Logan. I find many things to be more attractive than you."

"Sir Logan?" His voice lowered to a rough growl, and he turned her to face him. "I thought—" His voice trailed off, and he stopped all movement, just stood there staring intently into her eyes. When he spoke once more, his voice was firmer, more assured. "You must have remembered you are too good for me. Your mind and your body are at odds, my dear. You find me just as attractive as I find you."

His words stopped her cold. His description matched her quandary to perfection, but for one exception. Her mind fought him but, instead of firm resolve, teetered on a precarious ledge. She knew he would catch her, but could she allow herself to be caught?

She closed her eyes and whispered, "Yes. I am attracted to you. You are by far the most handsome man I have ever laid eyes on, and I want nothing more than to kiss you all the time."

Eleanor turned away from him, keeping her eyes closed against the pain in her heart as she said, "But so what? All that will happen from this mutual attraction is we kiss some more and avoid breaking a few more vases."

Logan draped his arms around her and nestled the back of her head in the crook of his neck. His warmth surrounded her in this cold, empty room, and his masculine scent filled her with longing for him. "You know full well where our attraction can lead. I want to marry you, not just play with you and discard you at my convenience."

Eleanor sighed, allowing herself to nestle into his warmth. "I know, and you have no idea how appealing that sounds, but we both know it cannot happen."

He breathed in a ragged breath and kissed the top of her head. "Stubborn woman. There is nothing holding you back but yourself." They stood together for several minutes, content to remain close. Her mind worked furiously all the while. No matter how hard she tried, she could not quite reach the answer he sought.

Even if she did agree to marry him, her parents would never approve. Nothing could come of their relationship but heartbreak.

Ever so slowly, he pulled away from her and said, "Well, that concludes our tour for the day. Is there anywhere else you wish to go?"

Eleanor turned to gape up at him. "You consider that a tour?"

He cocked his head and asked, "Shouldn't I?"

"I suppose it can count, but typical tours include a description of at least one room."

"Hmm. Right then." He led her from the ballroom down the familiar hallway and stopped before a set of doors. He opened it with a grand sweep of his arm. "This is the linen closet."

Eleanor could not help a wry smile from forming as she turned to him. "Thank you for the tour, I can see you planned that very well, especially ending on such an important room."

He grinned and said in mock affront, "Linen is not something to be taken lightly, you know." He led her back to the main part of the manor as it occurred to Eleanor that she had been too engrossed with the man beside her to focus on the tour. She could not remember any of the rooms, aside from the portrait gallery, ballroom, and linen closet.

He had spoken such sweet words to her and once again guaranteed her she could find happiness with him, but what did his guarantee matter? She could not wed him.

She left him at the bottom of the staircase and returned to her room as her stomach rumbled. She had forgotten lunch but would make herself wait until supper to find sustenance. She would lie down for a nap before she had to return downstairs.

****

Logan's troubled thoughts pestered him as he sat at his desk, attending to estate matters. While Ellie had warmed to him, she had returned to her former frigid nature in an instant. He never expected to find a lady he enjoyed spending time with, and now that he had, he could not bear the thought of losing her. Yes, Ellie had some prickly qualities, but she had many endearing ones as well. Beautiful women were easy to come by, but finding one with a personality to complement one's own was difficult. Impossible even.

Just as he finished with the last document, a soft knock sounded from the doorway. His butler led a gentleman in and bowed before departing. Logan's eyes widened in shock as his wastrel of a cousin, Lord Charles Thornwick, stood haphazardly before him. Whatever had motivated his cousin to seek him out today of all days deserved to be riddled with bullet holes.

Logan straightened in his chair, not bothering to rise, and asked, "What is it this time?"

Charles grinned and sauntered over to a nearby chair. "Who said I wanted anything? Can't I just stop by for a visit now that you have finally returned from the continent?"

Logan raised an imperious eyebrow at his cousin. As one of his only family members, Logan tried to stay on good terms with the man. Unfortunately, his cousin was barely tolerated at social functions anymore and was only accepted due to his title, fortune, and looks. Logan himself had never understood the appeal. While they were similar in appearance, his cousin was much too gregarious and shirked his duties, which might be why women fawned over him.

Today, as was the usual case when it came to Charles, was a day Logan did not care to spend engaging in chatter with the man. "Yes?"

Charles rolled his eyes and crossed his polished, booted feet. "I just needed to get away from town, so I thought of you."

Logan frowned. Charles must be avoiding something. Otherwise, he would never have departed London. "Well? Why?"

He sighed and shook his head. "Edwin."

This gave Logan pause. Edwin was not a troublemaker. "So? What has he done? I cannot imagine he has done any worse than you yourself have."

Charles scowled and shook his head. "Of course not. It's the exact opposite, actually. I had hoped we might mend fences since he is without Dear Daddy, but he will not give me the time of day, and worse yet, he has put it about town that I am a complete drunkard."

That was the precise rumor Logan himself had heard. "Well, aren't you?"

"Of course not!" He rose and crossed to a decanter. Pouring himself a drink, he turned and grinned. "While I do enjoy drink, I rarely drink to excess."

Well, that was news. Logan had never suspected the rumors about his cousin might be false. Granted, he would not put it past Charles to encourage the rumors to irritate his father. His eyes narrowed on his cousin's face and he scowled. Unless Charles was lying about his habits. Drunkards tended to do that.

"Normally, I would appreciate your visit, but now is not the time."

"Oh?" Charles took a sip of his scotch and raised an inquisitive brow.

"Yes." He rose, strode to the door, and opened it. "Now then, I trust you can see yourself out."

Undeterred by Logan's inhospitable mood, Charles shook his head. "No. Unless you can repair an axle on my carriage, I am afraid I will have to stay the night. And where are the servants anyway? I could not find a groom to save my life."

Logan groaned, once again closing the library door. "I have some news and some unusual requirements for you if you insist on staying." He returned to his seat and began to grudgingly fill in his cousin on the circumstances at Waking Hall. Logan did not appreciate the gleam of sheer joy that entered his cousin's dark gray eyes but felt confident the man would play along nonetheless.

Charles smiled. "I am elated I chose to visit this week. How exciting. I will just take my things to my room and pretend all is normal."

Logan leaned back and shook his head. "That is not possible. I am residing in those chambers. You may use your brother's room." He wanted Charles as far from Ellie as possible.

"Fine," Charles muttered. "I look forward to meeting this Miss Ashford. Although you might want to watch out. Women fall in love with me all the time."

Logan ignored him and returned to his work, which signaled the end of the meeting. His cousin jested, but Ellie could very well decide Charles's title was worth sacrificing herself for. Logan shuddered at the thought.

No respectable woman deserved his cousin.

****

Eleanor and Mrs. Westfield descended the stairs for dinner having agreed both ladies were famished. Their arrival at the landing was met by the scent of baked bread and roasted meat. Eleanor's stomach growled in response, and she bade it quiet down.

They turned toward the dining room when Eleanor spied an unknown gentleman, dressed in rich clothing and pleasant to look at. He was tall and thin with dark features and appeared to be on his way to supper as well. His coloring and build was similar to Logan's, and her stomach plummeted with the realization that he must be the duke. Somehow, she had convinced herself that she would never see the duke, but here he was, and yet she wished he wasn't.

The gentleman stopped when he spotted the ladies. Bowing, he kissed first Mrs. Westfield's hand and then Eleanor's. Despite his good looks, the brush of his lips on the back of her hand felt lifeless and cold, quite the opposite of Logan's warm touch.

His lips lingered on her hand as he raised his gray eyes to hers in a sensuous manner. "You must be Miss Ashford. The reports of your beauty have not done you justice."

The man must think himself charming, yet she felt nothing. She smiled anyway and curtsied. "And you must be the Duke of Waking."

His eyes froze on hers before he straightened and flicked a small speck from his otherwise impeccable jacket sleeve. "Of course. Who else could I possibly be?"

She took in his appearance once more and inwardly

shuddered while outwardly she smiled in welcome. He was handsome, and she would have been thrilled to meet him, but now Logan occupied her mind. "I trust you have recovered from your illness, Your Grace."

"Yes, my illness has gone on for nearly a fortnight. It was most troublesome."

A fortnight? As Eleanor tried to assimilate that piece of information, a red flag arose. His Grace should have never invited her here if he was sick, and she had been under the impression his illness had arose suddenly. Unless Logan had known and used the duke to lure her here.

"Well," Mrs. Westfield said, "I do believe dinner will be served shortly. No need to stand about dillydallying."

The duke agreed and offered his arm to Eleanor. She accepted and was led into the dining room as Mrs. Westfield trailed behind. As they entered the room, Eleanor's eyes met Logan's, and she was overtaken by the overwhelming attraction between them. She should be used to the feeling by now, but it still left her reeling. Having been led to a chair, she sank into it so she could focus on the napkin in front of her rather than those mesmerizing green eyes.

"Charles," Logan greeted without even the slightest smile.

Eleanor turned to the duke. "I had not realized your given name is Charles, Your Grace."

Lady Gammon suddenly had a coughing spell, and Lord Gammon's guffaw filled the room. Eleanor glanced from person to person but could not ascertain the cause of everyone's reaction. It must be an inside joke she was not privy to.

His Grace pulled out a chair at the head of the table, situated next to Eleanor, and sat down. He smiled at everyone and then said, "It is nice to be able to eat at a dinner table again. A fortnight is much too long to be ill."

Silence filled the dining room until Logan asked, "Has it been that long? No wonder you were quarantined." He turned to Mrs. Westfield. "How are you feeling today? I trust your head is better?"

"Oh yes, all I needed was a good night's rest." Her face darkened as she added, "Although I believe it might have been quicker if there were more servants to fetch things when required."

The group agreed as everyone shared their own frightful experiences with such a small staff. Instead of joining in, Eleanor chose to focus on her food. She was starving, after all.

"Slow down," His Grace whispered in her ear. "There's plenty more food."

Eleanor blushed with embarrassment for eating in such an unladylike manner, in front of a duke, no less. She placed her fork on the plate and took a sip of her rather dry red wine. "One never knows with so few staff. Where are they, anyway?"

"I would imagine they are in their homes."

What an unusual answer. She rephrased it. "Why are there only a handful of servants working at the manor?"

He refilled her wine glass, eyeing her with a cold look of disinterest. "I only recently returned from the continent."

"Ah." That much made sense. He must have let go most of his servants when he departed years before, but surely it did not take this long to fill the vacancies?

He waved his hand and said, "You are a ravishing creature, you know. I am surprised Logan has not snatched you up already."

The blood drained from her face so she took a drink of her wine. "Who says he hasn't tried?"

A curious light entered his eyes and he grinned. "So are you saying you don't want Logan?"

She turned her gaze to Logan and froze as the truth sank in. She did want Logan, and only Logan. Not this duke next to her that was once her ideal match. Yes, the duke had his title, money, and influence, but Logan held the greatest sway over her. He held her heart.

She toyed with her food as she tried to wrap her head around the sudden realization that, indeed, she loved Logan. Despite her rational side telling her love was impossible. She knew unequivocally she was in love.

The duke broke through her epiphany as he grinned in a lopsided manner and said, "You could marry me and be done with Logan, you know."

Eleanor laughed at his absurd suggestion. "I think I will take my chances with Logan."

"Interesting," he whispered before he returned his attention to his dinner plate.

Had she really just denied a duke? A week ago, she would have said yes without hesitation, not tell him she preferred his friend. No, the duke could not compare to Logan. No one could.

With the conclusion of dinner, Eleanor stood and professed to have a headache. Her bedroom was her safe zone, assuming Logan did not appear once more. A place where she needn't worry about doing anything foolish such as agreeing to marry Logan. Besides, she had a painting to finish.

****

The library was lit by a single taper which shed enough light to cast a faint glow in one corner of the room and leave the rest in unrepentant darkness. Logan sat in the lit corner, nursing his scotch and contemplating the shadows around him. Everyone had retired for the evening, but he was unable to sleep.

Who could sleep after such an aggravating supper? It wouldn't have been so bad, except Ellie had conversed at length with his cousin, and he had been forced to sit by and watch. There had been several times where he wanted to throw caution to the wind and tell her who the actual duke was, but he held himself back with the knowledge that she would love him. Hopefully.

"You cannot sleep either?" Charles's low voice rumbled from the doorway, and Logan turned to glare at him.

"No thanks to you."

Charles's steps were quiet as he found his way to the chair next to Logan. He crossed his right ankle over his left knee and turned his serious eyes on Logan. "I am doing you a favor, you know."

"Oh?" Charles would not fool Logan. He did this for his own entertainment, nothing more.

"What good is it if she agrees to marry you and regrets it later? Now, she can choose you over the biggest prize in the land—me." He smirked, stood, and helped himself to some of Logan's scotch.

There was a certain allure to what Charles said. If she did not chase after the supposed duke and continued to look favorably on Logan, then that meant she did want Logan. No one else. His pride would enjoy that, assuming she did not turn around and chase Charles. He shook his head. Of course she wouldn't. He knew his Ellie, and he knew she was not half as mercenary as she led everyone to believe.

"I suppose you desire my thanks for claiming to be me?" Logan asked, hoping to convey his irritation in his tone as he sipped his drink.

Charles chuckled and shook his head. "Let us not get carried away. I intend to irritate you as much as possible, so no thanks is necessary."

"Good, because I did not plan to thank you. How did you convince the ladies to believe you were I, anyway?"

"Well, it was all very simple," he said as he sat down. "Miss Ashford assumed I was he, er, you." He grinned into his glass. "I could not allow such an opportunity to pass by, so I agreed."

Logan could not fault Ellie for making such an erroneous assumption. Of course, now he had to deal with Charles for the duration of her visit. "Just promise me you will not compromise her or offend her in any way." That was the most he could hope for.

"I don't think I will be afforded the opportunity."

"Why is that?" Logan asked, leaning forward as a mixture of curiosity and apprehension descended.

"I think she is very much in love with you, but if I do ruin her, it will be for your own good."

Logan scowled as Charles's guffaw filled the room. He had begun to question his opinion of Charles's character, and then the man said that. "Very well. If she affords you the chance to ruin her, I am sure she will not mind the outcome. Marriage to a future marquess is almost as good as to a duke."

Charles paled, and this time Logan laughed. Charles arched an eyebrow and said, "Oh come now, we both know I would never be so foolish as to marry."

"Might I suggest you do not ruin Miss Ashford then?" Knowing Charles, it was only a matter of time before he compromised a lady and ended up leg-shackled. Yes, he gave it a year.

Chapter 9

Departing her room after a fitful night, Eleanor was not in the mood to deal with people. She held a letter for her cousin in one hand and her riding crop in the other. As much as she detested horses, they had their uses.

She entered the stables and waited for the groom to saddle her mare. Even the stables appeared devoid of servants, with only the one groom in sight. As she waited, she toyed with her riding crop but stopped when she saw the duke. He looked handsome, dressed in fashionable riding attire, and Eleanor hoped he would not wish to accompany her.

"Your Grace." She forced a smile to her face. "It appears there is but one groom."

"Of course there is." He chuckled as his gaze roamed over her body. Eleanor felt a chill sweep over her. Just why did he have to be the one to join her in the stables? "I suppose I will have to act as my own groom if I wish to ride with you. No point forcing you to wait."

She could not tell a duke she did not long for his illustrious companionship, so she agreed and waited for the groom to finish saddling her docile-looking mare. For a stable this size, it lacked in horses, but that was likely due to the duke's extended absence on the continent. His Grace emerged from a stall with his own stallion in tow, just after her groom finished with her mare.

They entered the courtyard, and the duke accepted the reins from the groom. He thanked the servant and waved him away. Now, Eleanor would have to ride with him. She had no other choice.

The sound of horse hooves broke through the quiet morning air. She looked up, and relief washed over her when she saw Logan returning from his morning ride.

"Good morning, my lady," Logan greeted Eleanor with a warm smile before coldly asking the duke, "Shouldn't you be resting, Your Grace? You cannot ride after such an *extended* illness."

The duke inclined his head and grinned. "I am sure my constitution has been restored enough to allow me a ride."

The tension was palpable between the two men, although Eleanor could not quite ascertain the cause of the tension in the first place. The best thing she could do was just separate the two. Logan was her first choice, but the duke was much closer to hand, so she turned to him and asked, "Your Grace, would you be so kind as to assist me in mounting my mare?"

He stepped to her side, helped her on to her steed, and then spoke in a loud enough volume for Logan to hear. "I would be more than happy to assist you in mounting *anything* you desire."

Eleanor had almost reprimanded him for his impertinence when she was silenced by the duke as he said, "I am a very virile male who can easily give you an enjoyable ride. That is, if you would agree to accompany me."

Her mouth fell open at his words. Innuendo was

common enough in the *ton*, but his words had skipped past innuendo and straight to vulgar.

"I think not," Logan said, his horse prancing beneath him.

His Grace gave him a wicked smile as he said, "You should remember your place, *Sir Logan*."

Eleanor surprised herself by rushing to Logan's defense. "I have no wish to ride with a cad such as yourself, Your Grace." Her stomach plummeted as she insulted a duke. It was unheard of, but she continued to insult him anyway. "It is clear that rank does not signify class. Thank you for your aid. Have a good ride."

****

Logan sent his cousin a triumphant glance as he turned his mount to catch up with Ellie, who had already departed the courtyard. The very idea that his cousin would presume to act as duke was aggravating, although it was proving useful in determining Ellie's feelings for Logan. He had almost leapt from his horse to kiss her when she dismissed the supposed duke.

"You are in a rush today, Ellie," Logan said as he caught up to her.

She smiled, and it felt as if a ray of sunshine peeked through the clouds just for him. "I have business to conduct, and we both know how much I enjoy horses."

"Ah, mailing a letter to your cousin?" He grinned when a stunned expression overtook her. "I must say you surprised me back there. It almost seemed as if you defended my lack of higher title."

She turned her face from him but not before he saw an alluring blush rise to her cheeks. The crisp morning air brought out the color in her cheeks but not nearly as much as her embarrassment. She returned her gaze to his and muttered, "Think nothing of it."

Logan would not allow such an important matter to drop, so he said, "I thought you would always defer to the higher title in any situation. What happened?"

"Yes, well, that was before—" She caught herself on a sharp intake of breath.

"Before what?" He focused his gaze on her and tried to compel her to answer.

Her horse continued forward as she sat immobile. Not that he was more mobile. Her eyes could mesmerize him no matter what happened around them.

She continued to stare at him, and he prompted, "Before?"

She sighed and dropped her gaze from his. "Before I came to care for you."

A rush of unadulterated joy overtook him as his heart swelled. In social settings, she was the gregarious sort, yet in matters of the heart, she was the shyest lady he had ever met. Her demureness had given him pause when he plotted his conquest of her heart. He had worried she would never admit her feelings, even if she did possess them.

He rode closer to her and took her hand in his. He placed a gentle kiss on its back and said, "I care for you also, quite possibly since the moment you landed on me in the mud."

Ellie blinked as a smile spread across her face. A twinkle appeared in her eye, and she said, "I am just glad you were the one that fell in the mud, not I."

She was so mischievous when she allowed herself to be. In fact, every part of her was intriguing to him. Mind, body, and soul. He wanted her, and sooner or later, she would be his.

They continued to chat the rest of the way to the village where they stopped to post the letter before riding back. Logan inquired after her painting, which she had finished the previous evening. Ellie seemed to glow whenever he remembered personal details about her, so he made sure to bring up such details in conversation regularly.

"Why do you choose fairy tale creatures?" he asked with his gaze trained on her. Each detail of her personality was important to him. He wanted to know all.

She paused to consider his question and then turned her sapphire blue eyes to his. "They symbolize an ideal to me. One of a world of purity which still allows for magic. I do not think I can fully explain how I feel, but an enchanting scene becomes so much more with their addition."

Logan nodded in understanding. "Sometimes it is necessary to have a simpler world to escape to. One set in black and white." His smile turned playful and he said, "Or whatever shade you choose."

"Yes, it doesn't matter how perfect a person's life may seem. There will always be something to escape from." They shared a mutual look of understanding as they neared the stables. "Thank you for accompanying me," Ellie said.

"It was an honor." He swung off his stallion and helped her dismount. His hands circled her waist, and he grinned when she emitted a small gasp. Her body responded to him every time he touched her. It was a promising sign.

He handed the horses off to the groom, then

extended his arm to her. "Shall we?"

Logan led her into the house and stopped at the base of the staircase. "Thank you for the pleasant ride."

He bowed low and kissed the back of her hand. Her dainty, gloved hand trembled in his, whether from the exertion of her ride or his presence. He preferred to believe the latter.

"You made my ride surprisingly tolerable." Her voice sounded strong, and her gaze held fast, yet her hand still shook.

"Only tolerable?" He gave her a mocking smile and shook his head. "I shall do better next time."

She smiled. Her eyes twinkled, and without her uttering a sound, he knew she would not mind a next time. She turned from him and slowly ascended the stairs. He watched until she disappeared.

He still felt the effects of his conversation with Ellie and would seek out Reuben. The fact that both he and Ellie had declared a mutual attraction and now shared their feelings was exhilarating and well worth imparting to his friend.

Upon entering the house, his butler directed him to the library where Reuben sat with Opal. The pair looked quite comfortable perched together on a settee in front of a crackling fire.

"Ah, Logan." Reuben and Opal began to rise before he stopped them.

"Do not stand on my account," he said as he shut the door behind him, in the off chance Ellie drifted by. "I have wonderful news to report."

"Let me guess," Opal said with a devious grin. "She professed her undying love for you?"

"Not exactly, but close enough." Logan went to

stand by the fire and leaned against the wall, inhaling the rich aroma. It was nice to be home. The servants knew to use cherry wood, as he appreciated the scent as it burned.

"What did I tell you, Reuben?" Opal asked her husband. "I knew it was but a matter of time. She practically salivated over him at dinner last night, you know."

Logan was surprised to hear that. All he noticed was the attention she gifted Charles.

"Of course you were right, my dear," Reuben murmured as he patted her hand. "But none of this matters unless she agrees to marry Logan without realizing he is a duke."

"That won't be a problem." Failure was not an option, especially when she gave him hope as she had earlier.

"I don't know," Reuben said as he pulled out a snuff box and took a pinch. "Lord Thornwick seemed awfully cozy with her last night."

Logan rolled his eyes and scoffed. "She sees right through him." He ended with a laugh, recalling the way Ellie rebuffed Charles that morning.

"But he claims to be a duke," Reuben said as he placed his snuff box back in his pocket. "I had a hard time keeping a straight face when he said he was you, I might add."

"As did I." Logan scowled. It was too early to drink, but when he remembered the previous night, he wished it wasn't. He had been positive as the night wore on that Ellie would spurn him for his cousin, but that morning had shed a new light on the situation, one that should allow him to sleep that night.

"Well, I for one think Lord Thornwick has done you a favor. What better way to test her than place a genuine duke before her?" Opal shifted so she could recline her head against Reuben's shoulder. She yawned and scowled. "My condition is the most exhausting phenomenon. I am afraid I require another nap."

Reuben patted her head as if she were a dog, and she tilted her head to smile lovingly up at him. As much as Logan approved of his friend's love match, sometimes it was sickening to watch.

Opal turned back toward him and said, "I do enjoy watching Miss Ashford around you, though. She remains silent in your presence, and whenever she looks at you, she blushes profusely. She seems like a different person around you."

Reuben nodded in agreement as he appeared lost in thought. "Now that you mention it, my dear, she does seem quieter. More subdued."

"My guess is she doesn't know how to handle her feelings for him. The change in her is remarkable though."

Logan quirked an eyebrow at Opal's deduction. He would not admit it, but Opal's observation raised his spirits and filled him with renewed vigor. In his heart, he knew Ellie loved him, even if she had only confessed to caring for him.

He straightened from the wall. "Maybe she is just more relaxed here. Either way, I can promise you we will have an understanding by the time she departs. Mark my words."

****

Eleanor changed into a pastel yellow gown in order

to arrive in time for lunch, the exchange between herself and Logan replaying in her mind all the while. She had told him she cared for him, and that was difficult enough. Imagine if she had confessed her love for him? Having never expected to develop feelings for someone, she had not realized how vulnerable a declaration would leave her. She was faintly comforted that he returned her feelings, but a certain awkwardness remained within her.

The more time spent with him only illustrated what her future could hold. Growing old with a gentleman who valued her personality had never been important to her, but now she feared she could not live without that requirement.

As she sat in front of her mirror, she gazed unseeingly at her reflection. In every childhood dream, she had envisioned a titled gentleman sweeping her off her feet into a marriage like the one her parents bore with their cold, quiet dignity, but now her dream had transformed into a vision of Logan. Once married to a baronet, her circles would not be as wide as if she were married to an earl. After all, her husband would not have a seat in parliament, and without a seat in parliament, who was to say Logan would even want to journey to London for the season every year?

Olivia added the final touches to Eleanor's hair and asked, "Is everything to your liking, my lady?"

Eleanor jumped. She had forgotten Olivia was there. Her gaze focused on the blonde ringlets framing her face. With a critical eye, she noted her hair was utter perfection with every curl placed in exact location to appear messy. She turned her head from side to side in an assessing manner and said, "I love it. You have done a tremendous job, Olivia." Olivia's eyes widened in surprise, but Eleanor continued to speak. "Tell me, what do you think is most important in life?"

Olivia swallowed and stuttered as she said, "Umm, I would have to say family, my lady. Earning a living is also important, but money won't keep one warm at night."

"If you are a man, it will." Eleanor laughed at her crude joke and then waved her hand. "However, I think you may be right." She stood and said over her shoulder as she exited, "I hope someday you find that happiness for yourself."

Eleanor stopped by her chaperone's room where Mrs. Westfield waited, ready for lunch. They strolled downstairs and were greeted by the enticing view of cucumber sandwiches with strawberries and cream for dessert. The meal was light but perfect for a sunny spring day.

The guests exchanged pleasantries while dining, and Eleanor tried her best to act like nothing had transpired between Logan and herself. She even managed to ask Logan how the horses fared and was proud of herself for not blushing when his eyes met hers. Clearly, it was just a matter of mastering her response to him so she did not make a spectacle of herself.

At a lull in the conversation, Mrs. Westfield turned to the duke and said, "Your Grace, I hear you just returned from the continent. Was there a specific reason, or did you miss home?"

The duke sent a sly smile to Logan before answering, "I decided it was high time to marry."

Mrs. Westfield's eyes took on an anticipatory

gleam, and she leaned in to ask, "Oh, is there anyone in particular? Or will you go to London for the rest of the season?"

"Well, I already offered for one lady's hand, but she declined."

Logan stiffened, and Mrs. Westfield leaned in again. Any further and she might very well topple over. Eleanor could only shake her head. The duke had not been serious when he asked her to marry him. Why would he get her chaperone's hopes up now?

"How tragic, Your Grace. Maybe the young lady will see reason given time."

The duke shook his head as a wounded expression graced his countenance. "I fear I will have to travel to London and face the hordes."

Mrs. Westfield's palpable excitement receded, and she returned to her food. Even a simpleton would be able to ascertain who the duke referred to, and Mrs. Westfield was far from a simpleton. Now, Eleanor would be forced to refute the idea that a duke had asked for her hand. How ridiculous.

As the luncheon drew to an end, Lady Gammon stood and addressed the group. "I have not been feeling the best of late, but today, I feel like my old self. I suggest we all adjourn to the parlor for some cards. Does anyone object?"

When no one negated the suggestion, she smiled and clasped her hands together in front of her bosom. "Marvelous. We need something to celebrate His Grace's timely recovery, and this should be just the thing."

Eleanor stood and managed a few steps before Logan stopped her. "My lady, might I have the honor of escorting you?"

"I would like nothing better." She smiled up at him as her stomach performed a somersault. His smile was overpowering. Their gazes locked in a moment of shared solitude, and the world around them disappeared.

His fingers grazed her cheek as he brushed an eyelash away from her skin. She shivered and looked away, unable to face the intensity of mutual feelings. Logan patted her hand and turned to escort her in an unhurried fashion to the parlor. They were the last of the group to enter the room, and only two seats remained, on a small Chippendale-style settee.

They sat, and Eleanor tensed when their thighs brushed. The barest whisper could be heard from the contact, but she swore it sounded as loud as a bell pealing in a quiet room. No one else noticed, and she scooted as far from him as discreetly possible. Her attempt at distancing herself left the barest of spaces between their legs. She kept her thigh tightly pinned in place, and if she relaxed at all, she would touch him. The knowledge that she was so near him was excruciating and exciting all at once, and she would never be able to focus now.

She sneaked a surreptitious glance at Logan, only to find him smiling at her obvious discomfort. He could move further from her if he chose, but his smirk suggested he was well aware of that and would not oblige her.

Lady Gammon shuffled the cards in a single adept move and said, "I thought we might play *vingt et un*. I shall deal first, unless someone objects." No one disagreed, and she dealt everyone a card.

Eleanor enjoyed parlor games, but she feared she might not concentrate properly with Logan at her side. She glanced at her card and exhaled. It was an ace, which was one of the best cards to be dealt in a game such as this.

"Charles," Logan said as he eyed his card. "How was your ride this morning?"

The duke appeared disinterested as he viewed his own card. "I was a bit chilled, but otherwise, not notable."

Lady Gammon leaned toward the table and admonished him with a stern frown. "Now, now, Your Grace, you must be careful so you don't return to your sickbed."

"Yes, that would be unfortunate indeed," Logan said in a neutral tone.

Eleanor raised her brow. She could have sworn Logan claimed to be friends with the duke, but the more she saw, the more she concluded he lied. The two did not get along and seemed to butt heads endlessly.

Lady Gammon dealt everyone another card. Eleanor received a six. She shook her head and eyed Logan. "I thought you said you two were friends?"

Charles raised his somber eyes to her and shook his head. "We are, my lady, but Logan disapproves of the way I act as of late."

"Only as of late?" Logan asked until he looked at Eleanor and blanched. "Yes, until recently, he has been above reproach."

"It is true," Opal said with an impish grin, "they practically grew up together. I am sure you could ask one anything about the other, and he would easily tell you."

Eleanor's pulse quickened as everyone stopped to look at her. She knew very little about Logan's childhood, aside from cursory information about his past. "Well then, Your Grace, tell me of Logan's family."

The duke's gray eyes lit with amusement and he smiled. "Well, my lady, Logan has very few family members still with us. His uncle is a marquess, and he has two cousins who are as different as night and day. His favorite cousin is Lord Thornwick. Have you heard of him, by chance?"

The color drained from Mrs. Westfield's face and she gasped. "No! And you claim Lord Thornwick is Sir Logan's *favorite* cousin? Why, he is barely tolerated!"

Logan could have at least mentioned his relatives were members of the peerage, and one was Lord Thornwick, no less. If one believed the gossips, Lord Thornwick's behavior had been poor since before his majority. If it weren't for the fact he was an earl, he would have been barred from polite society completely.

Lord Gammon snickered at Mrs. Westfield's outrage, and Lady Gammon asked Eleanor as she indicated her card, "Are you content, or would you like another?"

"Another, please." She waited to see which card she would receive and forgot about her leg. Her knee skimmed Logan's before she jerked it back into place, but the contact was enough to make her feel as if she had been burned. Lady Gammon dealt her another card, while everyone's eyes went to hers. Her cheeks heated. She must have gasped when she made contact with Logan. She needed to work on her control.

Her eyes settled on the three cards in front of her.

She now had an ace, a six, and a jack. If she played her ace as a one, she had seventeen points, and if as an eleven, she would exceed twenty-one and automatically lose. She stared at her cards and made up her mind. She might as well go for another card. She signaled Lady Gammon and received a five. She frowned as she did the math in her head. She had lost.

The duke hit twenty and inclined his head at Mrs. Westfield. "Lord Thornwick has quite the reputation, but I think all here would agree he has many redeeming qualities, doesn't he, Sir Logan?"

Mrs. Westfield shook her head and gave Logan a reproachful look. Logan smiled back in polite deference. "Yes. I only wish he were here with us now."

Lady Gammon revealed her other card. She had reached nineteen, which meant that everyone at the table lost but His Grace and Logan as they both had twenty.

Lady Gammon glanced about the table and asked, "Did we name the stakes? And did anyone else care to deal? I like dealing, so if no one objects, I will continue."

Logan waved his hand and scoffed. "We are playing as friends here. There is no need to place wagers."

"Isn't there?" Everyone's head swung to the duke who leaned back in his armchair. He smirked and eyed Logan. "I would suggest whoever wins this next round gets to accompany Miss Ashford on a stroll through the gardens."

Mrs. Westfield giggled. "What a marvelous idea!" She leaned toward the duke and whispered in a not-so-quiet voice, "Naturally, Your Grace, I hope you are victorious."

"What if I don't wish to take a stroll in the gardens?" Eleanor asked, heat rising to her face at such a presumptuous wager. While she would enjoy an outing with Logan, she did not desire to go anywhere with the duke.

Everyone ignored her and turned to face each other. Lady Gammon, as the dealer, could not win, and Lord Gammon along with Mrs. Westfield expressed their desire to not play that round. So, it was left to His Grace and Logan.

Eleanor leaned back against the settee as she kept her leg pinned in place and crossed her arms. She exhaled and waited for the outcome of the next round. Lady Gammon shuffled and dealt both gentlemen a single card. Logan received a nine, and His Grace a queen.

Eleanor waited for Lady Gammon to continue the game, but when nothing happened, she asked, "Well, what are we waiting for?"

His Grace stood and smiled lazily at her. "I had not realized you were in such a hurry for our stroll, Miss Ashford." He extended his arm, and Eleanor eyed it, not moving a muscle.

"Hold on, Your Grace. Let me fetch my parasol so I may chaperone you two." Mrs. Westfield beamed at them and rose to depart the room.

"We can take a groom," His Grace said before Mrs. Westfield could take a step. Mrs. Westfield sank back down and nodded. Her expression suggested she was pleased by the outcome of the wager, whether she was to chaperone or not.

Eleanor feared she had allowed her mouth to hang open. She clamped it shut and asked, "Didn't you need to deal more cards, Lady Gammon?"

"No, dear." Lady Gammon shot her a look of sympathy. "We determined whoever received the higher card would win. That way, we could resume the game."

How had she missed that? She was much too preoccupied with Logan whenever he was near. She shot Logan a dark look. Why had he allowed the duke to win? His Grace coughed, and she turned her attention back to him. He still stood before her with his arm stretched out to her. She accepted it, no matter how she despised the idea of a walk with him, and he led her from the parlor.

He glanced down the hall with a brooding frown and muttered something. She raised a questioning brow and asked, "Is something amiss, Your Grace?"

"I forgot there are no servants." He led her to the foyer and shook his head. "Hold on, my lady. I will find someone to accompany us."

She was not about to argue with the duke on the matter of a chaperone. She turned to inspect a painting below the grand staircase and smiled. If she were to guess, she would say it was a Titian. A young lady was portrayed with the most alluring smile. It was a true work of art, and Eleanor could easily enjoy it for hours.

"We are in luck, my lady, I have found someone."

Eleanor turned to find the duke at her elbow. Behind him hovered a nervous footman, and she nodded. He would do just fine.

The warm air embraced her as she stepped outside. She inhaled the clean scent of spring and swore she could detect a note of rain on the breeze. When she looked at the sky, however, there was not a cloud in sight.

He caught her elbow and led her down a graveled path toward the gardens. They walked slowly, neither speaking for several minutes until the duke asked, "Why do you like him?"

Eleanor caught herself before she could trip from the shock of his question. Her eyes darted to his, and she was unprepared for the somber look in his gray eyes. "I—" She swallowed and looked away. "There is something special about him. I think he is the first man to see past my beauty and accept me for me."

He remained silent as he directed her to a bench. She sat, and he turned to examine a caterpillar perched on the leaf of a tree. "So, if I accepted you for you, would you choose me over him?"

"Of course not!" she said, shocked by his forward question. She shook her head. "I meant no offense, Your Grace. I know you are superior to most, and you will have no trouble finding a lady in London."

He shrugged and turned to her. "I know. Women are easily replaceable. I just want to ensure you will not break Logan's heart."

Her jaw dropped open for the second time that day. "That is why you wished to walk with me?"

He grinned, and his eyes lit up as he nodded at her. "Yes, that, and I enjoy teasing Logan. It is one of my greatest sources of amusement. I guarantee he is inside fuming right now."

No wonder the duke had acted so interested in her. Suddenly, the dynamics between the duke and Logan made sense to her. "You can't possibly believe he is jealous?"

"Of course I can." His eyes scanned her face, and he said, "I believe Logan would move heaven and earth to be with you."

Eleanor blushed. She couldn't help it, but his words were so sweet and reassuring. She stood. Why continue this outing when she could return to Logan? "Thank you, Your Grace, for this enlightening stroll. I believe I should return to the house now."

He smiled and offered her his arm. He led her back to the manor, and as they reached the entryway, the door swung open to reveal Logan.

"What a surprise to find you here," the duke said with a smirk.

Logan's eyes looked like marble and his face a hard mask. It was fascinating to observe, really, but not in this moment. Right now, his anger was almost frightening. He stepped up to the duke and whispered something in His Grace's ear. The duke grinned in response and entered the house after performing a mocking bow.

Logan turned to Eleanor and growled, "Shall we take a stroll, Ellie?"

****

She smiled her enchanting smile and accepted his arm. The footman began to follow them, but Logan sent him a quelling glare which sent the footman running back to the house.

"You really need to calm down, Logan. Your anger is disproportionate to the situation."

"Who said I was angry?" He tried to slow the blood rushing in his ears. The entire time Ellie and Charles had strolled about his garden, he had worried about her. Lord Thornwick was known as a ladies' man and a reprobate. No matter what Charles had said the previous night, she was not safe with him. Of course, Logan liked to give his cousin the benefit of the doubt, but not when it came to Ellie.

"While I appreciate the fact that you are jealous, it is unnecessary."

Yes, he was jealous. He had told her the one person who could make him jealous was the duke, and that sentiment still remained true, even if the duke was Lord Thornwick, or anyone else, really. He shook his head and led her down the path. Until she was his, he was afraid any gentleman would make him jealous. He could not risk her with anyone, not when he cared as much as he did.

They rounded a bend in the pathway, and she left him to sit on a wrought-iron bench. The garden lay behind her, sprawling out in a manicured rectangle of green with a plethora of colors from the flowers. A row of apple trees lined the garden, which gave shade from above. She looked picturesque as she waited for him to join her, her ankles crossed and tucked neatly behind her. She was the most charming of all the blooms, besting every tulip, every azalea, and every violet in sight.

There was something wonderful about their budding relationship, something which bordered on impossible. His breath caught as his heart constricted. Could it be he loved her? He had never considered the possibility that he could fall for her and she remain indifferent. What if he could not win her as a baronet? He thought he could, but what if she had been swept away by a duke mere minutes before?

He took a seat next to her on the cold iron bench as a gust of wind tore through his hair. It was chillier outside than he had presumed. Their backs were to the garden, which left them with a glorious view of the pond and the manor, but he could not appreciate the scene. Not now.

He looked to his booted feet. He might as well find out what had transpired between the two. "Well, what did he say?"

Her voice was soft as it floated to him. "He said you would move heaven and earth to be with me."

He looked at her then. Her hands were clenched tightly in front of her, but the smile on her face belied her nervousness. "Did he?" He chuckled as relief washed over him. His rake of a cousin had walked with a renowned beauty and talked about Logan's love for her? It was astounding, yet the words were true. He would do anything for her, but what if that meant nothing to her? How could he live without her?

She shifted closer to him and laid her hand on his arm, drawing his attention back to her once more. "Was he correct? Do I truly mean that much to you?"

He looked down at her hand as it clutched the sleeve of his jacket. She had admitted she liked him, but love was something different. Love meant that she would sacrifice everything for him, just as he would for her.

He followed the elegant line of her hand to her arm and then to her face. Her eyes were shuttered as she waited for his response. The wind blew gently, and a tendril of her hair fell to her collarbone. It was so like her that even when mussed, she looked perfect. He inclined his head toward her and closed his eyes, silencing the nagging voices of doubt that plagued him. She must love him. She had to.

Had his cousin spoken the truth? He almost laughed out loud, because yes, Charles had. For Logan's heart brimmed with love for her. "Yes, Ellie. I love you." He didn't dare look at her. His heart was in the palm of her hand, and most likely, she would crush it.

He heard a rustle of fabric and felt her press against him. Her fingers touched his face, and he opened his eyes. Instead of the look of indifference he expected, there was enrapturement. "I love you, too."

A weight lifted from his shoulders, and a victorious smile tugged at his lips. Never had he understood joy as he did now. Pulling her to him, he inhaled the sweet scent of her.

Darkness washed over her clear eyes, and she stilled in his arms. "I love you…" Her voice faltered. She coughed and squared her shoulders. "But that may not be enough."

"Of course it is." He placed his finger to her lips and shushed her. "Remember, I will move heaven and earth for you." Her lips parted, and he shook his head. What more was there to say?

His lips descended on hers as the chill of the day receded with her nearness. She was sweet, delicate, and his. His heart swelled with the thought, even as his blood boiled to have her within his arms once more. Every motion she made, whether the press of her hand on his back, or the give and take of her tongue against his, caused him to want her more.

He kept his hands glued in place on her back lest he lose himself. Whatever she offered was enough for him because she had given him the most precious part of her. The thought made him smile, even as he kissed her, and he forced himself to end the kiss on that magical note.

"When shall our wedding take place?"

She sighed, laying her head against his chest. "It matters not. Sooner is better."

A chilling gust of wind hit him. The wind had picked up, as evidenced by the furious ripples on the pond before them. "Should we return inside?" As much as he appreciated her tucked away in his arms, he appreciated her health much more.

She stood and took a moment to set herself to rights. Once finished, he caught her hand in his and intertwined their fingers. They turned to the manor and strolled along in silence as a cloud passed over the sun, turning a brisk day even colder.

He wanted ever so much to warm her, to make her feel the depth of his passion for her. For this vixen with her many frigid tendencies had laid siege to his heart with her honesty and vulnerability. All her actions in the past had shielded that vulnerability from those around her, but he knew her, and he loved her.

His thoughts were interrupted as a tremor passed over her. Even with the sunlight streaming through the clouds, she grew colder. He grimaced as guilt ran through him. "I should not have kept you outdoors for so long."

She grinned as she batted her eyelashes at him. "At least you admit one thing you have done wrong."

What did she speak of now? He wrinkled his brow as he gazed down on her. Matters today had progressed quite swimmingly, at least he thought they had. "Were there others?"

"Yes." Her eyes sparkled with mischievous intent, and she said, "You toyed with me the entire time we played cards."

"I did no such thing." He remained seated near her on purpose, but that was all.

"You brushed your leg against mine on multiple occasions, and you did all manner of other bothersome things."

"From what I remember, you are the one that brushed your leg against mine." He leaned toward her as they walked and said, "I quite liked it, you know."

Just then, a clap of thunder rang out, and it started to rain. "Good lord," she muttered, glancing skyward.

He raised his eyes to the heavens. Fat droplets poured down on them from a sunny sky. The sky to the west, however, did not look as friendly.

He placed a kiss on the hand interlaced with his, and they ran back to the house before they could get too drenched. The entryway was devoid of people, which allowed Logan to place a small kiss on her before sending her to her room to dry off. He smirked as her hand left his and he said, "You know this means I won our bet."

Ellie scowled and nodded. "You should learn to stop when you're ahead." Then with a sweet smile up at him and a look in her eyes that suggested she was not displeased by his comment, she departed.

****

Eleanor dried off in front of the fireplace, her heart soaring with the day's events. Every movement she made felt lighter, as if she floated in a fairy tale. And wasn't she in a fairy tale, even if she would not marry a prince? Her knight in shining armor was superior to a prince, and he would move heaven and earth for her. Not only had he confessed his love for her, but he had also offered marriage. It was all so perfect.

A clap of thunder filled the room, and she turned to the window. The hue of the sky made her gray walls appear cheery in contrast. The tumultuous weather beckoned to her, so she pulled her chair over and watched the rain fall until a knock sounded on her door. Mrs. Westfield strode in, placing herself next to the window so she could face Eleanor. Her demeanor was grim, and the rhythmic tapping of her foot suggested she was agitated about something.

"Are you in love with him, also?" her aunt asked with a reproving frown.

Startled, Eleanor cocked her head and tried to appear unruffled. "What do you refer to?"

"I saw how you looked at him during our card game. I am not an idiot, you know." Mrs. Westfield scowled and shook her head. "To think, a duke would offer marriage right after meeting you and even win a stroll with you in a wager, but you would turn him down for *that*."

Eleanor bristled at her aunt's tone. All her life, she had tried to act in an exemplary fashion, but she couldn't now. Not when her future happiness was on the line. "I think Sir Logan is the one I shall marry."

"I thought you might feel this way." Mrs. Westfield sounded weary as she said, "Your parents will never allow such a match. You have been trained since infancy to be mistress of a grand household. Not some small estate far to the north."

"Don't you want me to be happy?" Her aunt, of all

people, had always cared for Eleanor. When Eleanor would fall and skin her knee, it was her aunt kissing it to make her feel better. Her aunt was the one to slip her a cookie when her mother placed her on a strict diet. Eleanor had always found an ally in her aunt.

"Of course I do." Her aunt softened. "But I know how your parents will react. They won't approve of him, even if I do."

"You do?" Eleanor's eyes widened in surprise.

"Of course I do. He's a likeable fellow and handsome as sin. You two would have some beautiful babies." Her lips dipped in a frown as she added, "But it's not my approval you require."

Eleanor turned back to the window and sighed. "Mother will not begrudge me my happiness. It's not as if he is some pauper. She will accept him." Her words sounded implausible, even to her own ears. Her mother had always set the minimum standard at an earl, with viscounts and barons some sort of consolation prize in case she failed.

Mrs. Westfield shook her head and spoke in a faint, sad voice. "You are so young." She strode to the door and turned to say, "Your parents spent a lot of money to ensure you make an advantageous match. There is no benefit to them if you marry this gentleman, and they will likely deny him your dowry. Your gentleman professes to love you now, but will he feel the same when you go to him without a dowry or penny to your name?"

The faint rustle of fabric could be heard as her aunt left. Eleanor's feeling of floating lessened with each patter of the rain, and the desire to cry welled up within her. Could Logan want her without a dowry? She shook her head as her spirits waned. He may profess his love for her, but no man wanted a penniless woman. One with an aunt she wished to support. Her mother was cold enough to withhold a chance of happiness from Eleanor, but could she be devoid of a heart?

She placed her head in her hands and allowed a tear to escape. Of course she could. Her mother had never been the sort to show emotion. Hell, Eleanor had barely known her mother existed until she turned five. Up to that point, her mother had been some vague entity that Eleanor was paraded before for the occasional inspection.

Eleanor rose and went to her bed. There, she lay down and tried to sort out her thoughts. As a young lady, she had very few options. She could not defy her parents unless she knew with absolute certainty that Logan would marry her, and if she did defy her parents and they disapproved, they could easily marry her to the first gentleman who would agree to a match.

The room began to darken as she reclined on the bed, and she breathed in a deep, reassuring breath. Each moment she spent in her room was torture. She should go to Logan and present him with her dilemma. If he still wanted her without a dowry, well, that would certainly lessen her worries, but if he did not want her...She shuddered. She would not dwell on that at present.

She stepped from her room, closed the door, and crept down the stairs. The halls were empty but still lit. She passed the smaller parlor and heard the voices of Lord and Lady Gammon. After pausing to listen for Logan's voice, she continued on her way. He must be in the library.

The wind blew, and the house creaked as it settled. She did not like venturing about large houses when she was all alone, especially at night. She reached the library and was dismayed to see it was unoccupied. He could be in the kitchens, but she rather doubted it. She departed from the library when a soft voice interrupted her thoughts and caused her to jump.

"My lady."

Eleanor whirled around to find the butler hovering in the hall. Her heart raced from the unexpected encounter. "I was just getting some milk."

"Of course, my lady." He bowed, and she hurried away to the kitchens. Her search for the night was finished. She would just have to wait until morning to talk to Logan. After filling a glass with milk, she returned to her room and shut the door behind her. Her little foray had accomplished nothing, and now she was bound to have a sleepless, tortuous night.

****

"Your Grace."

Logan was surprised by the voice calling to him from outside his room. He rushed to the door and opened it to find his butler on the other side. "What did I tell you about calling me by my title?"

His butler blanched and said, "I apologize, Your Grace, but I have information for you. It appears your lady was wandering the halls."

Logan cocked his head at the odd piece of information. "Did she look all right?"

"I cannot say for sure, but she looked a trifle peaked."

Logan nodded his appreciation. "Thank you, I believe I should check on the lady. It would be remiss of me as a host to allow her to suffer."

"Of course."

"You should go to bed now. There's no need for you to stay up so late." It was best if the household was asleep when he went to visit Ellie.

His butler closed the door, and Logan drew on a robe. His visit would be quick, but his concern necessitated he check on her, no matter the duration. She had not come down for dinner, which had perturbed him. Hopefully, she did not regret her declaration of love.

No one saw him as he went to her room, although he wouldn't care if he was seen, unless it was by the chaperone. That would not be pleasant. After knocking, he waited a moment until the door inched open to reveal two large blue eyes peering out at him. He frowned at the sight of her wan skin and the worry etched on her brow.

He slipped in, and she smiled with relief as she closed the door. The firelight played across her features and reminded him of the night they met. Even the scent of the rain drifting in through her window led him to reminisce, and suddenly, all he could see was his water nymph.

"I am so happy you are here. We have something very important to discuss."

"Of course, dearest, but first things first." He swept her into his arms and reveled in the feel of her. She was right where she belonged. He frowned as he realized she had her hands pressed against him. She gave a push, and he stepped back.

"This is serious. I must speak with you."

Her resistance was not the response he expected

from her, and he tensed. Her tone was foreboding, and he prepared himself for whatever dire news she would impart.

She turned from him and went to the windowsill. He pivoted to watch her but otherwise remained immobile as she traced the wooden ledge with her finger.

"My aunt came to visit me this afternoon. She guessed my feelings for you and told me I was foolish for loving you." Her breath caught. She looked so small and dainty as she shook her head and brought her arms around herself in a tight embrace. "She confirmed my fears. Mother and Father will never permit our union and, if we wed anyway, will likely refuse to deliver my dowry."

Silence descended as she continued to hug herself with her eyes shut tight, waiting for his answer. Her vulnerability had never been so evident, and he rushed to her side. Her dowry meant nothing to him. Nothing mattered, except that she love him, and he love her.

He needed to see her clearly when he asked her his next question, so he turned her to him. A small tear shone in the firelight as it made its way down her face. He brushed the tear away, while interlacing her hand in his. "Do you still wish to marry me?"

She nodded as another tear escaped. "I know my dowry is important, and I will understand if you no longer want me. If money were not a concern, I would suggest we elope, but no one is rich enough to throw aside twenty thousand pounds."

Her voice was hollow and disheartened. How long had she worried about this before seeking him out? "My sweet, darling Ellie. In the future, if you are worried about something, come to me immediately. Why worry when there is no reason?"

Her gaze met his, and she nodded. "I shall, if there is a next time."

"Of course there will be a next time, so long as you will have me. While your dowry would be agreeable, it is not necessary."

"But what of my aunt? Maybe my dream of supporting her is foolish, but I had always hoped…" Her voice trailed off, ending in a shudder which racked her body.

"I would gladly support such an important person in your life." And he would. He would do whatever necessary to ensure her happiness.

Her eyes turned up to his, and her face was transformed by relief. The corners of her lips tugged up in a smile, and he pulled her closer to him as his heart leapt. She laid her head on his shoulder, and he held her, each rise and fall of her chest reminding him to breathe lest he forget himself.

His moment of bliss cracked as he remembered the words she said. If they went to Gretna Green, he could wait to reveal his identity until they married. He was mildly concerned that if he revealed himself now, she would get angry with him and delay the wedding, and that would not do.

"My love," he murmured. At his words, she straightened, bringing her eyes to meet his. "You suggested we might elope. Were you in earnest?"

"Yes. It may be the only way we can marry."

"Then we will depart tomorrow." He nuzzled her neck as his heart raced. He would be a married man in a matter of days and to his Ellie, no less. He had never thought to long for his wedding day, but he did now.

She giggled as his lips skimmed her collarbone. "Stop it, you are tickling me."

Nuzzling her neck once more, he reveled in the feel of her writhing against him from his touches. He brought his lips to hers as a breeze drifted through the window and caused her to shiver. It would not do for her to get cold, so he guided her to the bed where the canopy sheltered them from the chill.

As he laid her down on the bed, he brought himself over her while continuing the kiss. She latched onto his robe and pulled him toward her, arching up to meet him in her eagerness. His hands roamed over her body, and when she made her throaty little sounds, he made sure to remember where he had touched to elicit such a response. When he finished tasting her as he wished, he returned to those spots, paying extra attention when she reacted so enticingly again.

Every part of her was fire, and the more she dropped her guard, the more passionate she grew. Each guttural sound she uttered drove him further into madness, nearer and nearer to the brink of complete abandon. Until, at last, he reined himself in, pulling up and away from this siren beneath him.

Her clouded eyes regarded him in dazed confusion at his abrupt departure. Her blonde hair lay about her in a puddle on the mattress, and he wished he could keep her just like that, forever in his mind.

"What are you doing?" she asked, her voice husky and lips swollen.

He smiled and stroked the side of her face. "I must leave. Otherwise I will be unable to."

Her lips curled into a smile, and she whispered,

"Stay with me."

"You do not understand what you ask of me." He could not breathe. Not when every fiber of his being waited for her answer. He longed to stay, even if it was just to hold her, but his nymph was not meant to simply hold, and it would be a torturous night indeed.

She placed her hand around the back of his neck and pulled him to her. "Of course I understand. Stay with me."

He was lost in those light blue orbs, and he allowed her to pull him to her. "I am yours to command, my love." Then, all rational thought left his brain and he kissed her.

Chapter 10

The luxurious sheets slipped in a tantalizing whisper against Eleanor's naked skin as she stretched and rolled over to find Logan had departed. It was best for everyone if the pair's indiscretions remained undiscovered, at least until they were properly married.

The sun had barely crested the horizon, but Eleanor was awake and energized. Her light blonde hair lay in a tumbled mess around her, and with her stretch, she could feel an oddly pleasant soreness from her night with Logan. Who knew a night with a man could be so delightful? She had asked Logan that exact question, and all he did was laugh while looking immensely pleased with himself.

She rolled out of bed, donned her robe, and noted the rumpled sheets on the floor. She would try to put them back in some semblance of order. Otherwise, Olivia would know something had happened. Before attempting to set things to right, Eleanor would first capture the moment in the only way she could, on paper.

She sat on a chair and propped her sketchbook on her lap. She traced the edges of the large canopied bed in all its soiled, amply used glory and relaxed at the familiar sound of her charcoal stick scratching against the paper. She didn't bother to capture the entire room, only the bed as if it were suspended in air.

The bed itself signaled such a major change in her life. She was ruined, and even if she wished to marry another gentleman, she couldn't. She was forever bound to Logan, for better or worse. Assuming he married her, of course.

She continued to trace the canopy of the bed and tried not to think about the chance she could be ruined. All her life, she had judged the ladies that were compromised, not that there were many, but she had never understood why they allowed a man to take their most precious commodity before the wedding. And now, here she was in the same predicament but with one exception. Logan would marry her.

They had a plan for their elopement, and it was perfect. They would leave after Mrs. Westfield retired for the evening, and her chaperone would not realize what transpired until morning, maybe even later. At that point, if Mrs. Westfield managed to alert Eleanor's parents, Eleanor would be too far gone for them to intercept.

Eleanor smiled as she surveyed her work. A cursory sketch of the bed was on the paper, and the rest of the details were engraved in her mind. Despite her ruination, she held no regrets. Logan was the one for her.

No other gentleman would understand her the way he did or could boast the numerous favorable qualities he had. In fact, he was almost too good for her. She almost laughed aloud at the thought. Who would have guessed, Miss Eleanor Ashford could think a gentleman too good for her? It was almost inconceivable, yet Logan was just that marvelous.

With a loud yawn, she returned her sketch back to

the desk and slipped into bed. The time was much too early to venture downstairs, and she found herself suddenly in need of sleep. She drifted off, feeling almost as if she were back in Logan's strong and capable arms. Warm and comfortable, she once again congratulated herself for her choice in suitor. She was in love and would choose his love in return over any title.

****

The clock struck half past ten when Eleanor woke, ready to face the day. Much to her dismay, the sheets were still in a puddle on the floor. She had forgotten to tidy before returning to her slumber. Before she could slide from beneath the canopy, a knock sounded and Oliva entered, looking refreshed and cheery.

"Good morning, my lady." Olivia stopped at the sight of the sheet on the floor, and her eyes came to rest on Eleanor. Suddenly self-conscious, Eleanor brought her hand to her head and realized why Olivia appeared so put-out. Her hair was a mess. Oliva must know what had transpired in that room.

Olivia turned from her with a small smile on her lips and rang the bell for tea. Neither said a word, not even when Eleanor slipped from the bed, wearing her robe. Olivia was no simpleton, and Eleanor had worn a dress the previous day which was impossible to remove without aid.

Olivia's grin intensified, and then she hurried to her task of seeing Eleanor dressed and ready for the day. Tea arrived shortly after, and the pair proceeded as usual, with one exception: Eleanor could not seem to focus on her hair or anything else for that matter. Her mind had been seized by Logan.

Every time she had considered Logan's suit, she had dismissed him for his lack of title. She remained firm in her resolve, even after he kissed her and made her feel like a princess in a fairy tale. She had not prepared herself adequately for that moment on the bench, when she learned the sheer intensity of his feelings for her.

In that moment, she knew she loved him, as much as he loved her. She also knew she could not let him go. Not for riches, or any other material force one might try to sway her with. After all, what were jewels in a lifetime of misery, but cold companions? She would trade such extravagances for the warmth of Logan's love any day.

Olivia slid a final pin in Eleanor's coiffure, and Eleanor stood. The clock chimed, indicating it was before luncheon. She already missed Logan's company and would go down to the library for a book. If she happened upon him, so be it.

The rain had stopped sometime last night, and as she stepped from her room, she inhaled. The house smelled of spring, with both the scent of wet earth and a promise of warmth. She drifted down to the library, and as she approached, the soft laughter of a woman and the corresponding answer of a man's deep voice carried to her. The door was wide open, and she entered to find Logan seated with Lord and Lady Gammon.

Her pulse quickened at the sight of Logan in his riding attire, but she hid her response with a demure curtsy. "Good morning."

"Good morning, my lady." Logan rose and bowed. He stepped to her side and placed a kiss on her hand as he whispered, "I trust you slept well."

Her cheeks heated to a startling temperature, and Eleanor could only nod. She was not ready for references about last night, so she glared at him. Truly, he deserved much more punishment than the angry look she shot him, but it would do for now.

Lady Gammon's lilting voice broke Eleanor's moment of agony as she said, "Logan, stop pestering the girl. I don't know what you have done to the poor thing, and I doubt I want to know." She pushed her husband away from her, beckoning Eleanor to join her. "Come, sit. We can have a coze before lunch."

Eleanor joined Lady Gammon on the sofa and gave her a grateful smile. The countess looked particularly pretty in a heather-green day dress this morning and must have caught up on some rest.

"Has your sickness abated?"

"For the most part," Lady Gammon said with an incline of her head. "My morning sickness started quite early on, you know. Some women are like that, while others experience no sickness whatsoever."

"How peculiar." Eleanor would have never guessed such a thing as morning sickness even existed. Maybe that was why pregnant women tended to stay hidden in the country.

"Oh yes," Lady Gammon murmured. She smoothed aside a wayward curl of her glossy dark hair and asked with interest, "Have you formulated a plan to win back your cousin yet?"

Eleanor sighed. "None other than what I have been doing. Someday, when I am in London, I will work up the courage to stop by for a visit."

Lady Gammon nodded her head in sympathy. "I was thinking on the matter last night. You mentioned you had insulted your cousin's sister-in-law. Might I suggest making amends with her first? That way your cousin will believe you feel remorseful."

Eleanor cringed and shifted in her seat at the uncomfortable notion. She had no desire to face Miss Farris, but she supposed she must. She glanced at Logan, deep in conversation with Lord Gammon, and softened. If she was to begin a new life with Logan, couldn't she also turn a new page in her dealings with those around her?

Eleanor regarded Lady Gammon with a scowl. "Very well, but if I am not in London in the near future"—which she had no intention of being—"then a letter will have to suffice."

"I think those terms are agreeable." Lady Gammon nodded toward the gentlemen and leaned nearer to Eleanor. "Now, how difficult do you imagine it would be to convince everyone to partake of some dancing tonight? I was thinking of arranging a little party after dinner."

"I am sure they would acquiesce if you ask them." Eleanor quite liked the idea of a small, intimate soiree.

Lady Gammon nodded. She appeared lost in thought as she turned once more to look at Logan and Lord Gammon. "How are things progressing between the two of you?"

Eleanor's cheeks heated again, and Lady Gammon laughed. "I had thought you blushed excessively when you greeted Logan. I am not about to ask what transpired between you, but have you decided to marry him? Has he asked?"

Eleanor glanced down to her hands neatly folded in her lap. She could confide in Lady Gammon, but should she? So far, the countess had seemed genuine in her interest toward Eleanor, so she squared her shoulders and looked the countess in the eye. "Yes, he offered, and I accepted, but I am worried my parents will not approve. They have always held much higher aspirations for me, you know."

Lady Gammon's eyes sparkled with excitement and she squealed. "Oh! I just knew this would happen. I am so very excited for the both of you." Then, she lowered her volume and whispered, "I cannot understand why your parents should disapprove of Logan. He has lofty connections and is quite rich. Yes, a baronet does not hold a seat in parliament, but that is only a minor issue."

"They will not approve, nonetheless. Logan has his estate, which I am sure affords a tidy income, but that will not impress them."

"Does that bother you?" Lady Gammon asked, her eyes fixed on Eleanor's.

Eleanor shook her head. When she first met Logan, his station had disqualified him from consideration, but she had realized she would prefer a simple life with him to a grander life with someone else. Again she shook her head. "No. I want him and no one else."

Lady Gammon nodded. "Do you remember when I told you Logan was rich?"

"Yes, but I am sure you exaggerated to help his suit. He is landed gentry. I know what that entails."

"Yes, well, it was not a lie." The door to the library swung open, and the ladies turned to see who entered. A nondescript gentleman hurried in, and Eleanor turned her attention once more to Lady Gammon who said, "Logan may not be the richest man in England, but he certainly is rich." She waved her hand around her and smirked. "In fact, I would say he is just as rich as the duke."

Eleanor gasped, her hand shooting up to cover her mouth. She had not expected Logan to hold *so* much wealth. No wonder he seemed so unconcerned about her dowry. She turned to look at Logan, who was deep in conversation with the unknown gentleman. His visage was austere, dark even, and a shudder passed over her. Something serious must have happened.

****

"Your Grace."

Logan whirled around with a thunderous scowl on his face. His steward approached with a smile, but when he saw Logan's expression, paled and clamped his mouth shut. "Be quiet," Logan hissed when his steward reached his side. He glanced sideways to Ellie only to find her staring at him with a look of shock on her face. She averted her eyes, and he knew the ruse was up. All the lengths he had gone to in order to keep his identity secret were ruined by two fatal words.

He would not be able to form a plausible excuse, and why should he when she would know the truth anyway? This was certainly not how he had wanted to tell her, but his ruse was finished.

"What is this about?"

The steward shifted uncomfortably at Logan's terse words and dark scowl. "There has been a fire, Your Grace."

A fire was one of the most disastrous things that could happen to an estate. "How bad?"

His steward began to sweat and pulled a handkerchief from his pocket. He mopped his brow and whispered, "Bad. I think it wise if you return with me."

His steward had always been the nervous sort but not to this extreme. Logan attempted to lighten his furious countenance. Ellie would not be pleased with this turn of events, but if a fire had ravaged one of his estates, he needed to go. His people needed him. "Fine. I will leave in short order. Until then, I am sure you could use some lunch. Please, go to the kitchens and avail yourself of whatever they have."

He turned to observe Ellie as she chatted with Lady Gammon. They shared a laugh at some comment while looking lovely seated together. Their coloring was a striking contrast of English beauty and a darker, exotic allure.

When he first met Ellie, she had struck him as beautiful, but her looks had failed to sway him. There were plenty of beautiful women in the world. Now that he had grown to know her, he could no longer say that. To him, she was the most beautiful woman, both inside and out.

"Have you forgotten I am here?"

Logan started. He turned to find Reuben at his arm with a sly grin on his face. With a look of chagrin, Logan said, "I am afraid I did."

Reuben chuckled. "I can hardly fault you. Go to her already."

The problem was, Logan was content to just observe her from afar. The more he thought of the upcoming conversation, the more his body behaved in a recalcitrant fashion. He would hope for an easy conversation where she would behave in a most understanding manner, but something told him she would be livid with him.

"Go on now," Reuben said, pushing Logan from his chair.

The gentle push was enough to force his limbs into action, and he went to her. He bowed before the ladies and extended his hand to Ellie. "My lady, would you care to stroll with me?"

She smiled and excused herself from Lady Gammon. She appeared quite docile as he led her from the room, which baffled him. He assumed she would be angry with him. Once he led her from the house and into the welcoming sunlight, he smiled a regretful smile and said, "I suppose you know the truth."

"Yes." She nodded. She continued speaking, as humor filled her clear blue eyes. "I don't understand all the secrecy, though."

He smiled as warmth filled him. She was so understanding, and here he had worried she would hate him. He led her to the gardens, back to the place where they had confessed their love for one another. "I wanted you to love me for me, not for some superficial reason."

She stooped down by the newly opened bright pink azaleas and looked up at him. "I can't say I blame you." She returned her attention to the flowers and bent over to enjoy their fragrance. Standing, she returned her arm to his and said, "I know how I treated you when we first met. I probably would have toned down details of myself if I were you, just out of spite."

He chuckled. That sounded like her. The air had warmed considerably, so he stopped their stroll at the bench beside the garden. He sat her down and inhaled a fortifying breath. He was not ready to impart his change in plans for their wedding, but there was no avoiding it.

****

His hand caressed her skin, and she had to stop herself from turning into his embrace. He would likely appreciate her boldness, but judging by the grim look on his face, now was not the appropriate time.

"I must leave."

Eleanor froze as his words hit her. She could not have heard him correctly. "You mean we leave tonight, right?"

He shook his head, and sorrow filled his eyes. "No. There has been a fire, and I must tend to the matter at once."

The hum of the birds disappeared as the world around her became muted. Fire could prove disastrous, depending on the extent of its damage, but they had plans. They were to depart for Gretna Green tonight. They were to marry, and she was ruined. Her pulse quickened at the thought and she inhaled a ragged breath. How could she have let this happen? He had used her, and this was his pathetic excuse to leave without facing the repercussions of his actions.

She shook her head and looked at the pond in the distance. "No. I will not allow you to throw me aside." Her voice was strong, but inwardly, she teetered on the very precipice of falling.

"I am not throwing you aside. I love you."

His voice was gravelly and deep. She should have been comforted by his words, but how many other women had heard the same thing and never seen their lover again? She was so very stupid. "If you love me, then you will take me to Gretna Green. Tonight."

He brought her hand to his lips and kissed it. "I am sorry, but this is for the best. There is no need to elope when we can marry by special license and avoid scandal."

She pulled her hand from his and placed it in her lap. Staring straight ahead, she tried to focus her thoughts, but the only ones to surface were from the scared girl within that knew she had made a grievous error. Now, she would return to her parents as damaged goods, and the only comfort they would offer was, once again, she had not measured up to Laura's standard. She had failed.

Years of training and emulation of her mother kicked in, and she remained stoic despite her inner turmoil. She wished to believe him and give him the benefit of the doubt, but optimism would not allow her to survive. Not if he abandoned her.

"When will you come for me?" Her voice was strong. At least she would make her mother proud for that reason.

"I should think two weeks."

She contemplated her well-manicured nails as she considered his words. "Very well. You shall have your two weeks, but after that, don't expect me to wait around for you."

He tensed beside her and scowled. "What do you mean?"

Finally, she turned to him. His dark green eyes held anger and the briefest flash of pain. That pain gave her hope. If her words could affect him so, maybe he did wish to come back for her. Yes, she could hope, but she must have her backup plan.

"If, in two weeks, you do not come for me, I will be forced to concede you no longer want me. In that event, I will move on."

Slowly, he smirked, but the smirk did not reach his

eyes. His eyes were dangerous, and he appeared quite menacing as he said, "In case you forgot, you are ruined. No one will have you."

She had not been caught in a compromising position, and as long as her night with Logan remained secret, she would succeed. The tenseness of their conversation had taken its toll on her, and instead of the neutral tones she hoped for, her voice was shaky as she said, "Virginities can be faked."

He inhaled sharply and turned her to him, gripping her shoulders in a tight hold. She thought he looked menacing before, but now there was real anger in his eyes. "You wouldn't dare. Even now you could carry my heir." He laughed when her eyebrow rose in surprise. "Yes, our one night together is enough. You might just be enceinte."

His words hit her like a blow. Was conceiving a child so easy? Well, it was his choice not to marry and not hers. If he worried she carried his heir, he would come back for her. She sent a frigid look to the hands that held her, and he slowly removed them. "I suggest we elope then, or if I truly am less important than your estate, you come to me within the next two weeks."

"You are being ridiculous. I love you, and I will return for you." He stood and looked down on her without a shred of remorse. "I must depart, but remember you are *mine*."

Her insides tensed as anxiety seized her. She remained calm, wanting to appear unruffled and indifferent. "We shall see."

He turned then and strode back to the manor. When he was out of sight, she slowly drew her legs to her chest and rested her chin on her knees. It was a terribly unladylike position and just what she needed. Because inwardly, she crumbled.

The Logan she knew and loved would come for her. He would marry her, and they would live happily ever after, but would he? He claimed she might carry his child, but was that a possibility? Lady Gammon had tried for years to conceive, so based on her example, Eleanor was without child.

She heaved a sigh and closed her eyes. He had spoken of marriage by special license, and now she wished she had paid more attention. It was hard to focus sometimes when one experienced hysterics. The bench called to her, and she almost lay down right there but resisted the urge. Rather, she rose and returned to the manor.

The scenery no longer held any appeal to her, and she focused on her breath while holding in the tears that threatened. She stopped by Mrs. Westfield's chambers and informed her chaperone of her desire to leave. Mrs. Westfield agreed, and Eleanor went to her room. She would nap and rein in her emotions. Otherwise she would lose all control and weep. She scowled as her head hit the pillow. These next two weeks would be long indeed.

Chapter 11

The Gammons waved them off, and the carriage pulled away from the ducal manor with Eleanor, Mrs. Westfield, and Olivia ensconced in its warmth. Eleanor sat facing the window, trying to keep a serene expression on her face. She did not see any of the scenery that passed because her thoughts were filled with Logan. After all they had been through, Logan deserved her trust. She resolved to believe he would come for her, despite the nagging doubt at the back of her mind that told her she was naïve.

She loved him, and if her cousin Laura was correct, love was something that could defy all odds. There was no harm in allowing herself to believe that, at least for the next two weeks. After that time had passed, she would have no choice but to move on. No matter how hard that would be, or how much she did not want to.

Soothed by her decision, Eleanor closed her eyes and dozed off despite the bumpy ride. She napped off and on for the rest of the uneventful trip and was grateful when they arrived at the Ashford estate. Servants swarmed the carriage, unloading the luggage in a buzz of activity. She had missed having a full staff of servants at her disposal and had never valued servants as much until her visit to Waking Hall.

She entered the house to the sound of familiar silence. She couldn't remember a time when her home had been loud. Even when Laura and Eleanor were in attendance, the place had been devoid of sound.

She rang for a bath and refreshments before sinking into the velvet cushions of her favorite armchair and surveying her room which had been decorated in various shades of pink. Before visiting Waking Hall, she thought her room suited her. Now, however, she felt it lacked in depth, maybe needing some gray to transform it.

The servants accomplished their tasks, and Eleanor found herself submerged in a steaming hot bath. Before meeting Logan, she had considered herself a socialite who somehow lacked certain basic emotions. Naturally, she had attributed her lack of caring to her mother, who displayed the same dearth of emotions as Eleanor. Now that she had come to love Logan, however, she knew she had erred in her estimation of herself. She was capable of a great deal more emotion than she had ever thought possible, and strangely, she liked it.

Her mother had taught her at a young age to trust no one and that emotions were unnecessary. At the very beginning of Eleanor's first season, she had yearned for some spark between herself and a gentleman, but nothing had ever happened. She never found a spark, and furthermore, she learned to distrust women.

Not that she trusted any besides Laura, but there was one certain lady who had reinforced the notion to Eleanor. This debutante had been upset that Eleanor was more popular than she and sent Eleanor a black vase filled with azaleas. In the language of flowers, a black vase with azaleas signified a death threat. The girl was not stupid enough to admit to the flowers, but Eleanor knew, and from that moment on, Eleanor gave up on her gender. She would have no friends, aside from Laura, and she would do her duty by marrying well.

She sighed from the memory and wrung the moisture from her hair. She stepped out of the tub and toweled dry. A servant helped her into a gown and braided her hair down her back.

Eleanor stopped in front of her mirror and looked at herself with a critical eye. While her outward appearance remained unchanged, internally she felt different. Logan had given her the freedom to change. The idea that she would not have to deal with the confines of the *ton* when she married Logan was so very freeing. How ironic that his lack of a higher title was the very thing that would liberate her most.

Picking up her skirts, she hurried downstairs for supper. Of course, she was the last to enter the dining room, and her entrance was not met with the welcoming greeting she had expected. Instead, she was met by a cold, disapproving stare from her mother and complete disregard from her father.

Eleanor slipped into her typical chair as her mother said, "Your aunt has apprised me of your situation." Eleanor's stomach lurched as her mother continued, "I do not know what you are thinking, turning down a duke. You should have accepted." She shook her perfectly coiffed head and said, "You will not marry this baronet. He is beneath you."

Eleanor's appetite disappeared and failed to return even as the servants placed plates of hot food in front of the assembled family members. Instead of reaching for her fork, she decided on a sip of wine for fortitude. "He is hardly a commoner, Mother." She took another sip and said, "He is quite rich, and I will marry no other."

Lady Ashford exhaled as her face remained a frozen mask. "That may be, but a baronet will not earn your father any votes in parliament." She laughed, which sent a shiver down Eleanor's spine. "Why even bother having a daughter if she gains nothing from her marriage?"

Frozen in place, Eleanor could not believe her ears. Her mother had always been on the frigid side but never heartless. Eleanor stood, her chair scraping against the floor with a loud screech. "You will regret those words, Mother."

She began to stride from the room when her mother said, "We depart for London in the morning. You may have failed to secure a duke, but we can find you a better match than a baronet."

Without uttering a response, Eleanor hurried out. She had told Logan they should elope, but his estate was more important. Her mother could be ruthless, and Eleanor was sure she had been serious about finding Eleanor a husband. Eleanor could stall for a little while, but if Logan did not act fast, she could be forced into an unwanted marriage to only God knew who.

Entering her room, she strode to her desk and pulled out some paper. Logan would need to know she had gone to London, assuming he would come for her. She thought he had said Briarthorn was located in Corningwall, so hopefully he would receive the missive without any interference. Her pride kept her from saying too much, other than to inform him of her change in location, and she signed it with a flourish.

She tucked the letter away in her desk. Hopefully, her mother would not find it. She did not need to alert her mother to just how rebelliously she planned on behaving. Olivia helped her into a nightgown, and she slipped into bed. She fell into a restless sleep filled with wary uncertainty of what would soon happen.

Chapter 12

Two weeks crept by as Eleanor settled into her townhouse in London. With each passing day, her nerves grew more and more agitated. Not only did the void of loneliness caused by Logan's absence increase daily, but her trust in him wavered. She immersed herself in her painting in order to keep away the gnawing worry, but even her paintings tended toward a darker theme.

He should have been here by now. Of course, she tried to come up with excuses for his absence, but she failed to convince herself of their credibility. Maybe her letter had been lost and he did not know where to find her, or perchance another emergency arose requiring his attention. She could almost believe the last excuse she created for him, which was that Logan had caught the duke's illness, but neither she nor Mrs. Westfield had become ill, and common sense dictated he had not as well.

She sighed and settled into her chair. Nothing held her attention, except her art. There, at least, she could rest her weary mind and just be. In answer to her ceaseless worry, Eleanor had created a bit of an art studio in one corner of her bedroom. She spent most of her time there, much to her mother's annoyance, and even now occupied the space. She had one canvas propped against the wall beside her in case she needed to cover the canvas she now worked on. No one could see her current art, no one but Logan.

She had smuggled her drawing of her soiled bed to London with her, and it had transformed into something she could be proud of. What once was a literal drawing of the bed was now a veritable sea of gray-blue satin and in its center, a nymph with blonde hair. She faced away from the viewer, allowing the smallest portion of her bare back to peek from the covers. Eleanor had poured her heart into the painting for Logan. For truly, every shadow and every line was made for him.

She stared at the canvas, lost in thought, until the door swung open. Her mother entered, bringing with her the cloying scent of lavender and an air of coldness. Eleanor tried her best to act unaffected by the intrusion, even as she shuddered. How terrible her mother's reaction would be to see Eleanor's artwork.

Lady Ashford strolled in with her usual reserved dignity and went to Eleanor's vanity. She picked up Eleanor's silver looking glass and eyed it for several moments before she turned to regard her daughter. "We have been invited to a ball tomorrow."

Her brows rose in astonishment. They had not been invited anywhere. She had begun to think they were ostracized from all of society.

Her mother's sharp eyes narrowed on her. "Wipe that expression from your face this instance. Do you wish to get wrinkles?" Eleanor did as told and waited for her mother to continue.

"It is vital you are positively flawless tomorrow night, and if the duke is in attendance, you will dance with him."

Eleanor continued to stare at her mother, keeping

her features flat. There was a time when she idolized the woman, back when she had been too young to know better. As she grew, so did her knowledge that her mother was not worthy of such a high pedestal. And now, she knew she would not turn into her mother, no matter what.

Her chance to break away from her mother's influence was at hand, her chance to turn into the exact opposite of the woman before her. Love was key to such a move, and it was imperative she convince her mother of Logan's suit, no matter how difficult.

She leveled her gaze at her mother and smiled as she spoke in a dispassionate voice. "Did you know Sir Logan is best friends with both the Duke of Waking and Lord Gammon? He is also nephew to a marquess."

"And?"

"And those are better connections than many members of the *ton* can boast. Most barons would be lucky to claim even one."

Without missing a beat, her mother sighed. "Yes, but a baron has a vote in parliament. The most we could hope from Sir Logan is to convince his friends or uncle to use their vote. It is not the same."

Eleanor set her paintbrush aside and rubbed at her temple. The clashing scents of lavender and paint fumes created an unsettling mixture. "You base my happiness on one vote here, one that cannot even be counted on. Who knows if this duke will cast his vote in favor of Father's issues?"

"It will be your job to change his mind, my dear."

Of course it would, even though the duke she met did not seem the swayable sort. "Shouldn't my feelings matter?"

"Don't be absurd." Her mother scoffed as she stepped to the striped pink and white bed. She took a seat and paused to consider Eleanor. Raising a delicate brow, she said, "You speak as though you imagine yourself in love with this Sir Logan."

Eleanor's heart sank. If admitting her feelings would help her situation, she would, but her mother would not be swayed by such emotions. Even now her mother's eyes had hardened beyond their icy indifference. Imagine if Eleanor confirmed the accusation?

Lady Ashford shifted and the bed creaked, drawing Eleanor's attention back as she said, "You do believe yourself in love, don't you? My sweet, sweet girl. You and I are not the sort to love. You might believe yourself to be in love now, but it will fade. What won't fade is a title and money."

Eleanor shook her head. She was not the same as her mother, and her love for Logan proved it. Of course, if he did not come for her, she might have to resort to the same actions her mother would take. Her waning spirits sank lower at the thought, and she shut her eyes to the horrid thought. She could not allow such a fate to happen. Not anymore. Not after she had tasted the sweetness of a future with Logan.

Reopening her eyes, she squared her shoulders and cocked her head to the side. "You would rather I choose a man that told me one woman was as good as another? He has no interest in me aside from my beauty, Mother."

"Of course you are replaceable. Why do you think young ladies are provided dowries? Even with your looks, if you did not have a dowry, you would have a difficult time making a good match. All because women are replaceable."

Eleanor froze as each biting word hit her. She could not believe what was said. No, Logan loved her and would not replace her so easily. After all, he had reassured her he did not care for her dowry. He wanted her no matter what. She bit her lip and shook her head as she looked her mother in the eye. "Sir Logan does not believe I am replaceable."

"He has to say something to convince you to choose him." Lady Ashford smiled, her smile not quite reaching her eyes. "Once you have provided him an heir, he will forget about you, just as your father forgot about me."

"What?" she asked, bewildered by the change in topic.

"Yes. Did I forget to mention that?" She *tsk*ed. "You are old enough to understand how a modern marriage functions. Whoever you marry will take a mistress, just as your father did one month into our marriage."

One month. The words sank in, and Eleanor shuddered. How could her father behave with such callous disregard for her mother's feelings? Logan would not consider taking a mistress, would he? Something in her told her he would not, and she smiled at her mother. "He will not, and I will marry him, Mother."

Her mother rose from the bed and crossed to the door, resting her slim hand on the knob while looking over her shoulder at Eleanor. "Really, Eleanor, you will not marry him." Her gaze turned scornful, and she spoke as she opened the door. "Laura would never have disappointed me so." Then she left the room, shutting the door with a firm click.

Eleanor scowled just to spite her mother, and then stopped herself. There was no point in behaving childishly. She stood from her stool and opened the window to her room. She needed air to clear her head.

Returning to her easel, she picked up the larger canvas from the wall and fitted it over the smaller painting. The larger canvas managed to leave enough space so the paint did not smudge. It was not the best conditions for drying wet paint, but it was better than someone seeing her work.

She stretched before ringing for her lady's maid. Once readied, she stepped from the house with Olivia as her companion. She would need a few things in order to attend a ball the following night. A ball could either prove exhausting, or maybe she would happen upon Logan. It could be he had no way of contacting her and haunted ballrooms in hopes of finding her. Her spirits rose at the thought.

Bond Street was packed with what appeared to be every member of the *ton* in attendance. Of course, no one approached her as she walked down the long row of shops. Everyone chose to believe the rumors that swirled around, but hopefully the dress she wore would dispel the juiciest untruth of her supposed pregnancy. Her day dress emphasized her slim waistline with a row of heavy buttons down the front. Any of the other rumors were much more difficult to disprove but were also not as ruinous.

As she walked through the crowd, she could feel the cold stares of past acquaintances on her. Funny how in the past, those same stares would have been eager smiles yearning for her approval. Her eyes roved the shops as she strolled past.

She entered a ribbon shop and perused the wares with disinterest, until her gaze alighted on a dark green silk ribbon. With a bittersweet sigh, she pulled it to her. The color was the exact shade of Logan's eyes, and she would keep it close to her henceforth until she could replace it with him.

She completed her purchase and went to the next shop and then the next, searching for nothing, yet unwilling to leave. With each shop, she grew more and more weary. What was the point of shopping when nothing held her interest? She turned with a disheartened sigh and began to exit the sweet shop, when she caught sight of Miss Farris.

Her pulse raced with the realization that now was the perfect time to make amends. She strolled to Miss Farris's side and surveyed the beauty. Her dark brown hair and bold blue eyes remained unchanged, but Miss Farris had gained at least ten pounds since Eleanor last saw her. Truthfully though, the extra weight made her look even lovelier.

Before Eleanor could greet Miss Farris, one of the debutantes, a Miss Fernly who had once tried to curry Eleanor's favor, spoke in a too-loud voice as her friend grinned wickedly beside her. "Why, if it isn't Miss Farris. Whatever are you doing in a sweet shop? This should be the last place you frequent."

Eleanor rolled her eyes as Miss Fernly's friend giggled. Why did women have to be so catty? The color drained from Miss Farris's face, and Eleanor's eyes narrowed. While she could not do anything about Logan, she could do something about this harridan.

She coughed to gain their attention. "Her figure hardly needs improvement." Her eyes roved over the slender, flat-chested girl that had spoken. "You are obviously unaware that gentlemen prefer curves on women."

Miss Fernly turned to Eleanor with a glare, although the only thing Eleanor noticed was Miss Farris's look of gratitude. Pride at her timely intervention coursed through her before the rude girl said, "Miss Ashford, what a pleasure." She smirked as she turned her venom on Eleanor. "I thought you would stay hidden away in the country until the delivery."

Eleanor gasped. While certain rumors followed her, no one dared say such damaging things to her face. Hiding her shock with a soft smile, she raised a condescending eyebrow at the chit. "You poor dear. You try so hard but are never quite up to snuff, are you?" Reaching over, she patted Miss Fernly's hand in commiseration before turning to Miss Farris and giving Miss Fernly the cut. "Miss Farris, would you care to stroll with me?"

Miss Farris agreed, although Eleanor could tell it was a tentative acceptance, and Eleanor led her from the shop. "I had hoped to run into you. Thank you for accompanying me."

Miss Farris nodded. "It would not have been beneficial to say no after you helped me, although I think that confrontation was more troublesome for you than for me."

"Don't be ridiculous." She inclined her head and smiled. "I was a bit surprised by her candor." Eleanor paused to take in a window display of various stockings and said, "Now I know this is a bit of a surprise, but I hoped to ask a favor of you."

"I doubt I will agree to your favor," Miss Farris said with an upraised eyebrow.

"Oh, just hear me out." Eleanor rushed on. "I behaved poorly when we first met. I thought I wanted something that you were trying to steal from me. As a result, I lashed out in an exceptionally cruel way." A feeling of deep regret accompanied her words. If she were in Miss Farris's shoes, she wouldn't forgive herself in one hundred years. "The favor I ask is that you forgive me."

Miss Farris stopped walking and turned to face Eleanor as her eyes turned a tumultuous blue. "You almost ruined my come-out ball." A scowl crept over her face and she said, "People still whisper about me, wondering if you spoke of me rather than Laura." She looked down at the wooded walkway. "Now to top it all off, I keep gaining weight."

"Truly. I am sorry for all of that. One's come-out ball is difficult enough without a scandal. I am sorry."

"Yes, well, it could have been better." She inspected her gloved hand and shook her head.

Eleanor scowled. When she had first orchestrated her attack on Miss Farris, it had all seemed so normal. Now, however, she could not understand what she had been thinking. No, she could. It was precisely the sort of thing her mother would have approved of. Any means was acceptable to gain a titled gentleman, and she had stooped to using *any* means. It was sickening.

She took Miss Farris's hand in hers and smiled when Miss Farris returned her gaze. "Don't be angry with me because of your weight gain. If anything, you should thank me."

Miss Farris appeared confused as she asked, "What do you mean by that?"

"I spoke the truth in that shop. Men love curves on women. You had none before, and now it appears your weight has settled into your bosom and hips. Both of which are places men like more rounded."

Miss Farris turned a hesitant gaze on Eleanor. "I have noticed a few looks from men, but assumed they were noting my expanding figure in a negative way."

They began to walk once more while Miss Farris remained deep in thought. They stopped in front of a shop near Eleanor's coach, and Eleanor asked, "So, is all forgiven?"

"I suppose so. I have always been terrible at holding a grudge."

"Thank you." A weight lifted from Eleanor's shoulders. Now, she could make amends with Laura.

With parting words, Eleanor left to return home, thankful for Miss Farris's forgiveness. She would attend the ball the following evening, and then visit Laura in hopes of a happy reunion, and if Logan appeared before then, well, she could readjust her plans.

****

The following night, Eleanor was once again dressed in all her finery in preparation for a ball. Her hair was done in an elaborate style piled high on her head, and she had donned a stylish gown of light blue that almost seemed to shimmer when she walked. She looked her best, but how else should she dress when she hoped Logan would sweep her away?

Right before her gown could be laced, she stopped Olivia and went to her jewelry box. There, she found her green ribbon, kissed it, and placed it within her camisole. He had to be there tonight. He just had to be.

The ride to the ball was filled with silence except for her mother's clipped words, which advised Eleanor to behave. She did not deign to respond and instead turned her attention to the cobblestones as they flew by. Still, her mother chatted on about Eleanor's need for propriety.

Engaging her mother in conversation right now would be futile, so Eleanor closed her eyes and breathed. The carriage rocked to a stop, and her mother ceased speaking. As they entered the decadent ballroom, Eleanor could feel all eyes drift to her. She squared her shoulders and held her head up high. Instead of cowering in a corner, she would spend her time drinking champagne and searching the crowd for Logan.

Her heart stopped when her eyes landed on a tall gentleman with the same colored hair as Logan. He was here. He really had been searching for her. She smiled. What a fool she had been to think he would not come for her. He turned his head, and the smile on her face faded. It was not him.

No matter how many times she scanned the crowd, she failed to spot him. Finally, she reached the conclusion that he was not there. The realization was too much to bear. She drank the rest of her champagne and searched the crowd for any welcoming face. She must do something to occupy herself. Otherwise she might just crumble into a mess of tears.

She spotted Miss Farris as the girl danced beneath the glittering candlelight of the ballroom. Miss Farris probably did not wish to speak to Eleanor, although she would benefit from some advice from Eleanor in terms of fashion. The girl was not dressed to her best advantage.

She turned to find the retiring room when a pleasant-looking young gentleman approached. She shuddered at the realization that her mother would still be able to find her a match, as long as there were fortune hunters in need of a dowry. "Lord Percival," she greeted as he grasped her hand in his.

"My lady." He bowed and placed a delicate kiss on the back of her gloved hand. "I am overjoyed by your return to society."

"Indeed." She did not desire to spend time with Lord Percival. In fact, she would rather spend the evening without a dance partner and alone than to engage in any dance with him. She scanned the crowd as she tried to formulate an excuse to end her conversation with him when her eyes alighted on the rude girl from Bond Street, Miss Fernly.

Eleanor whipped her fan out and smiled at him as she fanned her face. "I just had the most wonderful idea, my lord."

Lord Percival nodded. His eyes were trained on her décolletage, and he did not even bother to look at Eleanor's face as she addressed him. Annoyed, Eleanor felt justified in her suggestion. "Have you met Miss Fernly? She is the young lady next to the refreshment table."

That query caught his attention, and Lord Percival followed her nod to the indicated lady. With an unreadable expression, he said, "I do not believe so."

Eleanor leaned toward him and whispered, "It is rumored she has quite the sizeable dowry."

Lord Percival scoffed. "I doubt that. I would know

if she did."

"Well, she does." Eleanor whispered the rumored amount to him and smiled as his eyes grew round. He muttered a few words in parting and hurried away, intent on his new quarry. She exhaled the breath she hadn't realized she held and relaxed as she was once again left alone. She almost smiled when Lord Percival was introduced to the girl and led her on to the dance floor. She had never met two people more deserving of one another.

Eleanor left the ballroom and entered a hall decorated with more of the orchids that adorned the ballroom. She liked orchids, but tonight they did not hold their usual appeal. She spent a lengthy amount of time in the retiring room, and then made her way back to the ballroom. There, she found another glass of champagne and once again searched the crowd for Logan. Still, he was not there.

Her eyes remained glued on the doors to the ballroom, but Logan never entered. Several dances went by with Eleanor staring at the doorway, her ever-increasing feeling of anxiety building with the thought that he would not come for her. Surely, he would come. Just not tonight.

Someone coughed at her elbow, and Eleanor turned to find Miss Farris standing there. Miss Farris's cheeks were flushed with excitement, and she had never looked prettier. Eleanor smiled in greeting. "How has your night been?"

Miss Farris smiled a smile of pure enjoyment. "Most exhilarating, thank you. Have you not been dancing?"

Lifting her glass to her lips, Eleanor took a sip and

shook her head. "It appears I am somewhat of a pariah. I have been keeping myself busy with other things, though."

"How ironic that you should try to hurt my reputation, but you end up with the sullied name." Miss Farris laughed, and Eleanor could only shake her head. Miss Farris spoke the truth.

Eleanor scowled playfully and said, "Yes, but despite all that, I have managed to play matchmaker."

Miss Farris's eyes gleamed when Eleanor informed her who she had steered toward each other.

"How delightful. My brother warned me away from Lord Percival before I even had my come-out ball."

Eleanor nodded as she continued to observe the crowd. Still nothing. She turned to Miss Farris and said, "I do not wish to offend, but there is something you simply must allow me to help you with."

"Which is?"

"I believe we should meet at my dressmaker for a fitting," Eleanor said. Life was so much simpler if one spoke without artifice.

"Why? I have plenty of dresses."

Eleanor shrugged. "Yes, but you could use ones more suited to your figure."

Miss Farris glanced down in surprise at her own gown. "What is wrong with this one?"

"Nothing, really, it just doesn't flatter you the way it ought. You have a lovely figure, but it is not shown to its best advantage."

Miss Farris's fingers smoothed down the folds of her gown, and she tilted her head. "I suppose one visit cannot hurt. Gavin might not appreciate the cost, though."

Eleanor waved her hand and laughed. "Yes, but it is a small price to pay for your happiness." As the dance ended, a dark-haired gentleman approached Miss Farris to sweep her away. Eleanor observed them for a moment, a little envious of all the dancers spinning about.

Truthfully, she doubted she would care to dance much unless a certain gentleman was the one to escort her. She snared another glass of champagne. She should stop drinking, but what else was she to do? Scowling at the bubbles in her long-stemmed glass, she shook her head. Two weeks had passed. How long should she wait on him before giving up? Hopefully, she would never have to make that decision.

Chapter 13

Eleanor spent her morning in bed. The previous night had not gone well, at all. Her hope that Logan would find her at the ball and sweep her away had been shattered to pieces. Logan had not been in attendance and might never be.

Voices from the foyer drifted to her, and she eyed the mantel clock. She should have dressed and greeted the visitors who came to call that morning but instead chose to relax amongst the soft covering of her bed with a good book. Not that it held her attention, but it was the best excuse she could muster.

Her mother did not seem to care if she were present or not. Lady Ashford had sent a maid to see what delayed Eleanor, and Eleanor had simply sent the maid away without a reply. She knew her behavior bordered on petty, but there were very few times when she could rebel. It wasn't as if she could run away.

She tried to focus on her book and sighed. It was pointless. She rose and rang for her maid to help her dress. Olivia greeted her with a warm smile as she entered and helped Eleanor dress. Eleanor had already chosen her ensemble of a day dress of pastel purple and white, along with a small hat to perch daintily on her head. If there was one thing she excelled at, it was assembling a delightful outfit.

Once again, Olivia accompanied her into the

carriage and sat opposite Eleanor on the thick, padded seats. The day was dreary. The sky was overcast and promised rain, while a harsh wind threatened to carry away Eleanor's little hat. Olivia had pinned it well, as it remained glued to the top of her head. She congratulated Olivia on a job well done and settled in for the ride.

Bond Street was not its usual hub of activity. It was too early in the day for the wealthy class and too windy for most others. Eleanor was let out in front of her dressmaker's shop. She had arrived several minutes before the agreed-upon time when she would meet with Miss Farris and must now wait.

She stepped from the shop's entryway and went down the boardwalk. Her hat would stay pinned, but her hair was a different matter. She would have to rearrange her coiffure when she arrived at the dressmaker. After walking for a few minutes on the deserted street, she turned around and began her walk back.

Her walk brought her past a small jeweler's, where she stopped as her gaze lit upon the most lovely cameo necklace she had ever seen. The wind gusted stronger than ever, and she hurried into the jeweler's for closer inspection.

The proprietor of the shop greeted her with a small bow and his offer of assistance as she approached. If ever Eleanor would have pegged a man to be a jeweler, this would have been the one. He stood several inches shorter than Eleanor, with close cropped gray hair and spectacles perched on the end of his nose. He evidently could recognize a lady of quality and began to fawn over Eleanor. "My lady," he said as he rushed over, "is there anything I can help you with?"

Eleanor indicated the window display with her gloved hand. "I would like to see the cameo necklace please."

He nodded and rushed to do her bidding, pulling the displayed pendant from the shelf while taking the utmost care in its handling. "You have exquisite taste, my lady. This particular cameo is set in gold and carved from an opal."

Eleanor examined it under a nearby wall sconce. The craftsmanship was above reproach, while the cameo itself depicted the image of a beautiful Roman woman. The color of the opal gave the figure an ethereal quality, and Eleanor sighed as she realized the image could easily be a nymph. Such a lovely image deserved appreciation, and Eleanor knew she could be the one to do just that. With a small smile, she took a step back as she realized why she wanted to buy it. Aside from its beauty, she once again was searching for any small reminder or link to Logan.

"Thank you for showing this to me," Eleanor said, inhaling the musky scent of the shop. "I shall pass for now."

He nodded in understanding and said, "You know where to find it should you change your mind. I cannot imagine a lady it would complement more."

A wistful smile tugged at her lips as she departed the cozy shop into the gloomy street. Why had she not purchased the necklace? The answer was clear, in all its stark harshness. If Logan did not come for her, that necklace would serve as a terrible reminder of her broken heart.

The wind tore through her hair as she hurried along

the boarded walkway. The cold wind battered her, but wind was preferable to the way her heart felt. Heavy and cold.

Eleanor entered the dressmaker as the door slammed shut behind her. The walls were a light blue with white trim. Ornate white chairs were arranged on the side of the room with various sketches of the latest fashions on the walls. Her hair was a mess, and luckily, there were plenty of mirrors in the establishment. Eleanor set herself to rights just as Miss Farris joined her in the elegant establishment.

"Can you believe this weather?" Miss Farris said in a shocked tone. "I thought the carriage would tip over."

"Thank heavens that did not happen," Eleanor said with a kind smile as the proprietress of the establishment rushed into the room.

At the sight of Eleanor, she increased her speed and spoke in her heavy French accent. "Miss Ashford! What a delight to see you here. Did you have an appointment?" the pretty, diminutive woman asked with a crinkle of worry on her otherwise unlined brow.

Eleanor shook her head, knowing full well her business would never be turned away. "No, Mademoiselle Giraud, but we are in dire need of your help." With a wave of her hand, Eleanor indicated Miss Farris.

Her eyes followed Eleanor's hand, and Mademoiselle Giraud observed Miss Farris's attire. "I see." She *tsk*ed as she circled Miss Farris. "Yes, this will be no trouble at all. Follow me, please."

The two ladies trailed after the seamstress into a room meant for fittings. Miss Farris took her position on an elevated platform, and the mademoiselle began to take measurements. As she buzzed about in a positive tizzy of excitement, she said, "My lady, you have such a small waist. It is a shame to hide it. No, we must accentuate it."

"How can you accentuate it and keep with the current styles?" Miss Farris asked with a dubious frown.

Again, the mademoiselle *tsk*ed. "Normally, we tie just below the bosom with a ribbon or something else and the fabric falls here." She indicated the typical spot on Miss Farris and then said, "But with you, we use wider ribbon, and the skirts hug you more as they fall. You shall see."

Miss Farris's eyes gleamed with excitement as she endured the fitting. Her eyes lit even more from the kind remarks the mademoiselle made. By the end of the visit, not only had Miss Farris ordered several new gowns, but Eleanor could almost see a renewed confidence in her.

Mademoiselle Giraud agreed to send the gowns over upon completion, and Eleanor and Miss Farris left the shop. Braving the wind, the two hurried to a nearby café for a bit of tea. The café was normally bustling with activity at this time of day, but the wind had dissuaded many a casual shopper.

They chatted until the tea arrived, and then Eleanor finally dared ask the question uppermost in her mind. "How does Laura fare?" She made sure to act unconcerned, as if her query was polite nonsense, but internally she waited with trepidation.

Munching on a biscuit, Miss Farris rolled her eyes, swallowed, and said, "She is well. I try to avoid my brother and his new wife as much as possible, you know." She sighed and continued as Eleanor ate up her words. "The two cannot keep their hands off each other, and now that Laura is enceinte…"

Her words trailed off as Eleanor emitted a small shriek of shock. Eleanor covered her mouth in an attempt to hide her surprise, but it was too late. Miss Farris laughed and asked, "So, you did not know she is with child?"

Eleanor shook her head, and Miss Farris continued with avid excitement, "Oh yes. The doctor confirmed it a week ago, but she was certain much sooner."

"How did she know?" Eleanor asked as she leaned forward with interest. No one ever spoke of such a delicate topic, ever. Aside from Lady Gammon, of course.

"Well, she said her monthly courses never came, and then she was sick all the time." Miss Farris rolled her eyes. "It all sounds rather disgusting to me."

Miss Farris refilled her teacup as Eleanor tried to comprehend the information she just received. While she was happy for Laura, she was more concerned with the signs of pregnancy. Eleanor felt just fine, but her courses were normally on schedule. Thinking back, she did the math. Eleanor froze as realization hit her. Her palms grew damp, and the color drained from her face. Her insides knotted in a queasy ball as she realized her courses were an unheard-of week late.

Eleanor placed her porcelain teacup on its saucer with a shaky hand, cringing when the cup made a clinking sound. She could not be pregnant, could she?

Her silent musings were interrupted when Miss Farris said, "Are you feeling quite all right?"

Eleanor plastered a smile on her lips. "Of course."

There was still time for her body to disprove her fears, and until then, she would forget all about it. Eleanor changed topics to Miss Farris's interests and did her best to listen, despite the sickening feeling of dread that pestered her.

****

Logan had not anticipated his business would take so long to conclude and cursed his decision to leave Ellie for so long. After all, he could have kept to his original plan and eloped with her, but that would have been selfish. She deserved better than a hushed wedding followed by unavoidable scandal. He chuckled at the ironies of society. An elopement was deemed scandalous, but his special license to marry was perfectly acceptable.

The carriage jerked to a stop, and he smiled at the knowledge he would soon set matters to right. He would see her in mere moments. He departed from the carriage and a strong gust of wind hit him with a force that tore the breath from his body. He hurried to the grand house where a butler greeted him. The butler led him to a parlor frequented by numerous ladies, none of which were Ellie.

After the butler announced his identity, a slender, older version of Ellie stood to greet him. She curtsied in a sweeping, graceful movement and practically glowed with the knowledge that a duke stood in her sitting room. "Your Grace, what a delight," she gushed as she batted her eyelashes at him.

Logan's stomach revolted at her attempt to flirt with him. The smile on her face seemed almost alien to her, as if she needed to practice it just as her daughter practiced dancing. With a quick sweep of his gaze,

Logan spoke, not showing even the slightest hint of the disdain he felt for the woman. "I see your daughter, Miss Ashford, is not in attendance."

The smile vanished from her face, replaced by a worried expression. "No, Your Grace. I am afraid she is not in." She craned her neck to view the ornate, gilded clock set on a corner end table and said, "She should be home soon if you care to join us."

Logan glanced at the eager ladies in attendance and shuddered. As much as he desired to see Ellie, he could not bring himself to suffer so. "I think not. You may, however, take me to see Lord Ashford."

A calculating smile graced her lips, and she turned to lead him from the room, down the hall, and to the library. If fortune favored him, he would have seen Ellie the moment he entered the parlor, but he could at least conclude the formal part of his visit without her.

Matters with Lord Ashford were completed in a timely manner, and Logan was once more ensconced in his carriage. He had been a little surprised with how swiftly Lord Ashford had agreed to Logan's request to marry Ellie. Lord Ashford had not even bothered to consult his daughter. Ellie must have already apprised her family of her good fortune, which was why everyone was so quick to comply.

He was still disappointed Ellie had not arrived in time to see him, but he would return in a couple of days. Until then, he would just have to wait. If nothing else, he had at least accomplished one important task and that was to alert the *ton* that Ellie was his. Now, it was only a matter of time until she was back into his arms where she belonged.

****

Eleanor returned home and sneaked into her room. Her heart was hammering. Try as she might to ignore her fears, she could not stop her thoughts from returning to her missed cycle. The crackle of the fire was the only sound to interfere with her thoughts, but even its soothing warmth was not enough to calm her.

While beset with worry over Logan's absence, that worry was nothing compared to the despair she would experience if she was indeed pregnant. She would have to marry at once. If she did not, well, she would be hidden away in the countryside until the baby was born. She would be ruined beyond any chance at redemption, and not even a fortune hunter would have her.

Her choice to spend the night with Logan seemed so natural and felt so right, but of course, she should have abstained. All rational arguments pointed to that stark truth, but the more she considered the loss of that precious night with him, the more she failed to regret her actions.

How could she regret a night ensconced in the glow of shared love so strong as to still leave a tingling feeling in her chest? Nuzzled in the warmth of his arms that night, she had melted when he whispered sweet nothings to her, promises of times to come. How could she choose anything but belief in him?

Every ounce of her told her to trust him still, but what was she to do when she resided in a haze of uncertainty for not only her own, but a budding life's future? Logan had better hurry to her, or else she would have very few options indeed.

In an attempt to clear her mind, Eleanor crossed to her easel and drew a blank canvas from her desk. She sketched the view from her window in all its gloomy glory. She felt a new appreciation for the overcast sky, as its bleakness matched her spirit.

She performed a cursory sketch and then pulled out her paints, mixing black with a small amount of white. Achieving the precise gray of the sky was important. As the colors blended, she decided to add a tinge of blue to the palette. The blue transformed the humdrum color into an ideal hue of stormy potential, which allowed her to capture its uniqueness.

With each stroke of the brush, she relaxed, although Logan still haunted her. If her current luck held, he would never come for her, and she would stay forever cursed by unrequited love. She leaned toward the canvas and began to work on shaping a cloud when the fumes from the paint reached her. Nothing could have prepared her for the sudden onslaught of nausea that arose and prompted her to run for the chamber pot.

Her sickness abated, and Eleanor crawled back to the bed. She moaned as she lay down on the downy mattress. At least now she had her answer. Logan had impregnated her. Her worst fears presented themselves in the form of nausea and a missing groom. How disastrous.

A knock interrupted her thoughts, and Eleanor started in surprise at the abrupt sound. "Eleanor," her mother said, her voice muffled, yet as distant as ever.

Eleanor sat up in time to greet her mother who looked unusually happy.

"You haven't ruined everything after all," Lady Ashford said as she floated to stand before the bed. "His Grace, the Duke of Waking, was here."

Eleanor tried to hide her scowl, but it was no use. Her mother's eyes narrowed on her lips, but suddenly she did not care. She had more pressing matters to attend to than appeasing her mother. After all, an unwanted duke had deigned to call on her.

Lady Ashford's excitement dissipated, and she said, "Cheer up. You should have realized this would happen."

It was most unusual for a duke to drop by for a visit. In fact, it had never happened to the Ashfords. Eleanor uttered a noncommittal sound which her mother took as encouragement to continue. "I was naturally appalled that a duke should call when you were not receiving, but then the most extraordinary thing happened. He asked to speak with your father."

An unfamiliar gleam of approval was in her mother's eyes, and Eleanor understood precisely what her mother insinuated. "So, Father agreed to a marriage between myself and the Duke of Waking." A bitter taste filled her mouth. Why had His Grace asked for her hand in the first place? The last time she spoke with him, she had expressed her desire to marry his friend. Why would he disregard hers and Logan's wishes?

Her mother nodded, her expression returning to its former cheerful mien. Eleanor should have expected her parents to act this way, but it still hurt they cared so little for her preferences. She clenched her hands into fists and modulated the tone of her voice to a calm and cold tone. "So, you willingly sell me off to the highest title you can find despite my desire to marry a different man?"

A harsh mask settled onto her mother's face. "Your wishes are unimportant. You will marry this duke and you will be grateful when you are a duchess. This pathetic love match of yours is over, and you had best forget it."

With an indignant huff, Eleanor's mother departed the room. Not long ago, Eleanor would have been overjoyed by the news of the duke's interest, but that time had passed. A hot tear trickled down her face as she realized the repercussions of her mother's news. She had threatened Logan with finding a different man to marry, and now he would think she chose one of his best friends as her match. With a sob, she buried her head in her pillow and began to cry. Logan would never come for her now, not when he heard she was engaged to the very duke she had once desired to marry.

Chapter 14

Whipping his horse to a smooth canter, Logan sped through the unoccupied grounds of Hyde Park as he attempted to calm his mind. In relative terms, his problems were small, but he couldn't seem to ease his frustrations no matter what he did. Ever since going to visit Ellie, an unsettled feeling had lodged in his chest, making it almost impossible to gain clarity of mind.

Not that he blamed Ellie for her absence, but he just couldn't seem to wrap his mind around her behavior. He knew that she had been in London for some time now, yet she had not once written to him. He assumed they would communicate via missive, if not in person, yet she had not put forth any effort to contact him. At the very least, she could have sent a letter over the previous evening after his visit.

He shook his head as he guided his steed around a bend and set him in the direction of home. The trees were resplendent in their green leaves, which were no longer mere buds, and the dew of the morning had not yet disappeared. Such a day was ripe with promise.

As he rode, he glimpsed a couple through the trees and recognized Viscount Dunbar. He veered away from the couple in an attempt to avoid small talk, but not before noticing the shared smile between the viscount and his blonde companion. The couple's look spoke of a deep love for each other, which only sank the piercing feeling of loneliness further into his soul. There really was only one choice left to him, and that was to go visit Eleanor once more.

He returned home to his townhome a mere four blocks from the Ashfords and scowled as he entered his room. His house seemed lifeless and in desperate need of a blonde-haired vixen to grace its halls. He stopped in front of his bed and surveyed the room. Would she like his home? The townhouse did not concern him as much as his home in Briarthorn, as that estate held all his childhood memories.

Moving from the bed, he rang for a servant to draw a bath. No, Ellie would not mind the décor, and if she did, she would have free rein to change it. After all, his memories would remain even if the aging wallpaper did not.

Logan completed his ablutions and ate a hearty breakfast. The clock suggested the time was a bit early for a visit, but he was too antsy to wait at home. He could imagine the smile on Ellie's face when she saw him again, and that smile demanded he not keep her waiting.

Of course, as a duke, he could do better than just show up on her doorstep empty-handed. Thrusting his top hat on his head, he tucked his walking stick under his arm and left the townhouse. His carriage awaited him, and he directed his coachman to Bond Street.

He would find her the ideal gift, but choosing such a trinket was not as simple as he thought. Flowers were too typical, and she had more than enough clothes. His only other option was jewelry, but it had to be something special. Something to commemorate their love.

He stepped from his coach and scanned the shops. There seemed to be an unending amount of them. In the past, he sent someone to find appropriate gifts, but that was not acceptable this time. He continued to regard the shops until his eyes alighted on a jewelry store that seemed to beckon to him.

With sure steps, his strides ate up the distance to the store's entrance. He entered the well-lit shop and was greeted by the scent of an aging, musky interior. He had spent his entire life in homes that smelled similarly, and he chose to think of them as buildings that smelled of history, rather than mildew.

A short, older gentleman rushed out to greet Logan as he perused the wares on display. As the man took in Logan's attire, his smile grew broader and he said, "May I help you with something, my lord?"

Logan raised an eyebrow. What was worse? To point out a man's faux pas, or to leave it unaddressed? "You may address me as Your Grace."

The shopkeeper blanched as he stammered a hurried reply, "Of course, Your Grace. My apologies for my ignorance."

Logan ignored the kowtowing and said, "I require a gift for my future duchess. Something unique."

Nodding and appearing deep in thought, the shopkeeper leaned his chin into his hand as he considered Logan's request. After several seconds, he raised his index finger and said, "Give me one moment, Your Grace. I have just the thing." He rushed to the window display and pulled a piece from the case. He set out a velvet tray and draped a necklace over it. "Here is jewelry fit for an emperor, or a duchess."

Logan glanced down at the piece, which was a

cameo of a Roman goddess or other ethereal beauty. His breath caught as he smiled and picked it up to examine the craftsmanship in finer detail. He had never seen such an exquisite piece of jewelry before.

The shopkeeper continued speaking, despite Logan's inattentiveness. "That particular pendant belonged to the emperor, Napoleon Bonaparte. He held a special appreciation for such jewelry, and this one is an exceptional piece."

Logan nodded in agreement. He couldn't care less who had owned the cameo in the past, but he did care that the image could easily be Ellie. His water nymph was once more in his hands. Lifting his eyes from the image, Logan asked the shopkeeper the price and was apprised of the sum. Despite the high cost, he agreed and waited while the man wrapped the item.

The shopkeeper continued to speak as he secured the parcel. "You know, Your Grace, there was a young woman in here just yesterday that almost bought this. You are lucky it's still here."

Not caring to chitchat, Logan didn't reply until the cameo was in his hands, wrapped, and ready to go. "Thank you. If my lady approves, you may just see me here again." Logan ignored the speculative gleam that entered the jeweler's eyes, and departed, pleased with his choice and ready to see Ellie.

****

With his arrival at the Ashfords' townhouse, he began to regret his decision to visit at this time. Unlike the previous day where the sitting room held a small handful of guests, today it was packed. The butler announced his arrival while Logan once again searched the crowd. His search was futile as Ellie was not in attendance.

Lady Ashford stood to greet him with a proud smile. She rushed to his side and said, "Your Grace, what an honor." The volume of her voice increased as she added, "Two days in a row."

Logan bowed, albeit with great reluctance. Sometimes, good manners were most tedious. "Is Miss Ashford receiving guests today?"

Lady Ashford shook her head. "My dear daughter is under the weather."

"Did you tell her of my visit yesterday?"

"Of course, Your Grace." Lady Ashford simpered, batting her eyelashes at him while laying a gloved hand on his arm.

He shrugged her hand away. "And?"

She blinked. Logan could only assume she was unused to his treatment of her. "Naturally, she was overjoyed, Your Grace."

He nodded. That sounded accurate. "What ails her?"

Lady Ashford lowered her gaze and said, "I believe it is a megrim." She brought her eyes back to his and asked, "Would you like to meet with her? I'm sure she will come down for you."

"Yes." He glanced about the room, noting all in attendance listening with avid interest and added, "I will wait in a separate room, of course."

"Of course." Lady Ashford led him to a smaller parlor and curtsied before departing the room. He turned to a large, ornate longcase clock and settled in to wait.

****

Eleanor did not feel quite the thing and refused to

226

leave her bed, despite her mother's firm admonishments. Nothing could sway her to face the hordes of people that morning, and there would be hordes. A duke did not pay a visit without inspiring the masses to do the same.

So, instead of dressing and pasting a fake smile on her face, she slept. At least, she attempted sleep, but her nausea and incessant worries over Logan's whereabouts made that desire nigh on impossible. Her desires almost won, when she started with the sound of the brass knocker on the front door. Her room overlooked the streets, which meant she resided above the front door.

Many more knocks followed, until she gave up, propping herself up against several pillows and ringing for breakfast. Olivia soon entered with a tray of tea and toast. Eleanor could not stomach much else that morning.

"Thank you, Olivia."

Olivia bobbed a curtsy and left, leaving Eleanor to her breakfast. She munched on a piece of toast but stopped when the door swung open. "Mother?"

Hurrying to Eleanor's wardrobe, Lady Ashford shuffled through the gowns until she pulled out a powder blue one. "Get dressed. His Grace is here to see you."

"I will not," Eleanor said in as neutral a tone as she could muster. "I will not marry him and will not go down to meet him."

Lady Ashford stilled. "Yes, you will."

Eleanor shook her head as she crossed her arms across her chest. "No."

With an angry shriek, Lady Ashford grabbed one of Eleanor's wrists and began to drag her off the bed.

Eleanor cried out in panic, "Mother! What are you doing?"

Her mother stopped her physical assault and dropped Eleanor's wrist. "You cannot refuse to see a duke. It is unseemly."

She would not go down there. The duke should not have made this call in the first place. "Tell him I have contracted his own illness and must be quarantined." She scowled. "Actually, tell him whatever you wish or nothing at all. Either way, I will not go."

Her mother muttered a litany of unladylike words, and then said, "I may not be able to force you downstairs, but you will marry him." She spun on her heel and left Eleanor as abruptly as she came.

Eleanor shuddered. She quelled a hysterical laugh at the sheer absurdity of her predicament. She could not hide away in her room much longer, but she also could not marry anyone other than Logan. Her heart demanded that much of her.

****

Logan paced in the small parlor, listening for the sound of Ellie's approach. Finally, he heard light footsteps and stopped as the door opened. His welcoming smile disappeared when Lady Ashford entered, unaccompanied.

"Does she not wish to see me?"

Lady Ashford shook her head. "Of course she does, but she is not well, Your Grace. She says she has contracted your illness. Whatever that means."

Logan's eyes narrowed. She must not have overcome her anger toward him. After three weeks, she should have been overjoyed to see him, but evidently she was not. What could she hope to accomplish by claiming an imaginary illness? Nothing that he could deduce, and he was not one to pander to her silly whims by begging to see her. He was a duke, after all.

His mood sank to an angry sullenness, and Logan turned his attention back to Lady Ashford. "Tell her she may contact me if she wishes to. Otherwise, I will see her at our wedding."

He left then, not wanting to spend another minute in the house where her scent lingered, calling to him in faint whispers. No, he would go home and await a letter from her. Otherwise, she would have some explaining to do on their wedding day.

Chapter 15

Eleanor awoke the next morning to find her mother in a state of shock. His Grace had sent a missive that morning, explaining his desire to wed two weeks hence, and no one dared object. Except for Eleanor, naturally, but her complaints were met by deaf ears.

Within a day, word of the duke's interest in Eleanor reached the ears of the *ton*, and the Ashfords' drawing room turned into the most sought-after locale in all of London. Everyone conveniently forgot the gossip about her, instead attempting to curry the favor of a future duchess. Of course, Lady Ashford encouraged the rumors, which resulted in a steady stream of invitations.

Eleanor could only shake her head and smile her most polite and reserved smile. After all, people were idiots, but she could not shun the lot of them, even if she dearly wished to. One particular invitation stunned her more than the others, despite its relative simplicity. She was invited to attend a dinner party, held by none other than the earl she had insulted earlier in the season.

Her mother ordered Eleanor to attend with Mrs. Westfield as her chaperone, which was why she found herself stepping foot in the earl's lavish townhouse. Of course, the interior could not compare to the ducal manor, but it made a fair attempt with its deep burgundy walls and ornate carpeting. And then there were the candles. She had never seen so many tapers lit in a room this size. While the entrance hall was almost double the size of her bedroom, it did not need candles lining every wall.

"What an honor it is to see you again, my lady."

Eleanor's attention jerked to her host, who placed a gentle kiss on the back of her hand as he bowed. Tonight, the earl did *not* wear the same color as the servants.

He stood and said, "I really must thank you. Your thoughtful reminder of my attire several months ago has reinvigorated my attention toward fashion."

Eleanor held back an unladylike, derisive snort. A week ago, Lord Lamhurst still held a grudge, but now he thanked her. She smiled in response and said, "I try to help out whenever I can." Which was about the only response she could formulate to his surprising acknowledgement. Really now, what was the world coming to that an earl would thank her for an insult?

He turned to greet other guests, and Eleanor scanned the room. She stopped her perusal when she spotted her cousin, Laura. Laura's light brown hair was swept into an elegant French twist, and she wore a gown of deep purple. She appeared almost unchanged except for a becoming glow of happiness that surrounded her like an aura. Eleanor stepped toward her cousin and attempted a serene expression despite the nervous butterflies fluttering about in her stomach.

Laura turned with a welcoming smile as Eleanor drew near. The welcoming smile was evidently for anyone else and disappeared as she recognized Eleanor. Her eyes narrowed and she said, "Eleanor, I should have guessed you would be here. After all, it appears you have accomplished your mission and snagged a duke. Is he in attendance tonight, as well?"

Now was not the time or place to reveal her situation. She ignored her cousin's brusque tone and said, "Not that I am aware, but enough of me. I hear congratulations are in order."

A fleeting expression of surprise swept through Laura's violet eyes as she asked, "And you know this how?"

"Through Miss Farris, although it would have been preferable if you had told me yourself."

"Would it now?" Laura asked with averted eyes, and Eleanor's heart constricted at her indifference. They used to be so close.

The guilt returned to eat at her, and Eleanor whispered, "I know I have hurt you. Please, give me the chance to make amends. Miss Farris did, and I daresay we are something of friends now."

Laura inhaled a weary breath. "I heard the rumors, but I just cannot understand why I would want to give you a chance. Judging by your engagement to a duke, you have not changed much."

Eleanor opened her mouth to inform Laura of her desire to marry Logan, rather than the duke, when she saw Lord Farris approaching with a ferocious look on his face. Instead of telling Laura her secret, she clasped her cousin's hand in hers and brought her pleading eyes to Laura's. "Just give me a chance. Let me call on you tomorrow and explain matters. You can judge me afterward. Please."

Laura nodded, although her expression was a smidgen skeptical. "Fine. Tomorrow morning."

Eleanor's heart soared with renewed hope. While

her faith in Logan's rescue dwindled, at least she would get the chance to gain her cousin back. Unfortunately, it would have to wait until tomorrow, as judging by the look on Lord Farris's stern face, she wouldn't get much more time with Laura tonight.

"Thank you," Eleanor whispered as Lord Farris joined his wife's side and grasped Laura's small hand in his large one.

"Darling," he said with noticeable concern, "you look exhausted. Allow me to find a chair for you."

Laura nodded, and he led her through an impressive set of doors into what must be the dining room. The guests continued to mingle, some disappearing through the same set of doors Lord and Lady Farris had, while the rest remained until the butler announced supper, whereat the rest of the guests ventured into the dining room. While Eleanor hungered, she longed for sleep more than anything. Exhaustion overwhelmed her as of late, and tonight was no exception.

Eleanor was placed in a position of honor by the earl, which was far from her cousin. She made sure to chat with those around her, but between conversations, she couldn't stop the niggling doubt from creeping into her brain. Almost three weeks had passed since she sent her letter to Logan, and he should have been here by now. With barely over a week to her wedding to the duke, she was running out of time. She had no intention of marrying His Grace, but once she broke their engagement she would truly be ruined and no longer accepted in the *ton*.

Eleanor lost track of the number of courses served, but it seemed like an endless amount. At one point, she received fish, which almost caused her to run for the nearest chamber pot. Fortunately, dinner came to its conclusion, and Eleanor prepared to leave. The earl had planned some parlor games, but she was too exhausted to think, much less engage in conversation with others. Mrs. Westfield did not mind departing early, so the ladies slipped out into the warm night air to the sight of the carriage waiting for them.

The instant Eleanor's head hit the cushion in the cabin, she was asleep. The exhaustion from pregnancy was unlike anything she had ever experienced, so despite the bumpy ride, she slept the entire way home. She awoke to the feeling of Mrs. Westfield gently shaking her. Opening her eyes, she asked, "Oh dear, I fell asleep. Are we home?"

"Yes, dear. We just arrived." Concern filled Mrs. Westfield's eyes and she asked, "Are you coming down with something? It's unlike you to sleep so early."

"I think I must be." She yawned and smiled. "I had better go to bed and get some rest."

Mrs. Westfield agreed, and the ladies parted ways. Eleanor hated to lie to her aunt, but this was one secret she would keep to herself for as long as possible. Reaching her bed, she lay down and was once more lulled into a restful slumber.

****

Eleanor slept through the night and awoke feeling excited for her visit to Laura's. She ordered a servant to ready the carriage, dressed, and hurried out. Her mother was still abed, but she informed the butler of her plans and then rushed out the door.

Yet another day had passed without word from Logan, and now she had to make a choice. Should she apprise him of the child she carried or marry someone else? Logan must want his child. He did not seem the sort to father bastards, but could she go to him, groveling on her knees for him to take her?

The ride was short, and as the coach halted, Eleanor was given a view of Laura's townhouse. The white house had elegant Greek columns which supported a charming terrace. Vines crept up the lattice covering the majority of the front, as well as what Eleanor could see of the side. She stepped up the stairs to the entry and knocked on the brass lion's-head knocker.

The door swung open, and Eleanor followed the butler to a parlor where Laura was already seated. Not bothering to stand, Laura indicated a chair situated across the room from her for Eleanor to occupy. The walls were a light cream, and a large painting hung on a wall of a horse, which made Eleanor grimace in distaste.

"Have you been able to ride in London?" Laura had always made time to ride. Every single morning.

Laura's demeanor was reserved, but she allowed a small smile to grace her lips as she said, "Unfortunately, no. Riding is ill-advised when one is expecting."

"However do you survive? You always claimed riding relaxed you."

"Gavin helps me relieve some of my tension." Laura blushed and looked away. "But enough of me. Why are you here?"

After Eleanor's inadvisable night with Logan, she could imagine just how Gavin helped his wife. She shook her head. She needed to focus on mending her relationship with Laura, not wallow in self-pity. "I am sorry for all the pain I have caused you. I behaved abominably and regret my actions more than you will ever know."

Laura regarded her with raised brow and said in a skeptical voice, "Those words sound similar to the ones you wrote me in your letters. Tell me something that is not rehearsed. After all, words only mean so much."

So, Laura had read her letters? That was interesting, indeed. "I can tell you any number of things, but I doubt you will believe anything I say."

"Then why are you here?" Laura poured herself tea without bothering to offer some to Eleanor and lifted the cup, looking out at Eleanor with a raised brow.

Eleanor had dreamt of this moment since she first sent one of her weekly letters to Laura. She had planned an eloquent speech on the benefits of forgiveness and just how much she regretted her behavior, but now her speech seemed wrong. No, she would speak from her heart, and if that did not convince Laura, nothing would. "Allow me to tell you what I have done the past couple of months, and then you can tell me if you believe my sincerity or not."

"Very well." She leaned back and nodded. "You have my undivided attention."

Eleanor inhaled and then launched into her story. She started from the very first meeting with Logan and progressed to the house party. She told of her realization that she loved Logan and would marry no other. No detail was left out, not even her shocking night with Logan.

Laura gasped and placed a delicate hand over her mouth. "I cannot believe it." Her violet eyes rounded, and she poured Eleanor a cup of tea. "You mean to tell me you have fallen for a baronet and are now to marry a duke?"

Eleanor shuddered. "Yes. Logan swore he would come for me, but the more time ticks by, the more I fear he will not." She lowered her voice to a whisper. "The worst part is I am starting to question what transpired between us. Did I imagine things? Maybe his ardor was not as strong as I believed, and I fell for his tricks as any other young naïve lady would."

Her heart spasmed at the thought, and she averted her gaze from Laura's. Optimism was difficult to maintain in the face of such a harsh, unflattering reality. Silence settled between them, and Eleanor waited for Laura's criticisms. Only the most foolish young ladies were compromised before marriage, and Eleanor had always vowed to marry well. How could Laura not relish in the irony?

"Oh, Eleanor. You really have changed." Eleanor's gaze darted back to Laura's, and she was greeted by a reassuring, kind smile. "Your baronet should be here. I am sure he loves you but has been waylaid."

Logically, there was no way Laura would know that, but Eleanor needed that shred of hope. "There is one more thing." She swallowed and said, "I fear I might be enceinte."

"Oh dear."

"Indeed." Her situation would be so much simpler if she were not with child.

"This complicates matters." Laura leaned her chin into her hand and deliberated, and then brought her eyes back to Eleanor's. "You must go to him. There is no other option. If he doesn't want you, then—well, we will react accordingly."

"I cannot go to him." Eleanor shook her head, but inwardly, the idea that she could do something was so very appealing.

"Why not?"

"Oh, for heaven's sake. He lives in the northern region of England. I would be ruined if I traveled there by myself."

"And you will be ruined if you stay, unless you marry this duke, of course."

Eleanor paused. What her cousin said was true. She could not marry the duke, so unless she went to Logan, she would be ruined. Why not take her future in her hands and go to Logan, present him with his impending fatherhood, and grovel at his feet? "How will I leave without Mother noticing?"

Laura tapped her chin and then raised her finger in the air. "I will send her a note claiming you are under the weather. That will hold her off for at least a day or two."

The idea held merit, and the more Eleanor sat around, the more she worried. Doing something would ease her nerves. Otherwise, she didn't know how she would survive the following week. Raising her eyes to Laura's, Eleanor nodded, "I think this is the only option. When should I depart?"

"I would suggest immediately. I can lend you some clothes, and Gavin will make the arrangements. Of course you will take our coach as it is exceptionally smooth." She clapped her hands together and rose with a twinkle in her eye. "Let me go find him."

"Does this mean you are no longer upset with me?" Eleanor asked as she leaned forward in eager anticipation to hear the response.

"As if I could stay mad at you." Laura grinned. "It was only a matter of time before I forgave you, but your situation expedited matters." As she exited the room, she said with a sly grin, "To think, I shall hold a higher title than you." She shook her head. "What an extraordinary turn of events."

Laura departed, and Eleanor sank back into her chair. Yes, Laura would hold a higher title as a viscountess, but the realization did not have the impact Eleanor thought it would. Instead, the knowledge was met with indifference. She used to long for the title of countess, and now, the only thing that mattered was Logan. His love changed things.

Laura returned and preparations commenced. While Eleanor and Laura pilfered Laura's wardrobe for suitable clothing, Gavin readied the carriage. Gavin attempted to be the voice of reason and suggest she not go, but Eleanor's mind was made up. In response, he ordered a couple of extra footmen to accompany her for protection.

Eleanor had been unable to eat as her stomach roiled about anxiously, and when she climbed into the carriage, Laura handed up a basket full of ham and cheese sandwiches. With a few kind words and a hug, Eleanor was sent off to the far reaches of England. She had never dreamt such an excursion possible. Hopefully it would not be in vain.

Chapter 16

The ride seemed endless, and with each mile traversed, her doubts increased until she almost convinced herself to return to London. If Logan was at Briarthorn, it must mean he no longer wanted her. On the other hand, he deserved to know she was pregnant and at least be presented with the option to marry her. The problem was, Eleanor did not want to marry a man who only wanted her out of obligation, but she would have to for her child. A marriage of obligation was better than no marriage, even if he hated her for the rest of their lives together.

As the carriage pressed onward and the days crawled by, the voices in Eleanor's mind grew louder and louder. She needed a distraction, but aside from a couple of books Laura had provided her, she had nothing to do except sleep and look out the window. None were compelling options, but sleeping was the best of the three. Lying on her side, she closed her eyes and drifted off, hoping they would reach Briarthorn soon.

The night was perfectly still when the carriage pulled up to a castle-like structure. Eleanor was tired of traveling and ready to stretch her legs, but above all she just wanted her fears to end by seeing and talking to Logan. A full moon hung low in the sky, which gave an eerie glow to the courtyard, but she could not appreciate the sight due to her fragile nerves. The funny thing was Eleanor had always assumed she was too tough to fall prey to her feminine emotions, yet here she was, trying desperately to hide her hysterics.

The coachman helped her down from the carriage and rushed to the doorway, using the heavy brass knocker to alert the butler of their arrival. Eleanor stretched out her legs and gripped her skirts to hide the shaking of her hands. After several minutes waiting for the door to open, it finally swung wide to reveal a stout, older gentleman. "May I help you?" he asked as he peered into the darkness.

Eleanor stepped forward, not bothering to smile. "I need to see Logan."

"And you are?" he asked, looking down his nose at her.

She must look a fright after spending days in the coach. The last time she had been afforded the chance to freshen herself was that morning, and that was to splash some water on her face. Yes, she must appear frightful, but she still deserved respect. She drew herself to her full height and said in her most cultured voice, "I am Miss Eleanor Ashford."

Her words did not even faze the butler. "I am afraid His Grace is not in residence, but there is a nearby inn you can stay at."

At his words, Eleanor stiffened in shock. Had her ears deceived her? "What did you say?"

The butler spoke louder, accentuating his words as if speaking to a child. "His Grace is not here. You must go elsewhere."

A buzzing sound crept into her ears, blocking out all else around her. She clenched her hands together into tight, angry fists and tensed as she tried to make sense of what was happening. Logan claimed Briarthorn was his estate, although she supposed it could be the duke's, but when she asked the butler to find Logan, he assumed the Logan she referred to was the duke.

But then who was the duke she had met? This entire situation was much too confusing. She cleared her throat and asked in an attempt at clarity, "Who is Charles then?"

He raised his eyebrow. "I have no idea, my lady."

"Surely you must. Charles is a friend of Logan's." Her voice turned pleading as she said, "Please, you must know."

A sympathetic look passed over his otherwise impassive face, and he sighed. "I can only assume the Charles you refer to is Lord Thornwick, His Grace's cousin."

The buzzing returned to her ears. Logan claimed his cousin was Lord Thornwick, and Charles himself said Logan viewed Lord Thornwick as his favorite cousin. If Charles was not the duke, and this estate belonged to Logan, then the natural conclusion must be Logan was the duke.

"Bloody hell." She clenched her eyes shut as all the past interactions with Logan raced through her mind. Her body trembled, and even the knowledge that Logan loved her could not dispel the searing feeling of betrayal. He must have lied to her from the beginning. Yes, she formed certain assumptions on her own, but he failed to rectify her errors, and then he played on those assumptions in a most callous way.

What a fool she had been. All the clues were there,

staring at her in stark reality. His line that he was often mistaken for the duke, how he knew the Waking Hall so well, even his nonchalant attitude toward breaking precious pieces of pottery. How had she missed such ridiculous lies, other than to blame her foolish, misguided heart? And to think, she had traveled all the way to Briarthorn rather than wait in London to marry him.

She laughed a cynical, harsh laugh as her eyes reopened. Her gaze focused on the butler, who regarded her with a wary expression. Of course she did not act like a sane person, not in this moment. Not when her dream world burned to a mound of ashes before her feet.

Aside from Logan's trickery, Lord Thornwick, Lord Gammon, and Lady Gammon must have been involved. She had trusted those people, and for what? So they could manipulate her and help the duke bed her? At least he had not bedded her for sport. If any good came from this evening, it was to reassure her of Logan's intentions to marry her. He had not bedded her and thrown her aside as she worried.

"Are you quite all right, my lady?"

She narrowed her eyes at the butler, who still appeared a bit frazzled. She was in a calm state of fury, one where she would not be trifled with. "You shall ready a room and send a letter to His Grace notifying him of my location." When he appeared ready to deny her orders, she smiled, allowing her fury to show itself in that smile. "I will brook no arguments. His Grace would be most upset if you send me away."

He considered her words before nodding and leading her into the manor. The halls echoed with the sounds of their footsteps, and the light of his single taper afforded them enough light to see before them.

"We did not expect company, my lady, and will have to ready your chamber."

They rounded a bend in the hall, stopping at one of the many doors lining the corridor. He swung the door open, and she entered to find the furniture encased in white sheets and the scent one of general disuse. He pulled a sheet from an armchair near the cold hearth and then hurried to light a fire.

Eleanor sank into the chair after seeing a marvelous view of a tranquil river outside. She could not enjoy the scene of the moonlight striking the water, as she could not seem to dislodge her anger toward Logan and his cohorts. How could she? She closed her eyes, not bothering to open them even as the butler's steps receded from the room.

She remained immobile, unwilling to move from her current position. All her absurd dreams of a quiet life with the man she loved were dashed. She would live the life of a duchess. How Logan must have laughed when she refused his advances, claiming she required better than him. What an amusing joke she must have been for him and his friends. The unwitting lady tricked into loving a man, ripping her dreams to shreds for the man she would throw it all away for.

Strange, the humiliation over their antics faded in comparison to the hurt they instilled in her heart. She was the sort to guard against such pain, never trusting anyone, but she had trusted them, and they betrayed her. Could she have been a simple game to them? She did not wish to believe Logan capable of such callous actions, but what other reason could he have?

The butler returned to guide her to a pleasant bedchamber done up in olive and cream with a view of the river outside. He promised to send refreshments up soon, and then left her to her turmoil. She could not rest, not now. Fighting off the urge to break something, she resorted to pacing the short length of the room instead.

The butler had mentioned Logan was not in residence, and judging by the house, he had not stayed there in some time. Here was yet another lie she must contend with. Where had Logan gone? Was there even a fire?

Stopping her pacing, she leaned her hands on the cold windowsill and looked up at the gleaming moon before her. Love was supposed to be some simple, powerful emotion, yet her love for Logan was proving to be anything but, and it hurt. It hurt like the cleverest of barbs, except this one had teeth that flayed the very flesh from her soul.

Well, she had teeth of her own. She would marry Logan, but she would not make it easy for him. He could come to her here, in the far reaches of Northern England. She would marry him, but that did not mean she had to forgive him.

Chapter 17

The door swung shut behind Logan as he entered his club. There was a certain rightness to resuming the membership that had been so long neglected. He removed his hat as his gaze landed on his cousin, Lord Thornwick, seated alone at a table. Logan sat beside him, ordered a drink, and greeted his surprised cousin.

"Your Grace," Charles murmured before offering a sly grin. "Or should I address you as Sir Logan?"

Logan shook his head as he downed his aged port and ordered another. "She won't see me. I visited her twice, and she refused to see me both times."

Charles nodded. "Women are strange creatures. Was she mad at you when you left the house party?"

"No," he said as he leaned back, crossing his right ankle over his left knee. "She had taken the news of my identity quite well."

Charles's eyes flew to his in surprise. "You told her at the house party?"

"Not exactly, but she overheard my steward address me as 'Your Grace.' "

The noise of an argument rose nearby, and Charles grinned at him until the din died down. "Before I left Waking Hall, Lady Gammon and I chatted about your lady love. She was under the assumption that Miss Ashford believed you to be Sir Logan. Are you certain she knew?"

She had to know. They had conversed about his lie, and she said his lie was unnecessary. He thought her response odd at the time but concluded females were complex and would say nonsensical things.

"So you have tried to see her twice as the duke?" Charles asked with a gleam in his eye. "I cannot say I am flattered if she refused to see me twice. Perhaps you should return as Sir Logan."

"That should not be necessary. We are to marry this Saturday, you know."

"Ah, congratulations." Charles inclined his head. "She is likely upset, believing she will marry me. Not you."

"That can't be possible." Could it? Could she still think he was Sir Logan and Charles the duke? Such a belief would be absurd, and yet, she refused to see him. He shook his head. She couldn't.

They chatted over a couple more rounds, and then Logan rose. He returned home, despite the sinking feeling that bothered him since his conversation with Charles. Upon entering his house, his eyes fell on some letters in a silver salver. He picked up the stack and scanned the various invites until his eyes fell on a letter from his butler at Briarthorn.

Opening the missive, he searched the document before his good mood vanished. He swore loudly as he called for his horse to be brought around. His butler at Briarthorn was a trusted servant and would not report falsehoods. How was it he now reported a young lady's arrival that matched the description of Ellie?

He needed answers, and the Ashfords were going to give him some.

****

After a mad dash through London, he reached the Ashfords and knocked on the oak door. When the door swung wide, Logan entered without waiting for an invitation. "Where are Lord and Lady Ashford?"

The butler rushed to follow Logan and said, "Her ladyship is in the parlor, Your Grace."

Logan retraced the route to the parlor used to receive guests and entered to the sight of Lady Ashford and Mrs. Westfield reading books by the fireplace and sipping wine. "Lady Ashford." He bowed. "I must see your daughter. Now."

With a gasp of surprise, she rose to greet him. The color drained from her face and she swallowed. "Such a request is impossible, Your Grace. She visits her cousin and will not return 'til the morrow."

"Your Grace?" Mrs. Westfield's eyes widened. "You must be mistaken. This is Sir Logan." She placed her hand over her mouth and whispered, "You know, the one that Eleanor wishes to marry."

Mrs. Westfield needed to work on her whispering. The volume she used was only a minor decrease and audible to anyone in the surrounding radius. Lady Ashford speared her with a scathing glance, and Mrs. Westfield clamped her lips shut.

Mrs. Westfield did not appear to believe him a duke, and such a reaction did not bode well for Logan. Mrs. Westfield had been absent every time he visited as the duke, so if she did not know who he was, then Ellie must not either.

Lady Ashford rose and advanced on Logan. "Forgive my sister's confusion. We know you are the Duke of Waking."

Mrs. Westfield's eyes widened, and her

countenance turned excited. She hid her reaction by returning her gaze to her book. Her happy response to the news of his identity was as well-hidden as her whisper, which was poor indeed.

Returning his attention back to Lady Ashford, Logan scowled. He could not say why, but he did not trust Ellie's mother. Not one bit. "And how long has Miss Ashford visited her cousin?"

Lady Ashford gulped. "Not long at all, Your Grace."

He raised his eyebrow in patent disbelief. He would never receive a straight answer from her. He turned and departed the house without saying another word. He had one last visit to make before returning home which should give him the answers he so ardently desired.

Knocking on the front door of the Farris townhome, he waited impatiently for the door to open. Finally, it swung wide, and a butler greeted him. The time was well past traditional visiting hours, but he did not care. With an imperious expression, Logan said, "I am here to see Lady Farris."

"And you are?" the butler asked, giving Logan a cold once-over.

"The Duke of Waking."

The man gulped, then turned to lead Logan into the house. Logan didn't always enjoy his title, but moments like these accented how useful a ducal title could be.

"Let me see if she is in, Your Grace," he said as he led Logan to a small sitting room and departed to find Lady Farris. Logan crossed to a wall and found a small picture hung above a settee. Masterful brushstrokes depicted a scene with a weeping willow and a stream flowing next to it. With a start, he realized why the painting seemed so familiar. It was Eleanor's spot, and she had most likely painted it. "Where are you, my darling?" he asked as he stared at the nostalgic picture.

"Who are you talking to, Your Grace?"

Logan turned to find a small, lovely lady with a welcoming smile standing before him. Behind her stood the large frame of Lord Farris. "Never mind," he muttered, annoyed at being overheard. "I have been informed Miss Ashford is in residence. May I see her please?"

"Please, sit down." Lady Farris indicated a chair as she took a seat on an elegant, claw-footed sofa. She crossed her ankles and smiled at him.

Logan ignored her offer and said, "I must see Miss Ashford."

Lord Farris's expression remained impassive as he sat beside his wife. "You may be a duke, but you can have manners. I suggest you sit down."

Lady Farris placed her hand against her husband's sleeve before turning back to Logan. "I am afraid you cannot see her. She is indisposed."

Dealing with this family was frustrating, and Logan was growing annoyed. "I must ascertain her location immediately. If she is not here, then I can only assume she is at Briarthorn as my butler said."

Lady Farris's brow furrowed. "Did you say Briarthorn?"

"Yes." He scowled and ran a frustrated hand through his hair. "My estate in the northern region of England is called Briarthorn."

She stilled. "Do you know a Sir Logan, Your Grace?"

A sick feeling overtook him. How could he have muddled things up so much? He placed his head in his hands and laughed. "I am Sir Logan."

Her lips parted as if she wished to speak, but no sound issued forth.

He shook his head. "I acted as Sir Logan to make Miss Ashford fall in love with me. I thought she knew the truth, but now I see she does not."

"You mean *you* are the one she is in love with?" she asked, leaning forward in her chair with an avid expression of interest.

He nodded.

She turned to her husband and said, "Only Eleanor would manage to fall in love with a duke unwittingly." He chuckled, and she turned to give Logan the answer he was looking for. "I am sorry, Your Grace, she is not here. She left days ago for Briarthorn, afraid she was going to be forced into a marriage to you. Of course, she didn't realize you were the same man she wants to marry. It's unfortunate really. She could have avoided an enormous amount of trouble if she had known."

He nodded. He could have sworn she understood he was a duke when he left her at Waking Hall. How could such a massive misunderstanding transpire? He would have plenty of time to think on all of that when he rode up to Briarthorn. Standing, he smiled at first Lady Farris and then Lord Farris. "Thank you for clarifying this matter. I have a lengthy journey ahead and should get going."

Chapter 18

Eleanor settled into Briarthorn, reveling in all the opportunities it offered. She enjoyed the quiet which also presented her with a chance to think. As an uninhabited estate, only a few servants were around, but Eleanor quite enjoyed the lack of people. The butler at first had been a bit unapproachable but had warmed to her, although she still sensed he was skeptical about her visit. She couldn't blame him. He would see soon enough he was right to trust her. Then there was the cook and housekeeper, Mrs. O'Conner, who had made Eleanor feel welcome. An older woman, Mrs. O'Conner had worked at Briarthorn for many years and was more than happy to keep Eleanor company whenever she happened down to the kitchen.

After a morning walk along the river, Eleanor was famished and went down to the kitchen for some lunch. She entered the warm room and caught a whiff of the intended meal. Her stomach revolted at the scent, and she turned and ran from the room.

Her morning sickness had not abated in the slightest, and it was at its most touchy whenever she was around fish or paint. She managed to make it to a chamber pot, although her stomach was nearly empty. Mrs. O'Conner must have noticed her abrupt departure and soon found her as Eleanor sat by the chamber pot.

"Are you all right, dearie?"

"I think I am just a little under the weather," Eleanor said in a cheery voice, hoping Mrs. O'Conner would believe her.

"I am hardly a spring chicken, my lady. I can recognize when a lady is increasing." Mrs. O'Conner knelt beside Eleanor and placed a hand on her back in reassurance. "I am sure His Grace will make whatever amends he can once he arrives."

"He would be so lucky," Eleanor muttered as she rose. "Would it be possible to have something other than fish today?"

"Of course!" Mrs. O'Conner also rose and said, "You know Her Grace, the duke's mother, God rest her soul, was unable to stomach fish when she was with child, also."

Eleanor raised an eyebrow. She hadn't realized Mrs. O'Conner was quite *that* old. "So you knew Logan as a boy?"

Mrs. O'Conner led Eleanor to the dining room as she chatted. "Of course, I practically raised him. He was always such a sweet boy, forever trying to do the right thing. Now his cousin, Lord Thornwick, was a little hellion."

After directing Eleanor to take a seat at the large dining room table, Mrs. O'Conner continued regaling Eleanor with stories of Logan's childhood until Eleanor's stomach growled in angry defiance.

Mrs. O'Conner blushed. "Let me make you a sandwich, my lady."

Eleanor consented and was left alone in the large dining room to her thoughts. Hearing of Logan as a youth interested her. He must have been adorable, and hopefully he would pass that cuteness down to their child.

She rested her hand on her flat stomach and considered her future with Logan until she heard the faraway sound of voices. She rose from her seat and went to see where the sounds came from. A mixture of apprehension and anger filled her as she realized Logan must have arrived.

Rounding a bend in the lengthy hallway, Eleanor spotted Logan striding in her direction. Her stomach jerked at the sight of him. She had forgotten just how handsome he was. Her heart beat with renewed life, until she reminded herself she was still angry with him, and rightly so.

"What were you thinking, coming all the way up here by yourself?" He pulled her to him in an encompassing embrace, and she melted against him for the briefest of moments. She was home, at last.

Unfortunately, she could have felt at home in London if he had admitted his true identity in the first place. She could not focus in his arms, so she took a step back and crossed her arms before her. "What was I thinking? How about what were you thinking? What sort of a duke masquerades as landed gentry and doesn't bother to tell his intended that small detail?"

He scoffed. "You said you knew of the secret before I left Waking Hall. What more was I expected to do?"

"I knew of a secret, which was evidently the incorrect secret. Lady Gammon had informed me you are as rich as the duke. Isn't it amusing just how accurate those words are?"

"That is the secret you thought I kept from you? That I was rich?" The lines of his face softened, and he laughed. "I thought you already knew that."

She scowled. Why did everyone think that? Landed gentry were usually *not* one of the wealthiest in the kingdom. "Well, I did not."

His grin intensified, and her heart began to beat in an erratic tempo. His sinful mouth, coupled with those enigmatic green eyes were treacherous. "You would have married me without piles of money?"

"Naturally I assumed you had some money, otherwise you would have needed my dowry. I just assumed we might have to pinch pennies on occasion." She averted her eyes. Why were they having this conversation in the hallway? Shouldn't they at least speak in a less public area? "Your Grace."

He held up his hand. "My name is Logan to you."

"I will call you what I want." She stomped her foot to emphasize the point and raised her eyebrow at him. "All this time, you tricked me into believing you were a mere baronet, so forgive me if I don't listen to you."

He grinned at her again. "Technically speaking, I do hold the title of baronet, so it wasn't a complete lie."

How dare he look so cute with his dark hair set over his scintillating green eyes and luscious lips, and then say something so frustrating? "How is masquerading as a baronet anything other than a complete lie?"

All traces of humor left his face and he shook his head. "My actions were logical. Your quest to marry a titled gentleman is what led me to invent this little masquerade in the first place."

"I did not force you to do anything."

A movement down the hall caught Eleanor's attention. Someone must be eavesdropping, so she grabbed his hand and pulled him into the nearest room. She shut the door and enclosed them in a dimly lit, musty parlor. There were sheets draped over the furniture, and she sneezed from the general air of disuse.

She ignored his questioning brow at their hasty change of venue and asked, "Well, how did I force you to lie?"

He walked over to one of the covered pieces of furniture and pulled the sheet off. Sitting down, he crossed his legs and regarded her with an impassive look. "When we first met, I couldn't tell you I was a duke for fear you would claim I compromised you. You drew your own conclusions, and I went with them."

She glared at him, not wanting to concede his point, although she supposed it made sense. He continued his tirade while she remained silent. "I decided I should marry you, but only if I could make you love me. If you knew I was a duke, I would have never known if your feelings were genuine."

Her pride dictated she grow angry at his words, but deep inside, she knew he was right. "Why couldn't you have admitted who you are after I declared my feelings for you? Why wait?"

"I didn't want to anger you before we left for Gretna Green, not when I could wait until after the wedding."

"That decision worked so well for you." Another covered piece of furniture was beside Logan that looked like a chair, so she crossed over and uncovered it. She sat and ignored the dust that swirled around her. "That still doesn't explain why you changed our plans."

He sighed and shifted so he faced her. "Why face

the scandal of elopement when we could have a traditional wedding?"

"If I had known you were a duke, then your words would have made perfect sense. You never came back for me, despite the letter I wrote you, which is why I concluded this was your way of ruining me and leaving."

He stiffened, and his eyes darkened. "How dare you impugn my honor? I never received your letter, and I called on you twice. I would never stoop to such devious methods to bed a lady."

She ground her teeth. His skull was amazingly thick. "You mean when you visited as a duke?" She waved her hand and affected a casual demeanor. "Of course, how could I forget? You thought I knew. Never mind the fact that I did not know and assumed your cousin had decided to force me into an unwanted marriage."

Obviously, Logan did not feel he deserved blame. He shook his head. "If you had deigned to meet with me, you would have known the duke was I and not my cousin."

"So now it is my fault that I did not know you are a duke?"

He frowned. "Of course not. I am simply suggesting your actions created more trouble than they solved."

She stood and smoothed her skirts as she said, "I suppose you think I should have never come to Briarthorn."

"It would have saved us both a great deal of trouble if you hadn't," he said in response.

He reclined in his chair, with one ankle propped

over the other leg, and Eleanor could only shake her head. He did not understand. She required an explanation, of course, but she needed more. She needed him to understand what he had put her through. He might have been well-intentioned in his schemes, but she had lived for weeks in agony.

"I spent weeks waiting for you to come for me. You never did." She closed her eyes and turned from him. Admitting her feelings to him was painful. "I waited and waited. Eventually, I believed you would not come for me. Then, a duke shows up and requests my hand in marriage. If I had not come to Briarthorn, I would have been forced to marry him tomorrow."

"It was today."

"What?" She turned to him with a fierce scowl.

"We were supposed to marry today."

She flexed her fingers and breathed. "How is that relevant?"

"I thought you would like to know."

He smiled at her, and she threw up her hands in a show of frustration. "There is no talking to you. This entire situation is your fault, yet you do not accept responsibility as you ought, and then you don't even listen when I explain what I have been through. I am finished."

He stood, and his eyes turned a steely color she had never seen before. "You are at fault just as much as I. You came to Briarthorn and discovered my true identity, and then, rather than return to London for our wedding, you expected me to join you here."

She parted her lips. She would reveal her condition to him under happier circumstances. Once he knew, it would make perfect sense why she had not made the grueling journey a second time.

He stepped toward her and caught her arms in his hands. "You wanted to see if you could make your little marionette dance? Well, congratulations, you succeeded. I just hope you enjoy the fruits of your labor."

"What is that supposed to mean?" She tried to shrug out of his hold, but he kept her pinned in place. She should have been intimidated, but she couldn't. Not with him.

He smiled. "Well, now that I am here, we might as well stay here. This can be our honeymoon of sorts. I did win our bet, after all."

She didn't care and nodded her head in jerky little movements as she tried to tamp down her anger. "So be it. Let me know when and where our wedding shall take place, and I will be there." She turned from him and left him standing in place, keenly aware that he watched her retreat. She was hungry and tired, as her interaction with Logan had sapped the remainder of her energy.

As she entered her room, she spotted the tray of food laid out on her bed. Mrs. O'Conner must have guessed she would want a tray, and Eleanor would thank her later for the consideration.

She munched on a piece of bread and tried to calm herself. Logan thought he struck the winning blow by suggesting they remain at Briarthorn. Little did he know she would prefer to stay at this particular estate for a while, but now she knew better than to tell him so. Finishing off the food on her tray, Eleanor lay down for a nap. No good would come of being too sleepy to deal rationally with Logan.

****

Logan didn't know what had gone awry. He had envisioned a happy reunion between himself and Ellie, not this wretched spat that occurred. At the very least, he could have received some thanks for his trip across the entirety of England.

Striding to his chambers, he called for a bath and began to undress. He smelled of the road and should be grateful one of his daydreams had not turned out how he hoped. He could at least smell decent when he finally got to tup her again. He shook his head with dissatisfaction. What had passed between them had been so much more than a mere tup, although he was at a loss for words for how he should describe the physical aspect of their relationship.

In his many years, he had never experienced such a bond with a woman. With Ellie, the act of making love was an unidentifiable high without the inevitable crash that came in the afterglow of intimacy. She was not some vapid creature that could only satisfy him in bed, either. Her wit and humor amused him and kept him interested in her without fail. Even her responses in anger amused him, which was no small feat. Simply put, she intrigued him, and he needed her.

As the last of the servants trailed out, Logan stepped into his bathtub as the steam rose around him. He inhaled the vapors and relished the feeling of being home once more. Even though he had many other estates, this was the one he had grown up on and would spend many more years at. He shifted deeper into the water and closed his eyes. He planned on staying at Briarthorn, but now that Ellie knew there were other options available, would she choose to stay with him here?

Important topics such as these required a discussion between him and Ellie, but he would have a lifetime to do that. For now, he should try to repair the damage between them. Going into his masquerade to win her heart, he had known she was passionate and would just have to accept more spats like these would happen in the future.

He stepped from the tub, toweled off, and began to dress in a set of clothes one of the servants laid out. He would have to send for his valet now that he knew he would not return to London. He ignored the constricting cravat and left the room, but not before pocketing the gift he had purchased for her.

Logan found his butler directing a number of servants with the remaining items left to unpack from the coach. "Alban," Logan said, and the butler stopped what he was doing to attend to what Logan said. "Would you be so kind as to direct me to Miss Ashford's chambers?"

Alban looked at him askance. "Your Grace, she is a *lady*."

Brushing Alban's concerns of decorum aside with a brush of his hand, Logan said, "Yes, yes, and my future duchess. So tell me her location, and then send someone to alert the vicar that he must preside over a wedding tomorrow morning."

Nodding his head, the reproachful light in Alban's eyes did not diminish despite Logan's attempt to placate. "She is located in the West Room, Your Grace."

Logan turned on his heel and headed in the direction of Ellie's room. He was feeling better about his situation with her now that their wedding was in the near future. A faint smile even flickered on his face as he realized his problems with her were truly insignificant. Now he just needed to convince her of that.

He passed a door which led to the kitchens, and Mrs. O'Conner materialized with a smile. "Your Grace, what a delight to see you. Would you care for a sandwich?"

"In a little while. I must see to our guest first."

Her smile brightened. "Miss Ashford is such a delightful creature. You have chosen well."

He nodded as he began to walk once more but stopped as she continued speaking. Trying to hide his annoyance, he listened as she spoke.

"Try not to be too hard on her, Your Grace. A woman in her condition sometimes acts nonsensically." With her parting words of wisdom, Mrs. O'Conner turned to return to her kitchen, until Logan stopped her.

"In what condition?" he asked, dumbfounded.

"Why, increasing, of course." She cocked her head. "You did know she is with child, didn't you?"

Logan had never experienced an out-of-body moment quite like this before. His mind stopped its usual mechanisms, and he felt as though he had been hit with a sledgehammer. While his body remained grounded, his spirit floated above, examining him and discovering a new side he had not known existed. He was to be a father, and Ellie a mother. She would make a wonderful mother. He smiled as he thought of a smaller version of Ellie clinging shyly to her mother's skirts.

He moved forward then, unaware that his walk was more of a trot. If he was shocked by the news, imagine how Ellie must have felt. He rounded a corner, and his gaze landed on her door. Reaching the doorway, he raised his hand to knock but was interrupted when it swung open.

"Ellie," he breathed.

"Your Grace."

He winced. Her blue eyes were leveled on him in icy indifference. "Are you going somewhere?"

"As a matter of fact, yes." She stepped around him and began to make her way down the hall.

"Would you care for some company?"

"No, thank you."

He trailed after her and was beginning to think she would ignore him for the entirety of their walk, when suddenly she whirled on him. "What do you want from me?"

He stopped. He had come very near to running her over. "For starters, I should like very much to escort you on your outing."

She considered him for several seconds and then nodded. "Very well, but don't expect anything else from me."

He offered her his arm, but instead of taking it, she turned and began to walk once more. He couldn't help the grin that pulled on his lips. He followed all the way to the front door and down the gravel path. The sun had begun to descend, and an orange glow overtook the sky. The air was warm but not hot, and he savored the feeling of being home, with her.

She led him down to the river and turned to walk on its shoreline. He stopped her by asking, "Might I suggest we walk the opposite direction, my lady?"

"You may not. This is the direction I take when I

walk."

He grinned, and her gaze narrowed on him. She thrust her nose in the air and began to march away. She was behaving in a vexing manner, but he was just happy to spend time with her. He knew they would reach an accord soon, so why not enjoy his outing with her?

"I have something for you, but it lies in the opposite direction."

Again she stopped, but this time he could hear the distinct sound of pain in her words. "Why should I want anything from you when the one thing I truly desire you will not give?"

The gentle sound of the water lapping against the shoreline filled the silence. He had known she was angry, but this was something other than anger. This was hurt. "What do you mean?"

"I need more from you than a simple apology. I need you to understand the pain you have caused me."

His breath caught at her words. He had acted in a way that would benefit them both. Surely she understood that, didn't she? He stepped toward her but stopped when she held up her hand.

"Just don't." She shook her head. "Let me explain."

"Of course."

She breathed in a ragged breath. "I understand your actions, but that doesn't change how I felt." Her arms circled herself in a tight hug and she shut her eyes. "I didn't know where you were or when you would come for me. Then, out of nowhere, a duke wished to marry me. Naturally, I assumed it was the duke that I had met and not you. Mother wanted the match, but all I wanted was you."

He ached to go to her, to hold her in his arms, but when he moved to her side, she gave him a quelling look. He respected her wishes and stopped.

"I began to doubt you, and I let my fears convince me you had used me and no longer wanted me. Then, I discovered I was pregnant." She laughed. "Yes, Logan, you are to be a father." A solitary tear escaped from her eye, and she wiped it away. "That unforeseen complication changed everything. I could only assume that you did not care for me, and I would be sent away to birth your bastard in secret."

Her words shocked him. "I would never allow that to happen."

She turned to him and said, "How was I to know that? You weren't there. You may think that your little masquerade was innocent, but think of the pain it caused me because I didn't know. All the inner turmoil at defying my parents' desires and the dreams I had held since girlhood. These things may seem trivial to you, but I actually began to anticipate the change in my circumstances, as long as it was with you." Her voice caught, and he rushed forward. He ignored her protests and pulled her to him.

She was shaking, and he stroked her silken hair to calm her. Never in his wildest imagination had he thought she might suffer so. He had never wanted that for her. Never. "I am so sorry, my darling. I never intended for my actions to hurt you. So many things occurred due to both of our choices, but we are here now, and what matters is that I love you and you love me. I will never allow you to feel so much pain again, I swear."

She brought her head from his chest and gazed into his eyes. The orange glow of the setting sun tinted the world around them and made her appear even more beautiful. She sniffled, and he wiped a newly shed tear from her face. "Don't cry, Ellie. We are supposed to be happy now that we are together again."

"Of course I am, now that I know all is well." She smiled past the tears in her eyes and said, "You cannot imagine the doubts I dealt with on the way here. My primary concern was you would laugh at me for traveling all the way to Briarthorn and send me away. My other concern was you would marry me just for the baby."

"I could never send you away, but as for the baby—" He grinned and placed a kiss on the top of her forehead. "—I want you, and the baby is just an added boon." He hugged her to him in a tight embrace as his heart swelled. He could easily hold her just like this for the rest of time, but he had something else planned for her.

He disengaged himself from her and led her opposite to the way she had desired to go. Their feet barely made a whisper on the grass beside the river. He whistled a low, wondrous note and said, "Imagine, you are enceinte after only one magical night."

She giggled, and the sound filled him with joy. She was so precious to him, and no amount of disagreements or misunderstandings would lessen that.

They approached a wooded area, and she asked, "Are you sure you know where we are going?"

He smiled and continued to lead her through the trees until he spotted what he wished to show her. In front of him stood a small weeping willow, surrounded by lush green grass and wildflowers. The river lay nearby, and the castle could be seen above them. It was even more magical than he had envisioned. The setting sun cast a soft, otherworldly glow to the place, and Logan turned to look at Ellie's face.

She stood riveted in place, but he could not read what she felt. "Do you like it?" Logan asked, fearful of her answer.

"Do I like it? Oh, Logan, I love it." Ellie's eyes passed over two large rocks, situated next to the weeping willow. In time, the rocks would be overshadowed by the tree, but for now it would be just as wondrous a spot albeit without shade. She went to one of the rocks, sat, and looked back to Logan. "Is there a reason for two stones here?"

"Oh, the workers must have made a mistake." She blanched at his words before he chuckled and said, "Of course I planned that. How else are we to spend every moment together unless I have a rock to sit on?"

"How indeed?" she asked as her gloved hand trailed over the smooth rock. "Did you plan to test it today?"

He stepped over and sat on the rock next to her, and she asked, "When did you do this?"

"Roughly a week after I learned of your desire to have such a location at your future home."

She dropped her gaze from his, and he scowled. There she went, crying again. He laced his fingers with hers and tried to stop her tears. "Really, my love, there is no need to cry. All is well."

She smiled at him and shook her head. "I am so very happy. I cannot believe you have done all this for me." The corners of her eyes crinkled as she smiled at him. "It is the nicest thing anyone has ever done for me."

"If you like this, then hopefully you will like my other present for you."

"What more could I want?" Eleanor asked in a whisper.

He pulled a small black box from his jacket and opened the box for Eleanor's perusal.

Her eyes widened. "Where did you find this?"

"In London. I saw my water nymph carved in stone and knew it was meant for you."

Eleanor's eyes drifted to his. "Just as I fear I was meant for you. Thank you. You know, I love you, whether as the Duke of Waking or as Sir Logan, in London or here at Briarthorn. I just want to be with you."

"And I love you, my dear nymph." Rising, Logan turned her from him and placed the cameo on her. His hand brushed the nape of her neck, and he leaned in to settle a soft kiss on the back of her neck. "Shall we return?"

"I have something for you, as well." She turned, and they began to make their way uphill to the castle. "My gift is at the castle, though."

He raised an eyebrow and grinned. He liked the sound of that. "Oh really?"

She giggled. "This is an actual gift."

"Oh." His ardor was doused. "What is it?"

"You shall see."

They strolled up the hill and reached the castle. Logan counted the minutes until they reached her room because he felt like a parched man and she was water. He needed a kiss from her but out of sight of the servants.

They entered her room, and she made Logan close his eyes while she prepared his gift. After several moments, she bade him look, and he opened his eyes to the view of an easel with a small painting on it. He stepped to it and was afforded a rather scandalous view of his water nymph on a canopied bed.

"I love it." He exhaled as he observed the masterful details. Her back faced him with a sheet covering her except for the corner of her shoulder, and he knew it was Ellie.

She blushed and said, "It started as a literal representation of my bed after our night together, but I am afraid my imagination took over."

He pulled her to him and breathed in her alluring scent. "Really, this is the best wedding gift you could give me. Thank you."

Her hand went to the cameo on her neck, and she smiled up at him. "I think your gifts have far exceeded my small one."

"And I think there is one more gift you could bestow on me, my darling."

"Oh?"

"Yes." He began to nuzzle her neck and chuckled when she squirmed. "Although it is most ruinous in nature, you are already past redemption, so…"

"I think you can wait one more day, Your Grace."

He sighed and pulled away from her. "I suppose, if you insist."

"I do. We really do not have that long to wait."

"Fine." He placed a chaste goodnight kiss on her soft lips and went to the door. "Good night, my love."

"Good night."

Chapter 19

Eleanor woke early and selected the only gown that could possibly work as a wedding dress. It was a plain white day dress with a light pink overskirt. While it was not the typical wedding gown, it would work, especially since all her clothes were in London. She wore her cameo draped around her neck, but that was the only piece of jewelry to adorn her.

She could not stomach breakfast, and when the appointed time arrived, she went downstairs to meet her betrothed. As she descended the grand staircase, her eyes alighted on him and her palms dampened. He was dressed in evening wear and looked refined and handsome.

"Your Grace." She curtsied as she reached the landing.

A twinkle filled his green eyes, and he bowed over her hand. "Shall we, my lady?"

They ambled through the door and onto the drive. The sun shone, unhindered by a single cloud, and a gentle breeze played along her skin. They were not in a hurry, and strangely, Eleanor felt her wedding day was better like this as opposed to an enormous society show. Everything about this day was relaxed. It was perfect.

After entering the carriage, it jerked into motion, and she settled into the seat next to Logan. She peered up at him, only to find him as tranquil as she. "I wonder how my parents will react to all this. Mother must have had a fit when I was not there for our wedding day."

He grinned down at her. "I sent them a note before I departed London. I informed your mother that we would marry at my discretion. She likely is furious, but there is little she can do."

Her mother would be furious, indeed. Her mother would have planned an elaborate wedding breakfast and invited anyone who was anyone to attend. Of course, there would be a scandal, but that did not bother Eleanor. Nothing did on this magical day.

They arrived at the chapel, and Logan helped her from the carriage. They entered, and Eleanor stopped as her eyes adjusted to the change in light. She gasped as she viewed the interior. The church was beautiful. The architectural style was gothic, with large, stained-glass windows depicting various moments in Jesus's life. Although small, this chapel boasted more character and charm than many she had frequented in London.

Logan led her up the row of marble pews to the altar where the vicar waited. Logan spoke to him and then joined Eleanor as they waited for the vicar to summon a couple of witnesses. Several minutes ticked by before an older couple took a seat in the front pew.

The ceremony commenced, although Eleanor was unable to pay attention to anything but the feeling of Logan's large hand as it encompassed her own smaller one. After some time, they exchanged their vows, and Logan slipped a ring onto her finger. After a chaste kiss, Eleanor was stunned to discover the ceremony was over, and Logan was sweeping her into his arms and carrying her out to the carriage.

"Do you like it?" Logan indicated the ring on her

left hand.

"Of course," Eleanor whispered against him as she gazed at the ring he had placed there. It was simple but beautiful, boasting a large diamond surrounded by smaller sapphires. It twinkled when she moved her hand. Aside from its obvious beauty, it felt right, nestled there against her skin. Just as she felt right, tucked up against her husband.

"It is a family heirloom, but if you don't like it I can get you something different."

"Of course not," Eleanor said as tears began to threaten her eyes. She felt so happy, completely and unabashedly happy.

He lowered his mouth to hers in a much fiercer kiss than the one exchanged in the chapel. The feeling of his body against hers, and the intense sparks of attraction made her long for a quick carriage ride back. All those thoughts were swept aside as he continued to kiss her, but she pulled away long enough to say, "I love you, Your Grace."

"And I you, Your Grace."

Then, he returned his mouth to hers, and she was lost. Blissfully lost.

A word about the author...

Naomi Boom is an author with a newly discovered love for writing. Her inspiration struck when she was searching for the perfect historical romance novel to read. Nothing sounded appealing, so she decided she would write her own. That one novel has morphed into a series and hopefully many, many more.

She currently resides in Kansas with her family but has her eyes firmly planted on an acreage in eastern South Dakota. Once her husband retires from the United States Army, they will return to her home state.

Thank you for purchasing
this publication of The Wild Rose Press, Inc.

If you enjoyed the story, we would appreciate your
letting others know by leaving a review.

For other wonderful stories,
please visit our on-line bookstore at
www.thewildrosepress.com.

For questions or more information
contact us at
info@thewildrosepress.com.

The Wild Rose Press, Inc.
www.thewildrosepress.com

Stay current with The Wild Rose Press, Inc.

Like us on Facebook

https://www.facebook.com/TheWildRosePress

And Follow us on Twitter
https://twitter.com/WildRosePress